She returned to the clearing, with a flapping of wings. This time she flew right up to me. In her right claw, a small egg was clutched. She extended it.

I forced down my excitement. It had worked! I held out my right hand, after making sure it was steady. The egg dropped into it. I was somewhat startled by its warmth. It was of a size that fit well into my palm. I carefully placed it inside my jerkin, next to my chest.

"Thank you, mother," I thought to her. *"May your life be long, your food plentiful, and your children many."*

"And you," she said, *"long life and good hunting."*

"I am not a hunter," I told her.

"You will be."

Ace Books by Steven Brust

The Vlad Taltos Series
JHEREG
YENDI
TECKLA
TALTOS *(coming in March)*

THE REIGN IN HELL
BROKEDOWN PALACE

STEVEN BRUST

JHEREG

ACE BOOKS, NEW YORK

JHEREG

An Ace Book / published by arrangement with
the author and his agent,
Valerie Smith, Virginia Kidd Agency

PRINTING HISTORY
Ace edition / April 1983

ISBN: 0-441-38554-0

Ace Books are published by The Berkley Publishing Group,
200 Madison Avenue, New York, New York 10016.
The name "ACE" and the "A" logo
are trademarks belonging to Charter
Communications, Inc.
PRINTED IN THE UNITED STATES OF AMERICA

10   9   8   7

For my parents

Who understand professionalism
better than I ever will

Acknowledgments

My thanks to:
    Steven Bond
    Reen Brust
    Lee Pelton
    John Robey
      and
    John Stanley
      for being who they are.

And special thanks to Adrian Morgan, who set up the canvas and lent me her brushes.

—S.K.Z.B.

Let the winds of jungle's night
Stay the hunter in her flight.

Evening's breath to witch's mind;
Let our fates be intertwined.

Jhereg! Do not pass me by.
Show me where thine egg doth lie.

Pronunciation Guide

Adrilankha	ah-dri-LAHN-kuh
Adron	Ā-drahn
Aliera	uh-LEER-uh
Athyra	uh-THĪ-ruh
Baritt	BĀR-it
Brust	brūst
Cawti	KAW-tee
Chreotha	kree-O-thuh
Dragaera	druh-GAR-uh
Drien	DREE-en
Dzur	tser
Iorich	ī-Ō-rich
Issola	î-SŌ-luh
Jhegaala	jhuh-GAH-luh
Jhereg	jhuh-REG
Kiera	KĪ-ruh
Kieron	KĪ-rahn
Kragar	KRAY-gahr
Leareth	LEER-eth
Loiosh	LOI-ōsh
Lyorn	LI-orn
Mario	MAH-ree-ō
Mellar	MEH-lar
Morrolan	muh-RŌL-uhn
Norathar	NŌ-ruh-thahr
Rocza	RAW-tsuh
Serioli	sar-ee-Ō-lee
Taltos	TAHL-tōsh
Teckla	TEH-kluh
Tiassa	tee-AH-suh
Tsalmoth	TSAHL-mōth

Verra	VEE-ruh
Valista	vuhl-ISS-tuh
Yendi	YEN-dee
Zerika	zuh-REE-kuh

Prologue

There is a similarity, if I may be permitted an excursion into tenuous metaphor, between the feel of a chilly breeze and the feel of a knife's blade, as either is laid across the back of the neck. I can call up memories of both, if I work at it. The chilly breeze is invariably going to be the more pleasant memory. For instance . . .

I was eleven years old, and clearing tables in my father's restaurant. It was a quiet evening, with only a couple of tables occupied. A group had just left, and I was walking over to the table they'd used.

The table in the corner was a deuce. One male, one female. Both Dragaeran, of course. For some reason, humans rarely came into our place; perhaps because we were human too, and they didn't want the stigma, or something. My father himself always avoided doing business with other "Easterners."

There were three at the table along the far wall. All of them were male, and Dragaeran. I noted that there was no tip at the table I was clearing, and heard a gasp from behind me.

I turned as one member of the threesome let his head fall into his plate of lyorn leg with red peppers. My father had let me make the sauce for it that time, and, crazily, my first thought was to wonder if I'd built it wrong.

The other two stood up smoothly, seemingly not the least bit worried about their friend. They began moving toward the door, and I realized that they were planning to leave without paying. I looked for my father, but he was in back.

I glanced once more at the table, wondering whether I

should try to help the fellow who was choking, or intercept the two who were trying to walk out on their bill.

Then I saw the blood.

The hilt of a dagger was protruding from the throat of the fellow whose face was lying in his plate. It slowly dawned on me what had happened, and I decided that, no, I wasn't going to ask the two gentlemen who were leaving for money.

They didn't run, or even hurry. They walked quickly and quietly past me toward the door. I didn't move. I don't think I was even breathing. I remember suddenly becoming very much aware of my own heartbeat.

One set of footsteps stopped, directly behind me. I remained frozen, while in my mind, I cried out to Verra, the Demon Goddess.

At that moment, something cold and hard touched the back of my neck. I was too frozen to flinch. I would have closed my eyes if I could have. Instead, I stared straight ahead. I wasn't consciously aware of it at the time, but the Dragaeran girl was looking at me, and she started to rise then. I noticed her when her companion reached out a hand to stop her, which she brushed off.

Then I heard a soft, almost silky voice in my ear. "You didn't see a thing," it said. "Got that?" If I had had as much experience then as I do now, I would have known that I was in no real danger—if he'd had any intention of killing me he would have done so already. But I didn't, and so I shook. I felt I should nod, but couldn't manage. The Dragaeran girl was almost up to us now, and I imagine the guy behind me noticed her, because the blade was gone suddenly and I heard retreating footsteps.

I was shaking uncontrollably. The tall Dragaeran girl gently placed her hand on my shoulder. I saw sympathy on her face. It was a look I had never before been given from a Dragaeran, and it was, in its own way, as frightening as the experience I'd just been through. I had an urge to fall forward into her arms, but I didn't let myself. I became aware that she was speaking, softly, gently. "It's all right, they've left. Nothing is going to happen. Just take it easy, you'll be fine . . ."

My father came storming in from the other room.

"Vlad!" he called, "what's going on around here? Why—"

He stopped. He saw the body. I heard him getting sick and I felt ashamed for him. The hand on my shoulder tightened, then. I felt myself stop trembling, and looked at the girl in front of me.

Girl? I really couldn't judge her age at all, but, being Dragaeran, she could be anywhere from a hundred to a thousand years old. Her clothing was black and gray, which I knew meant she was of House Jhereg. Her companion, who was now approaching us, was also a Jhereg. The three who had been at the other table were of the same House. Nothing of any significance there; it was mostly Jhereg, or an occasional Teckla (each Dragaeran House bears the name of one of our native creatures), who came into our restaurant.

Her companion stood behind her.

"Your name is Vlad?" she asked me.

I nodded.

"I'm Kiera," she said. I only nodded again. She smiled once more and turned to her companion. They paid their bill and left. I went back to help clean up after the murdered man—and my father.

"*Kiera*," I thought to myself, "*I won't forget you.*"

When the Phoenix guards arrived some time later, I was in back, and I heard my father telling them that, no, no one had seen what had happened, we'd all been in back. But I never forgot the feel of a knife blade, as it is laid across the back of the neck.

And for another instance . . .

I was sixteen, and walking alone through the jungles west of Adrilankha. The city was somewhat more than a hundred miles away, and it was night. I was enjoying the feeling of solitude, and even the slight fear within my middle as I considered the possibility that I might run into a wild dzur, or a lyorn, or even, Verra preserve me, a dragon.

The ground under my boots alternated between "crunch" and "squish." I didn't make any effort to move quietly; I hoped that the noise I made would frighten off any beast which would otherwise frighten *me* off. The logic of that escapes me now.

I looked up, but there was no break in the overcast that blankets the Dragaeran Empire. My grandfather had told me that there was no such orange-red sky above his Eastern homeland. He'd said that one could see stars at night, and I had seen them through his eyes. He could open his mind to me, and did, often. It was part of his method for teaching witchcraft; a method that brought me, at age sixteen, to the jungles.

The sky lit the jungle enough for me to pick my way. I ignored the scratches on face and arms from the foliage. Slowly, my stomach settled down from the nausea that had hit when I had done the teleport that brought me here.

There was a good touch of irony there, too, I realized—using a Dragaeran sorcery to bring me to where I could take the next stop in learning witchcraft. I hitched the pack on my back, and stepped into a clearing.

This one looked like it might do, I decided. There were heavy grasses for perhaps forty feet in what was, very roughly, a circle. I walked around it, slowly and carefully, my eyes straining to pick out details. All I needed now was to stumble into a chreotha's net.

But it was empty, my clearing. I went to the middle of it and set my pack down. I dug out a small black brazier, a bag of coals, a single black candle, a stick of incense, a dead teckla, and a few dried leaves. The leaves were from the gorynth plant, which is sacred to certain religions back East.

I carefully crumbled the leaves into a coarse powder; then I walked the perimeter of the clearing and sprinkled it before me as I went.

I returned to the middle. I sat there for a time and went through the ritual of relaxing each muscle of my body, until I was almost in a trance. With my body relaxed, my mind had no choice but to follow. When I was ready, I placed the coals in the brazier, slowly, one at a time. I held each one for a moment, feeling its shape and texture, letting the soot rub off on my palms. With witchcraft, everything can be a ritual. Even before the actual enchantment begins, the preparations should be made properly. Of course, one can always just cast one's mind out, concentrating on the desired result, and hope. The odds of success that way aren't very good. Somehow, when done the right way, witchcraft is so much more *satisfying* than sorcery.

When the coals were in the brazier and placed just so, I put the incense among them. Taking the candle, I stared long and hard at the wick, willing it to burn. I could, certainly, have used a flint, or even sorcery, to start it, but doing it this way helped put me into the proper frame of mind.

I guess the mood of the jungle night was conducive to witchcraft; it was only a few minutes before I saw smoke rising from the candle, followed quickly by a small flame. I was also pleased that I felt no trace of the mental exhaustion that accompanies the completion of a major spell. There had been a time, not so long before, when the lighting of a candle would have left me too weak even for psionic communication.

I'm learning, Grandfather.

I used the candle, then, to start the coals burning, and laid my will upon it to get a good fire going. When it was burning well, I planted the candle in the ground. The scent of the incense, pleasantly sweet, reached my nostrils. I closed my eyes. The circle of crushed gorynth leaves would prevent any stray animals from wandering by and disturbing me. I waited.

After a time—I don't know how long—I opened my eyes again. The coals were glowing softly. The scent of the incense filled the air. The sounds of the jungle did not penetrate past the boundaries of the clearing. I was ready.

I stared deep into the coals and, timing my breathing, I spoke the chant—very slowly, as I had been taught. As I said each word, I *cast* it, sending it out into the jungle as far and as clearly as I could. It was an old spell, my grandfather had said, and had been used in the East for thousands of years, unchanged.

I agonized over each word, each syllable, exploring it, letting my tongue and mouth linger over and taste each of the sounds, and willing my brain to full understanding of each of the thoughts I was sending. As each word left me, it was imprinted on my consciousness and seemed to be a living thing itself.

The last sounds died out very slowly in the jungle night, taking a piece of me with them.

Now, indeed, I felt exhausted. As always when doing a spell of this power, I had to guard myself against falling into a deep trance. I breathed evenly, and deeply. As if sleep-walking, I picked up the dead teckla, and moved it to the edge of the clearing, where I could see it when I was sitting. Then I waited.

I believe it was only a few minutes later that I heard the flapping of wings near me. I opened my eyes and saw a jhereg at the edge of the clearing, near the dead teckla, looking at me.

We watched each other for a while, and then it tentatively moved up and took a small bite from my offering.

It was of average size, if female; a bit large, if male. If my spell had worked, it would be female. Its wing span was about the distance from my shoulder to my wrist, and it was a bit less than that from its snakelike head to the tip of its tail. The forked tongue flicked out over the rodent, tasting each piece before ripping off a small chunk, chewing, and swallowing. It ate very slowly, watching me watching it.

When I saw that it was nearly done, I began to compose my mind for psionic contact, and to hope.

Soon, it came. I felt a small, questing thought within me. I allowed it to grow. It became distinct.

"What is it you want?" I "heard" with surprising clarity.

Now came the real test. If this jhereg had come as a result of my spell, it would be female, with a nest of eggs, and what I was about to suggest wouldn't send it into an attack rage. If it was just a jhereg who was passing by and saw some carrion lying free for the taking, I could be in trouble. I had with me a few herbs which might prevent me from dying of the jhereg's poison—but then, again, they might not.

"Mother," I thought back to it, as clearly as I could, *"I would like one of your eggs."*

It didn't attack me, and I picked up no feeling of puzzlement or outrage at the suggestion. Good. My spell had brought her, and she would be at least receptive to bargaining. I felt excitement growing in me and forced it down. I concentrated on the jhereg before me. This part was almost a ritual in itself, but not quite. It all depended on what the jhereg thought of me.

"What," she asked, *"do you offer it?"*

"I offer it long life," I answered. *"And fresh, red meat without struggle, and I offer it my friendship."*

The animal considered this for a while, then said, *"And what will you ask of it?"*

"I will ask for aid in my endeavors, such as are in its power. I will ask for its wisdom, and I will ask for its friendship."

For a time then, nothing happened. She stood there, above the skeletal remains of the teckla, and watched me. Then she said, *"I approach you."*

The jhereg walked up to me. Its claws were long and sharp, but more useful for running than for fighting. After a full meal, a jhereg will often find that it weighs too much to become airborne and so must run to escape its enemies.

She stood before me and looked closely into my eyes. It was odd to see intelligence in small, beady snake eyes, and to have nearly human-level communication with an animal whose brain was no larger than the first joint of my finger. It seemed, somehow, unnatural—which it was, but I didn't find that out for quite some time.

After a while, the jhereg "spoke" again.

"Wait here," she said. And she turned and spread her batlike wings. She had to run a step or two before taking off, and then I was alone again.

Alone . . .

I wondered what my father would say, if he were alive to say anything. He wouldn't approve, of course. Witchcraft was too "Eastern" for him, and he was too involved in trying to be a Dragaeran.

My father died when I was fourteen. I never knew my mother, but my father would occasionally mutter something about the "witch" he had married. Shortly before his death, he squandered everything he had earned in forty years of running a restaurant in an effort to become even more Dragaeran—he bought a title. Thus we became citizens, and found ourselves linked to the Imperial Orb. The link allowed us to use sorcery, a practice which my father encouraged. He found a sorceress from the Left Hand of the Jhereg who was willing to teach me, and he forbade me to practice witchcraft. Then he found a swordmaster who agreed to teach me Dragaeran-style swordsmanship. My father forbade me to study Eastern fencing.

But my grandfather was still around. One day I explained to him that, even when I was full-grown, I would be too short and too weak to be effective as a swordsman the way I was being taught, and that sorcery didn't interest me. He never offered a word of criticism about my father, but he began teaching me fencing and witchcraft.

When my father died, he was pleased that I was a skilled enough sorcerer to teleport myself; he didn't know that teleports made me physically ill. He didn't know how often I would use witchcraft to cover up the bruises left by Dragaeran punks, who would catch me alone and let me know what they thought of Easterners with pretensions. And he most certainly never knew that Kiera had been teaching me how to move quietly, how to walk through a crowd as if I weren't there. I would use these skills, too. I'd go out at night with a large stick, and I'd find one of my tormentors alone, and leave him with a few broken bones.

I don't know. Perhaps if I'd worked a little harder at sorcery I'd have been good enough to save my father. I just don't know.

After his death, it was easier to find time to study witchcraft and fencing, despite the added work of running a restaurant. I started to get quite good as a witch. Good enough, in fact, that my grandfather finally said that he couldn't teach me any more, and gave me instructions in how to take the next step on my own. The next step, of course, was . . .

She returned to the clearing, with a flapping of wings. This time she flew right up to me, landing in front of my crossed legs. In her right claw, a small egg was clutched. She extended it.

I forced down my excitement. It had worked! I held out my right hand, after making sure it was steady. The egg dropped into it. I was somewhat startled by its warmth. It was of a size that fit well into my palm. I carefully placed it inside my jerkin, next to my chest.

"*Thank you, mother,*" I thought to her. "*May your life be long, your food plentiful, and your children many.*"

"*And you,*" she said, "*long life and good hunting.*"

"*I am not a hunter,*" I told her.

"*You will be,*" she said. And then she turned from me,

spread her wings, and flew out from the clearing.

Twice in the following week I almost crushed the egg that I carried around next to my chest. The first time I got into a fight with a couple of jerks from the House of the Orca; and the second, I started to carry a box of spices against my chest while working in the restaurant.

The incidents shook me up, I decided to make sure that nothing happened again that would put the egg in danger. To protect myself against the former, I learned diplomacy. And to take care of the latter, I sold the restaurant.

Learning diplomacy was the more difficult task. My natural inclinations didn't run that way at all, and I had to be on my guard all the time. But, eventually, I found that I could be very polite to a Dragaeran who was insulting me. Sometimes I think it was that, more than anything else, which trained me to be successful later on.

Selling the restaurant was more of a relief than anything else. I had been running it on my own since my father died, and doing well enough to make a living, but somehow I never thought of myself as a restaurateur.

However, it did bring me up rather sharply against the problem of what I was going to do for a living—both immediately and for the rest of my life. My grandfather offered me a half-interest in his witchcraft business, but I was well aware that there was hardly enough activity to keep him going alone. I also had an offer from Kiera, who was willing to teach me her profession, but Easterner thieves don't get good prices from Dragaeran fences. Besides, my grandfather didn't approve of stealing.

I sold the place with the problem still unresolved, and lived off the proceeds for a while. I won't tell you what I got for it; I was still young. I moved into new quarters then, too, since the place above the restaurant was going to be taken by the new owner.

Also, I bought a blade. It was a rather light rapier, made to my measurements by a swordsmith of House Jhereg, who overcharged me shamefully. It was just strong enough to be able to counter the attacks of the heavier Dragaeran sword, but light enough to be useful for the ripostes by which an Eastern fencer can surprise a Dragaeran swordsman, who probably doesn't know anything beyond attack-defend-attack.

Future unresolved, I sat back and tended my egg.

* * *

About two months after I had sold the restaurant, I was sitting at a card table, doing a little low-stakes gambling at a place that allowed Easterners in. That night I was the only human there, and there were about four tables in action.

I heard raised voices from the table next to me and was about to turn around, when something crashed into my chair. I felt a momentary surge of panic as I almost crushed the egg against the edge of the table, and I stood up. The panic transformed itself to anger, and, without thinking, I picked up my chair and broke it over the head of the guy who'd fallen into me. He dropped like a hawk and lay still. The guy who'd pushed him looked at me as if deciding whether to thank me or attack me. I still had the chair leg in my hand. I raised it, and waited for him to do something. Then a hand gripped my shoulder and I felt a familiar coldness on the back of my neck.

"We don't need fighting in here, punk," said a voice behind my right ear. My adrenalin was up, and I almost turned around to smash the bastard across the face, despite the knife he held against me. But the training I'd been giving myself came to the fore, and I heard myself saying, evenly, "My apologies, good sir. I assure you it won't happen again." I lowered my right arm and dropped the chair leg. There was no point in trying to explain to him what had happened if he hadn't seen it—and even less if he had. When there's a problem, and an Easterner is involved, there is no question about who is at fault. I didn't move.

Presently I felt the knife being taken off of my neck.

"You're right," said the voice. "It won't happen again. Get out of here and don't come back."

I nodded once. I left my money on the table where it was, and walked out without looking back.

I settled down somewhat on my way home. The incident bothered me. I shouldn't have hit the guy at all, I decided. I had let my fear take over, and I reacted without thinking. This would never do.

As I climbed up the stairs to my apartment, my mind returned to the old problem of what I was going to do. I'd left almost a gold Imperial's worth of coins lying on the table, and that was half a week's rent. It seemed that my only talents were witchcraft and beating up Dragaerans. I didn't think that there was much of a market for either.

I opened the door and relaxed on the couch. I took out the egg, to hold it for a while as a means of soothing my nerves—and stopped. There was a small crack in it. It must have happened when I banged against the table, although I'd thought it had escaped harm.

It was then and there, at the age of sixteen, that I learned the meaning of anger. A sheet of white fire flashed through me, as I remembered the face of the Dragaeran who had pushed the other into me, killing my egg. I learned that I was capable of murder. I intended to seek out that bastard, and I was going to kill him. There was no question in my mind that he was a dead man. I stood up and headed for the door, still holding the egg—

—And stopped again.

Something was wrong. I had a feeling, which I couldn't pin down, that was getting through the barrier of my anger. What was it? I looked down at the egg, and suddenly understood in a burst of relief.

Although not consciously aware of it, I had somehow gotten a psionic link to the being inside the egg. I was feeling something through it, on some level, and that meant that my jhereg was still alive.

Anger drained from me as quickly as it had come, leaving me trembling. I went back into the middle of the room and set the egg down on the floor, as softly as I could.

I felt along the link, and identified the emotion I was getting from it: determination. Just raw, blind purpose. I had never been in contact with such singleness of aim. It was startling that a thing that small could produce such high-powered emotion.

I stepped away from it, I suppose from some unreasoning desire to "give it air," and watched. There was an almost inaudible "tap, tap," and the crack widened. Then, suddenly, the egg split apart, and this ugly little reptile was lying amid broken shell fragments. Its wings were tightly drawn up against it, and its eyes were closed. The wings were no larger than my thumb.

It—*It? He,* I suddenly knew. He tried to move; failed. Tried to move again, and got nowhere. I felt that I should be doing something, although I had no idea what. His eyes opened, but didn't seem to focus on anything. His head lay on the floor, then moved—pitifully.

I felt along my link to him, and now felt confusion and a little fear. I tried to send back feelings of warmth, protection, and all that good stuff. Slowly, I walked up and reached for him.

Surprisingly, he must have seen my motion. He obviously didn't connect the movement with the thoughts he was getting from me, however, for I felt a quick burst of fear, and he tried to move away. He failed and I picked him up— gingerly. I got two things for this: my first clear message from him and my first jhereg bite. The bite was too small, and the poison still too weak for it to affect me, but he was certainly in possession of his fangs. The message was amazingly distinct.

"*Mamma?*" he said.

Right. Mamma. I thought that over for a while, then tried to send a message back.

"*No, Daddy,*" I told him.

"*Mamma,*" he agreed.

He stopped struggling and seemed to settle down in my hand. I realized that he was exhausted and then realized that I was, too. Also, we were both hungry. At that point it hit me—What the hell was I going to feed him? All the time I'd been carrying him, I'd known that he was going to hatch someday, but it had never really sunk in that there was actually going to be a real, live jhereg there.

I carried him into the kitchen and started hunting around. Let's see . . . milk. We'll start with that.

I managed to get out a saucer and pour a little milk into it. I set it down on the counter and set the jhereg down next to it, his head actually in the saucer.

He lapped up a little and didn't seem to be having any trouble, so I scouted around a little more and finally came up with a small piece of hawk wing. I placed it in the saucer; he found it almost at once. He tore a piece off (he had teeth already—good) and began chewing. He chewed it for close to three minutes before swallowing, but when he did, it went down with no trouble. I relaxed.

After that, he seemed more tired than hungry, so I picked him up and carried him over to the couch. I lay down and placed him on my stomach. I dozed off shortly thereafter. We shared pleasant dreams.

* * *

The next day, someone came to my door and clapped, around mid-afternoon. When I opened the door, I recognized the fellow immediately. He was the one who'd been running the game the day before and had told me not to come back—with a knife held against the back of my neck for added emphasis.

I invited him in, being the curious type.

"Thank you," he said. "I am called Nielar."

"Please sit down, my lord. I'm Vlad Taltos. Wine?"

"Thank you, but no. I don't expect to be staying very long."

"As you wish."

I showed him to a seat and sat down on the couch. I picked up my jhereg and held him. Nielar arched his eyebrows, but didn't say anything.

"What can I do for you, then?" I asked.

"It has come to my attention," he said, "that I was, perhaps, in the wrong when I faulted you for the events of yesterday."

What? A Dragaeran apologizing to an Easterner? I wondered if the world was coming to an end. This was, to say the least, unprecedented in my experience. I mean, I was a 16-year-old human, and he was a Dragaeran who was probably close to a thousand.

"It's very kind of you to say so, my lord," I managed.

He brushed it off. "I will also add that I liked the way you handled yourself."

He did? I didn't. What was going on here?

"What I'm getting at," he continued, "is that I could use someone like you, if you have a mind to work for me. I understand that you don't have a job at the moment, and—" He finished with a shrug.

There were several thousand questions I wanted to ask him, starting with, "How did you find out so much about me and why do you care?" But I didn't know how to go about asking them, so I said, "With all respect, my lord, I can't see what kind of things I can do for you."

He shrugged again. "For one thing, preventing the kind of problems we had last night. Also, I need help from time to time collecting debts. That sort of thing. I normally have two people who assist me in running the place, but one of them had an accident last week, so I'm shorthanded just at the moment."

Something about the way he said "accident" struck me as strange, but I didn't take any time out to guess at what he meant.

"Again with all respect, my lord, it doesn't seem to me that an Easterner is going to look very imposing when standing up to a Dragaeran. I don't know that I—"

"I'm convinced that it won't be any problem," he said. "We have a friend in common, and she assured me that you'd be able to handle this kind of thing. As it happened, I owe her a favor or two, and she asked me to consider taking you on."

She? There wasn't any doubt, of course. Kiera was looking out for me again, bless her heart. Suddenly things were a lot clearer.

"Your pay," he continued, "would be four Imperials a week, plus ten percent of any outstanding debts you are sent to collect. Or, actually, half of that, since you'll be working with my other assistant."

Sheesh! Four gold a week? That was already more than I usually made while I was running the restaurant! And the commission, even if it were split with—

"Are you sure that this assistant of yours isn't going to object to working with a hum—an Easterner?"

His eyes narrowed. "That's my problem," he said. "And, as a matter of fact, I've already discussed it with Kragar, and he doesn't mind at all."

I nodded. "I'll have to think it over," I said.

"That's fine. You know where to reach me."

I nodded and showed him to the door, with pleasant words on all sides. I looked down at my jhereg as the door snicked shut. "Well," I asked him, "what do you think?"

The jhereg didn't answer, but then, I hadn't expected him to. I sat down to think and to wonder if the question of my future were being settled, or just put off. Then I put it aside. I had a more important question to settle—what was I going to name my jhereg?

I called him "Loiosh." He called me "Mamma." I trained him. He bit me. Slowly, over the course of the next few months, I developed an immunity to his poison. Even more slowly, over the course of years, I developed a partial immunity to his sense of humor.

As I stumbled into my line of work, Loiosh was able to help me. First a little, then a great deal. After all, who notices another jhereg flying about the city? The jhereg, on the other hand, can notice a great deal.

Slowly, as time went on, I grew in skill, status, friends, and experience.

And, just as his mother had predicted, I became a hunter.

The Cycle

Phoenix sinks into decay
Haughty dragon yearns to slay.
Lyorn growls and lowers horn
Tiassa dreams and plots are born.
Hawk looks down from lofty flight
Dzur stalks and blends with night.
Issola strikes from courtly bow
Tsalmoth maintains though none knows
   how.
Vallista rends and then rebuilds
Jhereg feeds on others' kills.
Quiet iorich won't forget
Sly chreotha weaves his net.
Yendi coils and strikes, unseen
Orca circles, hard and lean.
Frightened teckla hides in grass
Jhegaala shifts as moments pass
Athyra rules minds' interplay
Phoenix rise from ashes, gray.

1.

**"Success leads to stagnation;
Stagnation leads to failure."**

I slipped the poison dart into its slot under the right collar of my cloak, next to the lockpick. It couldn't go in too straight, or it would be hard to get to quickly. It couldn't go in at too much of an angle, or I wouldn't have room left for the garrot. Just so . . . there.

Every two or three days I change weapons. Just in case I have to leave something sticking in, on, or around a body. I don't want the item to have been on my person long enough for a witch to trace it back to me.

This could, I suppose, be called paranoia. There are damn few witches available to the Dragaeran Empire, and witchcraft isn't very highly thought of. It is not likely that a witch would actually be called in to investigate a murder weapon and try to trace it back to the murderer—in fact, so far as I know, it has never been done in the 243 years since the end of the Interregnum. But I believe in caution and attention to detail. That is one reason I'm still around to practice my paranoia.

I reached for a new garrot, let the old one drop into a box on the floor, and began working the wire into a tight coil.

"Do you realize, Vlad," said a voice, "that it's been over a year since anyone has tried to kill you?"

I looked up.

"Do you realize, Krager," I said, "that if you keep walking in here without my seeing you, I'll probably die of a heart attack one of these days and save them the trouble?"

He chuckled a little.

"No, I mean it, though," he continued. "More than a year. We haven't had any trouble since that punk—What was his name?"

"G'ranthar."

"Right, G'ranthar. Since he tried to start up a business down on Copper Lane, and you quashed it."

"All right," I said, "so things have been quiet. What of it?"

"Nothing, really," he said. "It's just that I can't figure out if it's a good sign or a bad sign."

I studied his 7-foot frame sitting comfortably facing me against the back wall of my office. Kragar was something of an enigma. He had been with me since I had joined the business side of House Jhereg and had never shown the least sign of being unhappy taking orders from an "Easterner." We'd been working together for several years now and had saved each other's lives often enough for a certain amount of trust to develop.

"I don't see how it can be a bad sign," I told him, slipping the garrot into its slot. "I've proven myself. I've run my territory with no trouble, paid off the right people, and there's only once when I've had even a little trouble with the Empire. I'm accepted now. Human or not," I added, enjoying the ambiguity of the phrase. "And remember that I'm known as an assassin more than anything else, so who would want to go out of his way to make trouble for me?"

He looked at me quizzically for a moment. "That's why you keep doing 'work,' isn't it?" he said thoughtfully. "Just to make sure no one forgets what you can do."

I shrugged. Kragar was being more direct about things than I liked, and it made me a bit uncomfortable. He sensed this, I guess, and quickly shifted back to the earlier topic. "I just think that all this peace and quiet means that you haven't been moving as fast as you could, that's all. I mean, look," he continued, "you've built up, from scratch, a spy ring that's one of the best in the Jhereg—"

"Not true," I cut in. "I don't really have a spy ring at all. There are a lot of people who are willing to give me information from time to time, and that's it. It isn't the same thing."

He brushed it aside. "It amounts to the same thing when

we're talking about information sources. And you have access to Morrolan's network, which *is* a spy ring in every sense of the word."

"Morrolan," I pointed out, "is not in the Jhereg."

"That's a bonus," he said. "That means you can find out things from people who wouldn't deal with you directly."

"Well—all right. Go on."

"Okay, so we have damn good free-lance people. And our own enforcers are competent enough to have anyone worried. I think we ought to be using what we have, that's all."

"Kragar," I said, fishing out a slim throwing dagger and replacing it in the lining of my cloak, "would you kindly tell me why it is that I should *want* someone to be after my hide?"

"I'm not saying that you should," said Kragar. "I'm just wondering if the fact that no one is means that we're slipping."

I slid a dagger into the sheath on the outside of my right thigh. It was a paper-thin, short throwing knife, small enough to be unnoticeable even when I sat down. The slit in my breeches was equally unnoticeable. A good compromise, I felt, between subtlety and speed of access.

"What you're saying is that you're getting bored."

"Well, maybe just a little. But that doesn't make what I said any less true."

I shook my head. "Loiosh, can you believe this guy? He's getting bored, so he wants to get me killed."

My familiar flew over from his windowsill and landed on my shoulder. He started licking my ear.

"Big help you are," I told him.

I turned back to Kragar. "No. If and when something comes up, we'll deal with it. In the meantime, I have no intention of hunting for dragons. Now, if that's all—"

I stopped. At long last, my brain started functioning. Kragar walks into my office, with nothing on his mind except the sudden realization that we should go out and stir up trouble? No, no. Wrong. I know him better than that.

"Okay," I said. "Out with it. What's happened now?"

"Happened?" he asked innocently. "Why should something have happened?"

"I'm an Easterner, remember?" I said sarcastically.

"We get feelings about these things."

A smile played lightly around his lips. "Nothing much," he said. "Only a message from the personal secretary to the Demon."

Gulp. "The Demon," as he was called, was one of five members of a loose-knit "council" which, to some degree, controlled the business activities of House Jhereg. The council, a collection of the most powerful people in the House, had never had an official existence until the Interregnum, but they'd been around long before then. They ran things to the extent of settling disputes within the organization and making sure that things didn't get so messy that the Empire had to step in. Since the Interregnum they had been a little more than that—they'd been the group that had put the House back together after the Empire began to function again. Now they existed with clearly defined duties and responsibilities, and everyone who did anything at all in the organization gave part of the profits to them.

The Demon was generally acknowledged to be the number-two man in the organization. The last time I had met with someone that high up was in the middle of a war with another Jhereg, and the council member I'd spoken to had let me know that I'd better find a way to get things settled, or he would. I have no pleasant memories of that meeting.

"What does he want?" I asked.

"He wants to meet with you."

"Oh, crap. Double crap. Dragon dung. Any ideas why?"

"No. He did pick a meeting place in our territory, for whatever that's worth."

"It isn't worth a whole lot," I said. "Which place?"

"The Blue Flame restaurant," said Kragar.

"The Blue Flame, eh? What does that bring to mind?"

"I seem to recall that you 'worked' there twice."

"That's right. It's a real good place for killing someone. High booths, wide aisles, low lighting, and in an area where people like to mind their own business."

"That's the place. He set it up for two hours past noon, tomorrow."

"*After* noon?"

Kragar looked puzzled. "That's right. After noon. That

means when most people have eaten lunch, but haven't eaten supper yet. You must have come across the concept before."

I ignored his sarcasm. "You're missing the point," I said, flipping a shuriken into the wall next to his ear.

"Funny, Vlad—"

"Quiet. Now, how do you go about killing an assassin? Especially someone who's careful not to let his movements fall into any pattern?"

"Eh? You set up a meeting with him, just like the Demon is doing."

"Right. And, of course, you do everything you can to make him suspicious, don't you?"

"Uh, maybe *you* do. *I* don't."

"Damn right you don't! You make it sound like a simple business meeting. And that means you arrange to buy the guy a meal. And that means you *don't* arrange it for some time like two hours past noon."

He was quiet for a while, as he tried to follow my somewhat convoluted logic. "Okay," he said at last, "I agree that this is somewhat abnormal. Now, why?"

"I'm not sure. Tell you what; find out everything you can about him, bring it back here, and we'll try to figure it out. It might not mean anything, but . . ."

Kragar smiled and pulled a small notebook from inside his cloak. He began reading. "The Demon," he said. "True name unknown. Young, probably under eight hundred. No one heard of him before the Interregnum. He emerged just after it by personally killing two of the three members of the old council who survived the destruction of the city of Dragaera and the plagues and invasions. He built an organization from what was left, and helped make the House profitable again. As a matter of fact, Vlad," he said, looking up, "it seems that it was his idea to allow Easterners to buy titles in the Jhereg."

"Now that's interesting," I said. "So I have him to thank for my father being able to squander the profits from forty years of work in order to be spat upon as a Jhereg, in addition to being spat upon as an Easterner. I'll have to find some way to thank him for that."

"I might point out," said Kragar, "that if your father hadn't bought that title, you wouldn't have had the chance to join the business end of the House."

"Maybe. But go on."

"There isn't much more to tell. He didn't exactly make it to the top; it would be more accurate to say that he made it somewhere, and then declared the top to be where he was. You have to remember that things were pretty much a mess back then.

"And of course, he was tough enough, and good enough to make it stick. As far as I can tell, he hasn't had any serious threats to his power since he got there. He has a habit of spotting potential challengers while they're still weak, and getting rid of them. In fact—do you remember that fellow, Leonyar, we took out last year?"

I nodded.

"Well, I think that may have come indirectly from the Demon. We'll never know for sure, of course, but as I said: he likes to get rid of potential problems early."

"Yeah. Do you think he could see *me* as a 'potential problem?' "

Kragar thought that over. "I suppose he might, but I don't quite see why. You've been staying out of trouble, and, as I said before, you haven't really been moving very fast since the first couple of years. The only time there's been any problem was the business with Laris last year, and I think everyone knows that he forced it on you."

"I hope so. Does the Demon do 'work'?"

Kragar shrugged. "We can't say for sure, but it looks like he does. We know that he used to. As I said, he took out those two council members personally, back when he was getting started."

"Great. So in addition to whatever he could have set up, he might be planning to do the job himself."

"I suppose he could."

"But I still can't figure out—look, Kragar, with someone like the Demon, something like this wouldn't happen by accident, would it?"

"Something like—?"

"Like carefully arranging a meeting in just such a way as to arouse my suspicions."

"No, I don't think he—What is it?"

I guess he caught the look on my face, which must have been simply precious. I shook my head. "That's it, of course."

"What," he asked, "is what?"

"Kragar, arrange for three bodyguards for me, okay?"

"Bodyguards? But—"

"Make them busboys or something. You won't have any trouble; I own half interest in the place. Which, I might add, I'm sure the Demon is aware of."

"Don't you think he'll catch on?"

"Of *course* he'll catch on. That's the point. He knows that I'm going to be nervous about meeting him, so he deliberately set up the meeting with an irregularity to make me suspicious, so I'll have an excuse to have protection there. He's going out of his way to say, 'Go ahead and do what you have to, to feel safe, I won't be offended.' "

I shook my head again. I was starting to get dizzy. "I hope I don't ever have to go up against the son-of-a-bitch. He's devious."

"*You're* devious, boss," said Kragar. "I sometimes think you know Dragaerans better than other Dragaerans do."

"I do," I said flatly. "And that's because I'm not one."

He nodded. "Okay, three bodyguards. Our own people, or free-lance?"

"Make one of them our own, and hire the other two. There isn't any need to rub his nose in it, in case he recognizes our people."

"Right."

"You know, Kragar," I said thoughtfully, "I'm not real happy about this. He must know me well enough to know that I'd figure out what he was doing, which means this could be a setup after all." I held up my hand as he started to speak. "No, I'm not saying that I think it *is,* just that it could be."

"Well, you could always tell him that you can't make it?"

"Sure. Then, if he isn't planning to kill me now, he'd be sure to after that."

"Probably," admitted Kragar. "But what else can you do?"

"I can bitch a lot and go meet with him. Okay, that's tomorrow. Anything else going on?"

"Yeah," he said. "Some Teckla got mugged the night before last, a couple of blocks from here."

I cursed. "Hurt bad?"

Kragar shook his head. "A fractured jaw and a couple of

bruises. Nothing serious, but I thought you'd like to know."

"Right. Thanks. I take it you haven't found the guy who did it?"

"Not yet."

"Well, find him."

"It'll cost."

"Screw the cost. It'll cost more if all our customers get scared away. Find the guy and make an example of him."

Kragar raised an eyebrow.

"No," I said, "not that much of an example. . . . And find a healer for that Teckla—on us. I take it he was a customer?"

"Everyone around here is a customer, one way or another."

"Yeah. So pay for a healer and reimburse him. How much did the guy get, by the way?"

"Almost two Imperials. Which could have been the Dragon Treasury, to hear him tell it."

"I suppose so. Tell you what: Why don't you have the victim come up and see me, and I'll pay him back personally and give him a talk about crime in the streets and how bad I feel, as a fellow citizen, of course, about what happened to him. Then he can go home and tell all his friends what a nice guy Uncle Vlad the Easterner is, and maybe we'll even pull in some new business out of the deal."

"Sheer genius, boss," said Kragar.

I snorted. "Anything else?"

"Nothing important, I guess. I'll go arrange for your protection tomorrow."

"Fine. And make it good people. As I say, this has me worried."

"Paranoia, boss."

"Yep. Paranoid and proud."

He nodded and left. I wrapped Spellbreaker around my right wrist. The two-foot length of gold chain was the one weapon that I didn't change, since I had no intention of ever leaving it behind me. As its name implied, it broke spells. If I was going to be hit with a magical attack (unlikely, even if this *was* a setup), I'd want it ready. I flexed my arm and tested the weight. Good.

I turned to Loiosh, who was still resting comfortably

on my right shoulder. He'd been strangely silent during the conversation.

"*What's the matter?*" I asked him psionically. "*Bad feelings about the meeting tomorrow?*"

"*No, bad feelings about having a Teckla in the office. Can I eat him, boss? Can I? Huh? Huh?*"

I laughed and went back to changing weapons with an all-new enthusiasm.

2.

"There is no substitute for good manners—except fast reflexes."

The Blue Flame is on a short street called Copper Lane just off Lower Kieron Road. I arrived fifteen minutes early and carefully selected a seat that put my back to the door. I'd decided that if Loiosh, working along with the people we had planted here, couldn't give me enough warning, the difference it would make if I were facing the door probably wouldn't matter. This way, in case the meeting was legitimate, which I strongly suspected it was, I was showing the Demon that I trusted him and negating any feelings of "disrespect" he might get from seeing that I had brought protection. Loiosh was perched on my left shoulder, watching the door.

I ordered a white wine and waited. I spotted one of my enforcers busing dishes, but couldn't identify either of the free-lancers. Good. If I couldn't spot them, there was a good chance that the Demon couldn't. I sipped my wine slowly, still chuckling slightly over the meeting I'd had earlier with the Teckla (what was his name?) who'd been mugged. It had gone well enough, though I had had to work to avoid bursting out laughing from my trusty jhereg familiar's constant psionic appeals of "Aw, c'mon, boss. *Please* can't I eat him?" I have a nasty familiar.

I kept a tight control on the amount of wine I was drinking—the last thing I needed right now was to be slowed down. I flexed my right ankle, feeling the hilt of one of my boot-knives press reassuringly against my calf. I nudged the table an inch or so away from me, since I was sitting in a booth and couldn't position my chair. I noted the locations of the spices on the table, as objects to throw, or things to get in the way. And I waited.

Five minutes after the hour, according to the Imperial Clock, I received a warning from Loiosh. I set my right arm crosswise on the table, so that my hand was two inches away from my left sleeve. That was as close as I wanted to come to holding a weapon. A rather large guard-type appeared in front of my table, nodded to me, and stepped back. A well-dressed Dragaeran in gray and black approached and sat down opposite me.

I waited for him to speak. It was his meeting, so it was up to him to set the tone; also, my mouth was suddenly very dry.

"You are Vladimir Taltos?" he asked, pronouncing my name correctly.

I nodded and took a sip of wine. "You are the Demon?"

He nodded. I offered wine and we drank to each other's health; I wouldn't swear to the sincerity of the toast. My hand was steady as I held the glass. Good.

He sipped his wine delicately, watching me. All of his motions were slow and controlled. I thought I could see where a dagger was hidden up his right sleeve; I noticed a couple of bulges where other weapons might be in his cloak. He probably noticed the same in mine. He was, indeed, young for his position. He looked to be somewhere between eight hundred and a thousand, which is thirty-five or forty to a human. He had those eyes that never seemed capable of opening to more than slits. Like mine, say. Kragar was right; this was an assassin.

"We understand," he said, swirling the wine in his glass, "that you do 'work.' "

I kept the surprise off my face. Was I about to be offered a contract? From the Demon? Why? Perhaps this was just an effort to get me off my guard. I couldn't figure it. If he really wanted me for something, he should have gone through about half a dozen intermediaries.

"I'm afraid not," I told him, measuring my words. "I don't get involved with that kind of thing."

Then, "I have a friend who does."

He looked away for a moment, then nodded. "I see.

Could you put me in touch with this 'friend?' "

"He doesn't get out much," I explained. "I can get a message to him, if you like."

He nodded, still not looking at me. "I suppose your 'friend' is an Easterner, too?"

"As a matter of fact, he is. Does it matter?"

"It might. Tell him we'd like him to work for us, if he's available. I hope he has access to your information sources. I suspect this job will require all of them."

Oh, ho! So that's why he'd come to me! He knew that my ways of obtaining information were good enough that even he would have trouble matching them. I allowed myself a little bit of cautious optimism. This just might be legitimate. On the other hand, I still couldn't see why he'd come personally.

There were several questions I very badly wanted to ask him, such as, "Why me?" and "Why you?" But I couldn't approach them directly. The problem was, he wasn't going to give me any more information until he had a certain amount of commitment from me—and I didn't feel like giving him that commitment until I knew more.

"Suggestions, Loiosh?"

"You could ask him who the target is."

"That's exactly what I don't want to do. That commits me."

"Only if he answers."

"What makes you think he won't answer?"

"I'm a jhereg, remember?" he said sarcastically. *"We get feelings about these things."*

One of Loiosh's great skills is throwing my own lines back at me. The damnable thing about it was that he might be simply telling the truth.

The Demon remained politely silent during the psionic conversation—either because he didn't notice it, or out of courtesy. I suspected the latter.

"Who?" I said aloud.

The Demon turned back to me, then, and looked at me for what seemed to be a long time. Then he turned his face to the side again.

"Someone who's worth sixty-five thousand gold to us," he said.

This time I couldn't keep my expression from showing.

Sixty-five thousand! That was . . . let me see . . . over thirty, no, *forty* times the standard fee! For that kind of money I could build my wife the castle she'd been talking about! Hell, I could build it twice! I could bloody well retire! I could—

"Who are you after?" I asked again, forcing my voice to stay low and even. "The Empress?"

He smiled a little. "Is your friend interested?" He was no longer pronouncing the quotation marks, I noted.

"Not in taking out the Empress."

"Don't worry. We aren't expecting Mario." As it happened, that was the wrong thing for him to say just then. It started me thinking . . . for the kind of gold he was talking about, he *could* hire Mario. Why wouldn't he?

I thought of one reason right away: The someone who had to be taken out was so big that whoever did the job would have to be eliminated himself, afterwards. They would know better than to try that on Mario; but with me, well, yes. I wasn't so well protected that I couldn't be disposed of by the resources the Demon had at his disposal.

It fit in another way, too: It explained why the Demon had shown up personally. If he was, in fact, planning to have me take a fall after doing the job, he wouldn't care that I knew that he was behind it and wouldn't want a lot of other people in his organization to know. Hiring someone to do something and then killing him when he does it is not strictly honorable—but it's been done.

I pushed the thought aside for the moment. What I wanted was a clear idea of what was going on. I had a suspicion, yes; but I wasn't a Dzur. I needed more than a suspicion to take any action.

So the question remained, who was it that the Demon wanted me to nail for him? Someone big enough that the man who did it had to go too. . . . A high noble? Possible—but why? Who had crossed the Demon?

The Demon was sharp, he was careful, he didn't make many enemies, he was on the council, he—wait! The council? Sure, that had to be it. Either someone on the council was trying to get rid of him, or he finally decided that being number two wasn't enough. If it was the latter, sixty-five thousand wasn't enough. I knew who I'd be going after, and he was as close to untouchable as it is possible to get. In either case, it didn't sound hopeful.

What else could it be? Someone high up in the Demon's organization suddenly deciding to open his mouth to the Empire? Damn unlikely! The Demon wouldn't make the kind of mistakes that led to that. No, it had to be someone on the council. And that, as I'd guessed, would mean that whoever did the job might have a lot of trouble staying alive after: he'd have too much information on the fellow who had given him the job and he'd know too much about internal squabbles on the council.

I started to shake my head, but the Demon held his hand up. "It isn't what you think," he said. "The only reason we aren't trying to get hold of Mario is because there have to be certain conditions attached to the job—conditions that Mario wouldn't accept. Nothing more than that."

I felt a brief flash of anger, but pushed it back down before it showed. What the hell made him think he could stick me with conditions that Mario wouldn't accept? (Sixty-five thousand gold, that's what.) I thought a little longer. The problem was, of course, that the Demon had a reputation for honesty. He wasn't known as the type who'd hire an assassin and then set him up. On the other hand, if they were talking about sixty-five thousand, things were desperate in some fashion already. He could be desperate enough to do a lot of things he otherwise wouldn't do.

The figure sixty-five thousand gold Imperials kept running through my head. However, one other figure kept meeting it: one hundred and fifty gold. That's the average cost of a funeral.

"I think," I told him at last, "that my friend would not be interested in taking out a member of the council."

He nodded in appreciation of the way my mind worked, but said, "You're close. An ex-member of the council."

What? More and more riddles.

"I hadn't realized," I said slowly, "that there was more than one way to leave the council." And, if the guy had taken that way, they certainly didn't need my services.

"Neither had we," he said. "But Mellar found a way."

At last! A name! Mellar, Mellar, let me see . . . right. He was awfully tough. He had a good, solid organization, brains, and, well, enough muscle and resources to get and hold a position on the council. But why had the Demon told me? Was he planning to kill me after all if I turned him down? Or was he taking a chance on being able to convince me?

"What way is that?" I asked, sipping my wine.

"To take nine million gold in council operating funds and disappear."

I almost choked.

By the sacred balls of the Imperial Phoenix! Absconding with Jhereg funds? With *council* funds? My head started hurting.

"When—when did this happen?" I managed.

"Yesterday." He was watching the expression on my face. He nodded grimly. "Nervy bastard, isn't he?"

I nodded back. "You know," I said, "you're going to have one bitch of a time keeping this quiet."

"That's right," he said. "We just aren't going to be able to for very long." For a moment his eyes went cold, and I began to understand how the Demon had gotten his name. "He took everything we had," he said tightly. "We all have our own funds, of course, and we've been using them in the investigation. But on the kind of scale we're working on, we can't keep it up long."

I shook my head. "Once this gets out—"

"He'd better be dead," the Demon finished for me. "Or every two-silverpiece thief in the Empire is going to think he can take us. And one of them will do it, too."

Something else hit me at that point. I realized that, for one thing, I could accept this job quite safely. Once Mellar was dead, it wouldn't matter if word got out what he'd tried. However, if I turned it down, I was suddenly a big risk and, shortly thereafter, I suspected, a small corpse.

Once again, the Demon seemed to guess what I was thinking.

"No," he said flatly. He leaned forward, earnestly. "I assure you that if you turn me down, nothing will happen to you. I know that we can trust you—that's one reason we came to you."

I wondered briefly if he were reading my mind. I decided that he wasn't. An Easterner is not an easy person to mind-probe, and I doubted that he could do it without my being aware of it. And I was *sure* he couldn't do it without Loiosh noticing.

"Of course, if you turn us down and then let something slip . . ."

His voice trailed off. I suppressed a shudder.

I did some more hard thinking. "It would seem to me," I said, "that this has to be done soon."

He nodded. "And that's why we can't get Mario. There's no way we can rush him."

"And you think you can rush my friend?"

He shrugged. "I think we're paying for it."

I had to agree with that. There was, at least, no time limit. But I had never before accepted "work" without the understanding that I had as much time as I needed. How much, I wondered, would it throw me off to have to hurry?

"Do you have *any* idea where he went?"

"We strongly suspect that he headed out East. At least, if I were pulling something like this, that's where I'd go."

I shook my head. "That doesn't make sense. Dragaerans out East are treated about the same as Easterners are treated here—worse, if anything. He'd be considered, if you'll pardon the expression, a demon. He'd stand out like a Morganti weapon in the Imperial Palace."

He smiled. "True enough, but we have the fewest resources there, so it would take a while for word to get back to us. Also, we've had the best sorceresses from the Left Hand looking for him since we found out what happened, and we can't find him."

I shrugged. "He could have put up a block against tracing."

"He definitely has done that."

"Well, then—"

He shook his head. "You have no idea of the kind of power we're pouring into this. We could break down any block he could put up, no matter how long he's been planning it, or who the sorcerer is who put the block up. If he was anywhere within a hundred miles of Adrilankha we'd have broken it by now, or at least found a general area that we couldn't penetrate."

"So, you can guarantee that he isn't within a hundred miles of the city?"

"Right. Now, it's possible that he's in the jungle to the west, in which case we'll probably find him within the next day or two. But I'd guess he'd bolted for the East."

I nodded slowly. "So you came to me, figuring that I can operate out there easier than a Dragaeran."

"That's right. And, of course, we know that you have an extremely formidable information network."

"My information network," I said, "doesn't extend to the East." That was almost true. My sources back in my ancestral homeland were few and far between. Still, there wasn't any reason to let the Demon in on everything I had.

"Well, then," he said, "there's an additional bonus for you. By the time this is over, you'll probably have something where you didn't before."

I smiled at his riposte, and nodded a little.

"And so," I said, "you want my friend to go out to wherever Mellar is hiding and get your gold back?"

"That would be nice," he admitted. "But it's secondary. The main thing is to make sure that no one gets the idea that it's safe to steal from us. Even Kiera, bless her sweet little fingers, hasn't tried *that*. I'll add that I take this whole thing very personally. And I will feel very warmly toward whomever does this particular little job for me."

I sat back, and thought for a long time, then. The Demon was politely silent. Sixty-five thousand gold! And, of course, having the Demon owe me a favor was better than a poke in the eye with a Morganti dagger by all means.

"Morganti?" I asked.

He shrugged. "It has to be permanent, however you want to do it. If you happen to destroy his soul in the process, I won't be upset. But it isn't necessary. Just so that he ends up dead, with no chance of anyone revivifying him."

"Yeah. You say that the Left Hand is working on locating him?"

"Right. The best they've got."

"That can't be helping your security any."

He shrugged. "They know who; they don't know why. As far as they're concerned, it's a personal matter between Mellar and me. You may not realize it, but the Left Hand tends to take less of an interest in what the council is doing than the lowest pimp on the streets. I'm not worried about security from that end. But if this goes on too long, word will get out that I'm looking for Mellar, and someone who notices that the council is having financial trouble will start counting the eggs."

"I suppose. Okay, I suspect that my friend will be willing to take this on. He's going to need whatever information you have about Mellar as a starting point."

The Demon held his hand out to the side. The body-guard, who had been standing politely (and safely) out of earshot, placed a rather formidable-looking sheaf of papers in it. The Demon handed these over to me. "It's all there," he said.

"All?"

"As much as we know. I'm afraid it may not be as much as you'd like."

"Okay." I briefly ruffled through the papers. "You've been busy," I remarked.

He smiled.

"If there's anything else I need," I said, "I'll get back to you."

"Fine. It should be obvious, but your friend is going to have all the help he needs on this one."

"In that case, I presume you're going to continue with your searching? You have access to better sorcerers than my friend has; you could keep going on that front."

"I intend to," he said drily. "And I should also mention something else. If we happen to run into him before you do and see an opportunity, we're going to take him ourselves. I mean no disrespect by that, but I think you can understand that this is a rather special situation."

"I can't say I like it," I said, "but I understand." I wasn't at all happy about it, in fact. Sure, my fee would be safe, but things like that can cause complications—and complications scare me.

I shrugged. "I think you can understand, too—and *I* mean no disrespect by *this*—that if some Teckla gets in the way, and my friend thinks the guy's going to bungle it, my friend will have to put him down."

The Demon nodded.

I sighed. Communication was such a fine thing.

I raised my glass. "To friends," I said.

He smiled and raised his. "To friends."

3·

"Everyone is a predator."

"Work" comes in three variations, each with its own effect, purpose, price—and penalty.

The simplest is not used often, but happens enough to have acquired the term "standard." The idea is that you want to warn an individual away from a certain course of action, or toward another. In this case, for a fee that starts at fifteen hundred gold and goes up from there depending on how hard the target is, an assassin will arrange for the selected individual to become dead. What happens after that doesn't much matter to the killer, but as often as not the body will eventually be found by a friend or relative, who may or may not be willing and able to have the person revivified.

Revivification costs heavily—up to four thousand gold for difficult cases. Even the easiest takes an expert sorcerer to perform, and it is never a sure thing.

In other words, the victim will wake up, if he does, with the knowledge that there is someone out there—and he usually knows who—who doesn't really care if he lives or dies and is willing to expend at least fifteen hundred gold Imperials to prove this.

This is rather chilling knowledge. It happened to me once, when I started pushing into the territory of a fellow who was just the least bit tougher than I was. I got the message, all right. I knew just what he was telling me, without any room for mistakes. "I can take you any time I want, punk, and I'd do it, too, only you aren't worth more than fifteen hundred gold to dispose of."

And it worked. I was returned to life by Sethra Lavode, after Kiera found my body lying in a gutter. I backed off. I've never bothered the guy since, either. Of course, someday. . . .

Now you should understand, to begin with, that there are some rather strict laws concerning the circumstances under which one person may legally kill another, and they involve things like "authorized dueling area," "Imperial witnesses," and the like. Assassination just never seems to qualify as a legal taking of a life. This brings us to the biggest single problem with the kind of job I've just mentioned—you have to be sure that the victim doesn't get a look at your face. If he were to be returned to life and he went to the Empire (strictly against Jhereg custom, but . . .), the assassin could find himself arrested for murder. There would follow an inquisition and the possibility of conviction. A conviction of murder will bring a permanent end to an assassin's career. When the Empire holds an execution, they burn the body to make sure no one gets hold of it to revivify it.

At the other extreme from simply killing someone and leaving his body to be found and, possibly, revivified, is a special kind of murder which is almost never done. To take an example, let us say that an assassin whom you have hired is caught by the Empire and tells them who hired him, in exchange for his worthless soul.

What do you do? You've already marked him as dead—no way the Empire can protect him enough to keep a top-notch assassin out. But that isn't enough; not for someone low enough to talk to the Empire about you. So what do you do? You scrape together, oh, at least six thousand gold, and you arrange to meet with the best assassin you can find—an absolute top-notch professional—and give him the name of the target, and you say, "Morganti."

Unlike any other kind of situation, you will probably have to explain your reasons. Even the coldest, most vicious assassin will find it distasteful to use a weapon that will destroy a person's soul. Chances are he won't do it unless you have a damn good reason why it has to be done that way and no other. There are times, though, when nothing else will do. I've worked that way twice. It was fully justified both times—believe me, it was.

However, just as the Jhereg makes exceptions in the cases where a Morganti weapon is to be used, so does the Empire. They suddenly forget all about their rules against the torture of suspects and forced mind-probes. So there are very real risks here. When they've finished with you, whatever is left is given to a Morganti blade, as a form of poetic justice, I suppose.

There is, however, a happy middle ground between Morganti killings and fatal warnings: the bread and butter of the assassin.

If you want someone to go and you don't want him coming back, and you're connected to the organization (I don't know any assassin stupid enough to "work" for anyone outside the House), you should figure that it will cost you at least three thousand gold. Naturally, it will be higher if the person is especially tough, or hard to get to, or important. The highest I've ever heard of anyone being paid is, well, excuse me, sixty-five thousand gold. Ahem. I expect that Mario Greymist was paid a substantially higher fee for killing the old Phoenix Emperor just before the Interregnum, but I've never heard a figure quoted.

And so, my fledgling assassins, you are asking me how you make sure that a corpse remains properly a corpse, eh? Without using a Morganti weapon, whose problems we've just discussed? I know of three methods and have used all of them, and combinations, during my career.

First, you can make sure that the body isn't found for three full days, after which time the soul will have departed. The most common method for doing this is to pay a moderate fee, usually around three to five hundred gold, to a sorceress from the Left Hand of the Jhereg, who will guarantee that the body is undisturbed for the requisite period. Or, of course, you can arrange to secrete the body yourself—risky, and not at all pleasant to be seen carrying a body around. It causes talk.

The second method, if you aren't so greedy, is to pay these same sorceresses something closer to a thousand, or even fifteen hundred of your newly acquired gold, and they will make sure that, no matter who does what, the body will never be revivified. Or, third, you can make the body unrevivifiable: burn it, chop off the head . . . use your imagination.

For myself, I'll stick with the methods I developed in the course of my first couple of years of working: hours of planning, split-second timing, precise calculations, and a single, sharp, accurate knife.

I haven't bungled one yet.

Kragar was waiting for me when I returned. I filled him in on the conversation and the result. He looked judicious.

"It's too bad," he remarked when I had finished, "that you *don't* have a 'friend' you can unload this one on."

"What do you mean, friend?" I said.

"I—" he looked startled for a minute, then grinned.

"No, you don't," he said. "You took the job; you do it."

"I know, I know. But what did you mean? Don't you think we're up to it?"

"Vlad, this guy is *good*. He was on the *council*. You think you can just walk up to him and put a dagger into his left eye?"

"I never meant to imply that I thought it was going to be easy. So, we have to put a little work into it—"

"A little!"

"All right, a lot. So we put a lot of work into the setup. I told you what I'm getting for it, and you know what your percentage is. What's happened to your innate sense of greed, anyway?"

"I don't need one," he said. "You've got enough for both of us."

I ignored that.

"The first step," I told him, "is locating the guy. Can you come up with some method for figuring out where he might be hiding?"

Kragar looked thoughtful. "Tell you what, Vlad; just for variety this time, *you* do all the setup work, and when you're done, *I'll* take him out. What do you say?"

I gave him the most eloquent look I could manage.

He sighed. "All right, all right. You say he's got sorcery blocked out for tracing?"

"Apparently. And the Demon is using the best there is to look for him that way, in any case."

"Hmmm. Are we working under the assumption that the

Demon is right, that he's out East somewhere?''

"Good point." I thought about it. "No. Let's not start out making any assumptions at all. What we *know*, because the Demon guaranteed it, is that Mellar's nowhere within a hundred-mile radius of Adrilankha. For the moment, let's assume that he could be anywhere outside of that."

"Which includes a few thousand square miles of jungle."

"True."

"You aren't going out of your way to make my life easy, are you?"

I shrugged. Kragar was thoughtfully silent for a while.

"What about witchcraft, Vlad? Do you think you can trace him with that? I would doubt that he thought to protect himself against it, even if he could."

"Witchcraft? Let me think—I don't know. Witchcraft really isn't very good for that sort of thing. I mean, I could probably find him, to the extent of getting an image and a psionic fix, but there isn't any way of going from there to a hard location, or teleport coordinates, or anything really useful. I guess we could use it to make sure he's alive, but I suspect we can safely assume that, anyway."

Kragar nodded, and looked thoughtful. "Well," he said after a time, "if you have any kind of psionic fix at all, maybe you can come up with something Daymar could use to find out where he is. He's good at that kind of thing."

Now there was an idea. Daymar was strange, but psionics were his specialty. If anyone could do it, he could.

"I'm not sure we want to get that many people involved in this," I said. "The Demon wouldn't be real happy about the number of potential leaks we'd have to generate. And Daymar isn't even a Jhereg."

"So don't mention it to the Demon," said Kragar. "The thing is, we have to find him, right? And we know we can trust Daymar, right?"

"Well—"

"Oh, come on, Vlad. If you ask him not to talk about it, he won't. Besides, where else can you get expert help, on that level, without paying a thing for it? Daymar enjoys showing off; he'd do it for free. What can we lose?"

I raised my eyebrow and looked at him.

"There is that," he admitted. "But I think the risk involved in telling Daymar as much as we have to tell him is pretty damn small. Especially when you consider what we're getting for it."

"If he can do it."

"I think he can," said Kragar.

"All right," I said, "I'm sold. Quiet a minute while I figure out what I'm going to need."

I ran through, in my mind, what I was going to have to do to locate Mellar, and what I'd have to do so that Daymar could trace him afterwards. I wished I knew more about how Daymar did things like that, but I could make a reasonable guess. It seemed that it would be a pretty straight-forward spell, which really should work if Mellar had no blocks against witchcraft.

I built up a mental list of what I'd need. Nothing out of the ordinary; I already had everything except for one small matter.

"Kragar, put word out on the street that I'd like to arrange to see Kiera. At her convenience, of course."

"Okay. Any preference on where you meet?"

"No, just some—wait!" I interrupted myself, and thought for a minute. In my office, I had witchcraft protections and alarms. I knew these were hard to beat, and I wasn't happy about taking any chances at all of this information leaking out. The Demon would be upset, anyway, if he knew that I was dealing with Kiera. I didn't really like the idea of having one of his people see me talking with her in some public place. On the other hand, Kiera was . . . well, Kiera. Hmmm. Tough question.

Hell with it, I decided. I'd just shock the staff a little. It'd be good for them. "I'd like to meet her here, in my office, if that's all right with her."

Kragar looked startled and seemed about to say something, but changed his mind, I guess, when he realized that I'd just gone over all of the objections myself. "All right," he said. "Now about Daymar. You know what kind of problems we have reaching him; do you want me to figure out a way?"

"No, thanks. I'll take care of it."

"All by yourself? My goodness!"

"No, I'm going to get Loiosh to help. There, feel better?"

He snickered and left. I got up and opened the window.

"Loiosh," I thought to my familiar, *"find Daymar."*

"As Your Majesty requests," he answered.

"Feel free to save the sarcasm."

A telepathic giggle is an odd thing to experience. Loiosh flew out the window.

I sat down again and stared off blankly for a while. How many times had I been in this position? Just at the beginning of a job, with no idea of where it was going, or how it would get there. Nothing, really, except an image of how it should end; as always, with a corpse. How many times? It isn't really a rhetorical question. This would be the forty-second assassination I'd done. My first thought was that it was going to be somewhat different than the others, at some level, in some way, to some degree. I have clear memories of each one. The process I go through before I do the job is such that I can't forget any of them—I have to get to know them too well. This would certainly be a problem if I were given to nightmares.

The fourth one? He was the button man who would always order a fine liqueur after dinner and leave half the bottle instead of a tip. The twelfth was a small-time muscle who liked to keep his cash in the largest denominations he could. The nineteenth was a sorcerer who carried a cloth around with him to polish his staff with—which he did constantly. There is always something distinct about them. Sometimes it is something I can use; more often it is just something that sticks out in my memory. When you know someone well enough, he becomes an individual no matter how hard you try to think of him as just a face—or a body.

But if you take it back a level, you once more wind up with the similarities being important. Because when they come to me as names mentioned in a conversation, over a quiet meal, with a purse handed over which will contain somewhere between fifteen hundred and four thousand gold Imperials, they *are* all the same, and I treat them the same: plan the job, do it.

I usually worked backwards: after finding out everything I could about his habits, and following him, tracking him, and timing him for days, sometimes for weeks, I'd decide where I wanted it to happen. That would usually determine the time and often the day as well. Then it was a matter of starting from there and working things so that all of the factors came together then and there. The execution itself was only interesting if I made a mistake somewhere along the line.

Kragar once asked me, when I was feeling particularly mellow, if I enjoyed killing people. I didn't answer, because I didn't know, but it set me to thinking. I'm still not really sure. I know that I enjoy the planning of a job, and setting it in motion so that everything works out. But the actual killing? I don't think I either consciously enjoy it or fail to enjoy it; I just do it.

I leaned back and closed my eyes. The beginning of a job like this is like the beginning of a witchcraft spell. The most important single thing is my frame of mind when I begin. I want to make absolutely sure that I have no preconceived notions about how, or where, or anything. That comes later. I hadn't even begun to study the fellow yet, so I didn't have anything to really go on. The little I did know went rolling around my subconscious, free-associating, letting images and ideas pop up and be casually discarded. Sometimes, when I'm in the middle of planning, I'll get a sudden inspiration, or what appears to be a sudden burst of brilliance. I fancy myself an artist at times like this.

I came out of my reverie slowly, with the feeling that there was something I should be thinking about. I wasn't really fully awake yet, so it took me awhile to become aware of what it was. There was a stray, questing thought fluttering around in my forebrain.

After a while, I realized that it had an external source. I gave it some freedom to grow and take shape enough for me to recognize it, and discovered that someone was trying to get into psionic contact with me. I recognized the sender.

"Ah, Daymar," I thought back. *"Thank you."*

"No problem," came the clear, gentle thought. *"You wanted something?"* Daymar had better mental control, and more power, than anyone I'd ever met. I got the feeling from him that he had to be careful, even in mental contact, lest he burn my mind out accidentally.

"I'd like a favor, Daymar."

"Yes?" He had a way of making his "yes" last about four times as long as it should.

"Nothing right now," I told him. *"But sometime within the next day or so, I expect to need some locating done."*

"Locating? What kind of locating?"

"I expect to have a psionic tag on a fellow I'm interested in finding, and I'll want some way to figure out exactly where he is. Kragar thinks you can do it."

"Is there some reason why I couldn't just trace him now?"

"He has a block up against sorcery tracing spells," I told him. *"I don't think even you can get past them."*

I was damn sure Daymar couldn't get past a block that was holding off the best sorcerers of the Left Hand, but a little judicious flattery never hurt anything.

"Oh," he said. *"Then how do you expect to put a tag on him?"*

"I'm hoping he didn't protect himself against witchcraft. Since witchcraft uses psionic power, we should be able to leave a mark on him that you can find."

"I see. You're going to try to fix him with a witchcraft spell, and then I locate him psionically from the marks left by that. Interesting idea."

"Thank you. Do you think it will work?"

"No."

I sighed. Daymar, I thought to myself, someday I'm going to. . . . *"Why not?"* I asked, with some hesitation.

"The marks," he explained, *"won't stay around long enough for me to trace them. If they do, they'll also be strong enough for him to notice, and he'll just wipe them out."*

I sighed again. Never argue with an expert.

"All right," I said, *"do you have any ideas for something that would work?"*

"Yes," he said.

I waited, but he didn't go on. Daymar, I said to myself, some day I'm *definitely* going to. . . . *"What is it?"*

"The reverse."

"The reverse?"

He explained. I asked a few questions, and he was able to answer them, more or less.

I began thinking of what kind of spell I'd have to do to get the kind of effect he was talking about. A crystal, I decided, and then I'd start the spell out just like the other one, and then. . . . I remembered that Daymar was still in contact with me—which, in turn, brought up another point that I really ought to clarify, given whom I was dealing with.

"Are you willing to do the locating for me?" I asked.

There was a brief pause, then: *"Sure—If I can watch you do the witchcraft spell."*

Why am I not surprised? I sighed to myself once more. *"It's a deal,"* I said. *"How do I get in touch with you? Can I count on finding you at home if I send Loiosh again?"*

He thought about that, then: *"Probably not. I'll open up for contact for a few seconds on the hour, each hour, starting tomorrow morning. Will that do?"*

"That will be fine," I said. *"I'll get in touch with you before I start the spell."*

"Excellent. Until then."

"Until then. And Daymar, thanks."

"My pleasure," he said.

Actually, I reflected, it probably was. But it wouldn't have been politic to say so. The link was broken.

Sometime later, Loiosh returned. I opened the window in answer to his knocking. Why he preferred to knock, rather than just contact me, I don't know. After he was in, I closed it behind him.

"Thanks."

"Sure, boss."

I resumed reading; Loiosh perched on my right shoulder this time, and pretended to be reading along with me. Or, who knows? Maybe he really did learn to read somehow and just never bothered to inform me. I wouldn't put it past him.

The job was under way. I couldn't really go any further until I had some idea of where Mellar was, so I turned my attention to who he was, instead. This kept me occupied until my next visitor arrived, a few hours later.

4.

"Inspiration requires preparation."

My receptionist, in the two years he'd been with me, had killed three people outside the door of my office.

One was an assassin whose bluff didn't quite work. The other two were perfectly innocent fools who should have known better than to try to bluster their way past him.

He was killed once, himself, delaying another assassin long enough for me to escape heroically out the window. I was very relieved when we were successful in having him revivified. He fulfills the function of bodyguard, recording secretary, buffer, and whatever else either Kragar or I need. He may well be the highest-paid receptionist on Dragaera.

"Uh, boss?"

"Yes?"

"Uh, Kiera is here."

"Oh, good! Send her in."

"That's Kiera the Thief, boss. Are you sure?"

"Quite sure, thank you."

"But—okay. Should I escort her in, and keep an eye—"

"That won't be necessary" (or sufficient, I thought to myself). *"Just send her in."*

"Okay. Whatever you want."

I put down the papers and stood up as the door opened. A small Dragaeran female form entered the room. I recalled with some amusement that I had thought her tall when we had first met, but then, I was only eleven at the time. And, of course, she was still more than a head taller than I, but by now I was used to the size difference.

She moved with ease and grace, almost reminiscent of Mario. She flowed up to me and greeted me with a kiss that would have made Cawti jealous if she were the jealous type. I gave as good as I got, and pulled up a chair for her.

Kiera had a sharp, rather angular face, with no noticeable House characteristics—the lack of which was typical for a Jhereg.

She allowed me to seat her and made a quick glance around the office. Her eyes clicked from one place to another, making notes of significant items. This wasn't surprising; she'd taught me how to do it. On the other hand, I suspected that she was looking for different things than I would be.

She favored me with a smile.

"Thanks for coming, Kiera," I said, as warmly as I could.

"Glad to," she said softly. "Nice office."

"Thanks. How's business been?"

"Not hurting, Vlad. I haven't had any contract jobs in a while, but I've been doing all right on my own. How about you?"

I shook my head.

"What is it, problems?" she asked, genuinely concerned.

"I went and got greedy again."

"Uh, oh. I know what that means. Somebody offered something too big to pass up, eh? And you couldn't resist, so you're in over your head, right?"

"Something like that."

She slowly shook her head. Loiosh interrupted, then, flapping over to her and landing on her shoulder. She renewed their acquaintance, scratching under his chin. "The last time that happened," she said after a while, "you found yourself fighting an Athyra wizard, right in his own castle, as I recall. That kind of thing isn't healthy, Vlad."

"I know, I know. But remember: I won."

"With help."

"Well . . . yes. One can always use a little help."

"Always," she agreed. "Which, I imagine, brings us to this. It must be something big, or you wouldn't have wanted to meet here."

"Perceptive as always," I said. "Not only big, but nasty. I can't risk anyone catching wind of this. I'm hoping no one saw you come in; I can't risk being seen with you and having certain parties guess that I'm letting you in on what's going on."

"No one saw me come in," she said.

I nodded. I knew her. If she said no one had seen her, I had no reason to doubt it.

"But," she continued, "what are your own people going to say when they find you've been meeting me in your own office? They'll think you've finally gone 'into the jungle,' you know." She was smiling lightly; baiting me. She knew her reputation.

"No problem," I said. "I'll just let it slip that we've been lovers for years."

She laughed. "Now there's an idea, Vlad! We should have thought of that cycles ago!"

This time I laughed. "Then what would *your* friends say? Kiera the Thief, consorting with an Easterner? Tut, tut."

"They won't say anything," she said flatly. "I have a friend who does 'work.' "

"Speaking of which—"

"Right. To business. I take it you want something stolen."

I nodded. "Do you know of a certain Lord Mellar, House Jhereg? I think he's officially a count, or a duke, or some such."

Her eyes widened, slightly. "Going after big game, aren't you, Vlad? You certainly *are* in over your head. I know him, all right. I've helped him out a couple of times."

"Not recently!" I said, with a sudden sinking feeling.

She looked at me quizzically, but didn't ask what I meant. "No, not in the last few months. It wasn't anything big, any of the times. Just sort of an exchange of favors; you know how it goes."

I nodded, quite relieved. "He isn't a friend, or anything, is he?"

She shook her head. "No. We just did a few things for each other. I don't owe him."

"Good. And speaking of owing, by the way . . ." I placed a purse on my desk in front of her. It held five hundred gold Imperials. She didn't touch it yet, of course.

"How would you like to have me owe you still another favor?"

"I'm always happy to have you in my debt," she said lightly. "What does he have that you want?"

"Any of a number of things. A piece of clothing would be good. Hair would be excellent. Anything that has a long association with him."

She shook her head once more, in mock sadness. "More of your Eastern witchcraft, Vlad?"

"I'm afraid so," I admitted. "You know how we are, always like to keep our hand in, and all."

"I'll bet." She took the purse and stood up. "Okay, you're on. It shouldn't take more than a day or two."

"No hurry," I lied politely. I stood as she left, and bowed her out.

"How long do you think it will actually take her?" asked Kragar.

"How long have you been sitting there?"

"Not too long."

I shook my head in disgust. "I wouldn't be surprised if we had it tomorrow."

"Not bad," he said. "Did you talk to Daymar?"

"Yes."

"And?"

I explained the outcome of our conversation. He shrugged over the technical details of the witchcraft, but caught the gist of it. He laughed a bit when I explained that Daymar had managed to include himself in the spell.

"Well, do you think it will work?" he asked.

"Daymar thinks it will work; I think it will work."

He seemed satisfied with this answer. "So nothing happens until we hear from Kiera, right?"

"Right."

"Good. I think I'll go catch up on my sleep."

"Wrong."

"What now, Oh Master?"

"You're getting as bad as Loiosh."

"What's that supposed to mean, boss?"

"Shut up, Loiosh."

"Right, boss."

I picked up the notes on Mellar that I'd been reading and handed them to Kragar. "Read," I said. "Let me know what you think."

He ruffled through them briefly. "There's a lot here."
"Yeah."
"Look, Vlad, my eyes are sore. How about tomorrow?"
"Read."
He sighed and started reading.

"You know what strikes me, Vlad?" he asked a bit later.
"What?"
"There's been something funny about this guy since he first showed up in the organization."
"What do you mean?"
He paged through the notes quickly and continued. "He moved too fast. He made it from nowhere to the top in just over ten years. That's damned quick. I've never heard of anyone except you moving that quickly, and you have the excuse of being an Easterner.

"I mean, look," he went on. "He starts out protecting a little brothel, right? A muscle. A year later he's running the place; a year after that he has ten more. In eight years he's got a territory bigger than you have now. A year after that, he wipes out Terion and takes his place on the council. And a year after that, he grabs up the council funds and vanishes. It's almost as if he had the whole thing figured out when he started."

"Hmmm. I see what you're saying, but isn't ten years a long time to set up one job?"

"You're thinking like an Easterner again, Vlad. It isn't a long time if you expect to have a two-thousand- or three-thousand-year lifetime."

I nodded and thought over what he'd suggested.

"I can't see it, Kragar," I said finally. "How much gold was it that he got?"

"Nine million," he said, almost reverently.

"Right. Now, that's a lot. That's one hell of a lot. If I ever have a tenth of that in one place at one time I'll retire. But would you throw away a position on the council for it?"

Kragar started to speak, stopped.

I continued, "And that isn't the only way to get nine million gold either. It isn't the best, the fastest, or the easiest. He could have gone free-lance and done a lot better than that over those same ten years. He could have held up the Dragon Treasury, and doubled it at least, and not be taking any more risk than he is with this thing."

Kragar nodded. "That's true. Are you saying that he wasn't after the gold?"

"Not at all. I'm suggesting that he may have developed a sudden need to have a few million and this was the only way to get it in a hurry."

"I don't know, Vlad. Just looking at his whole history, it sure seems like he had this planned out from the start."

"But why, Kragar? No one works his way up to a seat on the council for money. You have to be after power to do something like that—"

"You should know," said Kragar, smirking.

"—and you don't throw away that kind of power unless you have to."

"Maybe he lost interest in it," he said. "Maybe he was just after the thrill of getting to the top, and after he made it, he went after a new thrill."

"If that's true," I remarked, "he's going to get his thrills, and then some. But doesn't that go against your He-Planned-It-All-From-the-Start theory?"

"I suppose it does. I'm beginning to get the feeling that we don't have enough information; all we're doing is guessing."

"True enough. So how about if you start collecting the information, eh?"

"Me? Look, Vlad, my boots are in the shop this week getting new soles. Why don't we hire a flunky and get him to do the legwork for us, okay?"

I told him where he could hire the flunky and what he could have him do.

He sighed. "All right, I'm going. What are you going to be working on?"

I thought for a minute. "A couple of things," I said. "For one, I'm going to try to think up a good reason for someone to suddenly decide to leave the council in such a way as to get the whole Jhereg down on his ass. Also I'm going to check in with Morrolan's spy ring and contact some of our own people. I want to dig up as much information as I can, and it wouldn't hurt to have both of us working on it. After that—I think I'll visit the Lady Aliera."

Kragar was about halfway out the door, but as I finished speaking, he stopped and turned around. "Who?" he asked, incredulous.

"Aliera e'Kieron, House of the Dragon, Morrolan's cous—"

"I know who she is, I just couldn't believe I heard you straight. Why not ask the Empress, while you're at it?"

"I have a few questions about this guy that I want to check out, and they're just the kind of thing she's good at. Why not? We've been friends for quite a while."

"Boss, she's a *Dragon*. They don't *believe* in assassination. They consider it a *crime*. If you go up to her and—"

"Kragar," I interrupted, "I never said that I was going to go up to her and say, 'Aliera, I'm trying to assassinate this guy, how would you like to help set him up?' Give me credit for a little finesse, all right? All we have to do is find some reasonable excuse for her to be interested in Mellar, and she'll be happy to help out."

"Just a 'reasonable excuse,' eh? Just out of curiosity, do you have any idea how to find an excuse like that?"

"As a matter of fact," I said nastily, "I do. Easiest thing in the world. I just give you the assignment."

"Me? Dammit, Vlad, you've already got me working on background, as well as trying to figure out a nonexistent event to provide an insufficient reason for a vanished Jhereg to do the impossible. I can't—"

"Sure you can. I have confidence in you."

"Go suck yendi eggs. How?"

"You'll think of something."

5.

"There are dangers in eyesight too keen."

The only significant thing that happened the rest of the day
was the arrival of a courier from the Demon, along with a
rather impressive escort and several large purses. The full
sixty-five thousand Imperials. It was official now; I was
committed.

I gave Kragar the purses to put into safekeeping, and
went home for the day. My wife, I'm sure, knew that something was up, but didn't ask about it. I had no good reason
for not mentioning anything to her, but I didn't.

The next morning I found a small envelope on my desk. I
slit it open and several human, or Dragaeran, hairs fell out.
There was also a note which read, "From his pillow.—K."
I destroyed the note and reached out for psionic contact
with my wife.

"Yes, Vlad?"

"Are you busy, sweetheart?"

"Not really. Just practicing a little knife-throwing."

"Hey! I wish you wouldn't do that!"

"Why not?"

"Because you can already beat me seven out of ten times."

*"I'm going for eight out of ten. You've been getting uppity
lately. What's up? Do you have some 'work' for me?"*

"No such luck. Drop on by and I'll tell you about it."

"Right away?"

"As soon as it's convenient."

"Okay. I'll be over shortly."

"Fine. Meet me in the lab."

"Oh," she said, understanding, and the link was broken.

I left word with my receptionist that I wasn't going to be taking any messages for the next two hours and walked down a few flights of stairs. Loiosh rode complacently on my left shoulder, looking around as if he were conducting an inspection. I came to a small room in the basement and unlocked the door.

In this building, locks are next to useless as a means of actually keeping people out of places, but they are effective as a way of saying "Private."

It was a smallish room, with a low table in the exact center and several mounted lamps along the wall. I kindled these. In a corner of the room was a small chest. The middle of the table held a brazier, with a few unburned coals in it. I dumped these out and got more from the chest.

I focused, briefly, on one of the candles and was rewarded by a flame. I used it to light the others, then put out the lamps.

I checked the time and found that I still had a little while before I could contact Daymar. I checked the placement of the candles and watched the flickering shadows for a moment.

Removing a few more items from the chest, including a piece of incense, I set them on the table next to the brazier, placing the incense among the coals. Next, I took a candle and held the flame next to a coal. A moment of concentration, and the fire spread evenly and quickly. The smell of incense began to introduce itself to the various nooks and corners of the room.

Soon Cawti arrived and greeted me with a sunshine smile. She was an Easterner, a small, pretty woman with dzur-black hair and fluid, graceful movements. If she'd been a Dragaeran, she might have been born into the House of the Issola, and taught them all something about "courtliness." And something about "surprise," as well.

Her hands were small, but strong, and could produce knives out of nowhere. Her eyes burned—sometimes with the impish delight of a mischievous child, sometimes with the cold passion of a professional killer, sometimes with the rage of a Dragonlord going into battle.

Cawti was one of the deadliest assassins I had ever met.

She and her partner, then a defrocked Dragonlord, had
made one of the most sought-after teams of killers in the
Jhereg, going under the somewhat melodramatic names of
"The Sword and the Dagger." I had deemed it a high honor
when an enemy of mine had considered me worth the ex-
pense of hiring the team to take me out. I'd been quite surprised when I woke up afterwards and found that they
hadn't managed to make it permanent. For that, thank
Kragar's alertness, Morrolan's speed and fighting ability,
and Aliera's rather exceptional skill in healing and
revivification.

Some couples fall in love and end up trying to kill each
other. We'd done it the other way around.

Cawti was also a competent witch, though not quite as
skilled as I. I explained to her what was going to be needed,
then we made small talk.

"Boss!"

"Yes, Loiosh?"

"I hate to interrupt—"

"Like hell you do."

"But it's time to contact Daymar."

"Already? Okay, thanks."

"Well, I suppose you're welcome."

I reached out, thinking of Daymar, concentrating, remembering the "feel" of his mind.

"Yes?" he said. He was one of few people whose voice I
could actually hear when we were in contact. In the other
cases it was because I knew them well enough for my imagination to supply the voice. With Daymar it was simply the
strength of the contact.

"Would you mind showing up?" I asked him. *"We'd like
to get started on this spell."*

*"Fine. Just let me. . . . Okay, I've got a fix on you. I'll be
right there."*

*"Give me a minute first, so I can turn off some protections
and alarms. I don't want to have forty-eleven things go off
when you teleport in."*

I ordered our teleport protections taken down for a few
seconds. Daymar appeared in front of me—floating, cross-
legged, about three feet off the floor. I rolled my eyes;
Cawti shook her head sadly. Loiosh hissed. Daymar
shrugged, and stretched his legs down; stood up.

"You left off the thunderclap and the lightning flash," I told him.

"Should I try again?"

"Never mind."

Daymar stood roughly 7 feet, 3 inches tall. He had the sharp, well-chiseled features of the House of the Hawk, although they were somewhat gentler, softer, than those of most Hawklords I've met. He was incredibly thin, looking almost transparent. It seemed that his eyes rarely focused, giving him the appearance of looking past whatever he was observing, or at something deep inside it. We had been friends since the time I had almost killed him for mind-probing one of my people. He'd done it out of curiosity, and I think he never understood why I objected.

"So," Daymar asked, "who is this you want located?"

"A Jhereg. With luck, I should have what you wanted for the trace. Will this do?"

I handed him a small crystal I'd taken from the chest. He inspected it carefully, although I'm damned if I know what he was looking for. He nodded and gave it back to me.

"I've seen better," he remarked, "but it will do."

I set it carefully down on the right side of the brazier. I opened the envelope I'd gotten from Kiera and removed about half of the dozen or so strands of hair. These I set on top of the envelope on the left side of the brazier; the others I would save in case I had to try the spell again.

It was interesting, I reflected, how much a witchcraft spell resembles an assassination, as opposed to either of them being similar to sorcery. To use sorcery, all you do is reach out through your link to the Imperial Orb, grab some power, shape it, and throw it. With witchcraft, however, you have to plan carefully and precisely so that you don't end up searching around for some implement you need, right at the moment of using it.

The room began to get smoky with the lingering scent of incense. I took my position in front of the brazier; Cawti automatically stood to my right, and I motioned Daymar to stand at my left, and back. I let my mind drift and linked up mentally with Cawti. It was not necessary for there to be physical contact between us for this to happen, which is one reason why I like to work with her. One of the clear advantages witchcraft enjoys over sorcery is that more than one witch can participate in a single spell. I felt my power diminish and increase at the same time; which is strange to say and even stranger to experience.

I laid a few leaves on the coals, which obliged by making the proper hissing sounds. They were large, broad leaves from the Heaken tree, which only grows out East. They had been prepared by being soaked in purified water for a number of hours, and by diverse enchantments. A large gout of steam-smoke rose up, and Cawti began chanting, low and almost inaudible. As the leaves began to blacken and burn, my left hand found the envelope and the hairs. I rolled them around on my fingertips for a moment. I felt things start to happen—the very first sign of a witchcraft spell starting to have any kind of effect is when certain senses begin to feel sharper. In this case, each hair felt distinct and unique to my fingertips, and I could almost make out tiny details on each one. I dropped them onto the burning leaves, as Cawti's chanting became more intense, and I could almost pick out the words.

At that moment, a sudden rush of power flooded my mind. I felt giddy, and I would certainly have lost my end of the spell if I had actually begun it. A thought came into being, and I heard Daymar's pseudo-voice say, *"Mind if I help?"*

I didn't answer, trying to cope with more psychic energy than I'd ever had at my disposal before. I had a brief urge to answer, "No!" and hurl the energy back at him as hard as I could, but it wouldn't have done more than hurt his feelings. I observed my own anger at this unasked-for interference as if it were in a stranger.

Any spell, no matter how trivial it really is, involves some degree of danger. After all, what you're really doing is building up a force of energy from your own mind and manipulating it as if it were something external. There have been witches whose minds have been destroyed by mishandling this power. Daymar, of course, couldn't know this. He was just being his usual helpful, meddlesome self.

I gritted my teeth and tried to use my anger to control the forces we had generated, to direct them into the spell. Somewhere, I felt Loiosh fighting to hold onto his control and take up what I couldn't handle. Loiosh and I were so deeply linked that anything that happened to me would happen to him. The link broadened, more and more power flooded through it, and I knew that, between the two of us, we'd either be able to handle it, or our minds would be burned out. I would have been as scared as a teckla if my anger hadn't blocked it—and the rage I felt was sustained, perhaps, by my knowledge of the fear underlying it.

It hung in the balance, and time stretched to both horizons. I heard Cawti, as if from a great distance, chanting steadily, strongly, although she must have felt the backwash of forces as much as I. She was helping, too. I had to direct the energy into the spell, or it would find release some other way. I remember thinking, at that moment, *"Daymar, if you've hurt my familiar's mind, you are one dead Dragaeran."*

Loiosh was straining. I could feel him, right at his limit, trying to absorb power, control it, channel it. This is why witches have familiars. I think he saved me.

I felt control had come, and fought to hang onto it long enough to throw it into the spell. I wanted to rush through the next part, but resisted the temptation. You do *not* rush through any phase of a witchcraft spell.

The hairs were burning; they merged and combined into a part of the steam and smoke and they should still be tied to their owner. I fought to identify exactly which isolated puff of smoke held the essence of those burning hairs and therefore was an unbreakable bond to my target.

I lifted my arms until my hands were at the outermost perimeter of the grayish-white cloud. I felt the fourway pull of energy—me to Daymar to Loiosh to Cawti and back. I let it flow out through my hands, until the smoke stopped rising—the first visible sign that the spell was having an effect. I held it there for an instant and slowly brought my hands closer together. The smoke became more dense in front of me, and I flung the energy I held at and through it. . . .

There is a cry of "charge" and five thousand Dragons come storming at the place the Eastern army is entrenched. . . . Making love to Cawti that first time—the moment of entry, even more than the moment of release; I wonder if she plans to kill me before we're finished, and I don't really care. . . . The Dzur hero, coming alone to Dzur mountain, sees Sethra Lavode stand up before him, Iceflame alive in her hand. . . . A small girl-child with big brown eyes looks at me and smiles. . . . The energy bolt, visible as a black wave, streaks toward me, and I swing Spellbreaker at it, wondering whether it will work. . . . Aliera stands up before the shadow of Kieron the Conqueror, there in the midst of the Halls of Judgment, in the Paths of the Dead, beyond Deathsgate Falls. . . .

And with it all, at that moment, I held in my mind everything I knew about Mellar, and all of my anger at Daymar, and above it all, on top of everything, my desire, my will, my hope. I flung it at the small cloud of steam-smoke rising from the brazier; I reached through it, beyond it, within it, toward the one who was tied to it.

Cawti chanted strongly, with no break in her voice, in words I still couldn't quite make out. Loiosh, within me, part of my being, was searching and hunting. And Daymar, away from us, and yet a part of us too, stood out as a beacon of light, which I grabbed, and shaped, and pushed through.

I felt a response. Slowly, very slowly, an image formed in the smoke. I forced energy into it as it began to grow distinct. I forced myself to ignore the face itself, which was only a distraction at this point. And, with agonizing slowness, I . . . lowered . . . my . . . right . . . hand . . . and . . . began . . . dropping . . . control . . . of . . . the. . . spell. . . .

Piece by minute, fractional piece, Loiosh picked up the threads of control, accepted them, handled them. Exhaustion was my enemy then, and I fought it back. The jhereg had taken the power, and was handling it all, by the green scales of Barlen!

I allowed myself to look at the image for the first time, as my right hand found the small crystal. The face was middle-aged and showed features reminiscent of the House of the Dzur. I carefully raised the crystal to eye level, dropped the last threads of control over the spell, and held my breath.

The image was steady; I had trained Loiosh well. Cawti was no longer chanting. She had done her part and was now just supplying power for the last stage of the spell. I studied the image through the crystal, closing my left eye. It was, of course, distorted, but that didn't matter; the image appeared through it enough to be identified.

A moment of intense concentration; I reached for the energy Cawti and Daymar were offering and burned the face into the container before my eye. My right eye was blinded for a moment, and I felt slightly dizzy as I bore down on it, trying to use up all of the excess power we had built up.

I heard Cawti sigh and relax. I sagged against the back wall, and Loiosh sagged against my neck. I heard Daymar sigh. There was now a milky haze within the crystal. I knew, without trying it, that by an act of will the haze could be cleared and Mellar's face would appear in it. More important, there was now a connection between Mellar, wherever he might be, and the crystal. The chances of his ever detecting this link were so small as to approach nonexistent. I nodded my satisfaction to Cawti, as we stood there for a few minutes catching our collective breath.

After a time, I blew out the candles, and Cawti lit the lamps along the wall. I opened the vent to let the smoke out, along with the smell of the incense, which now seemed cloying and sweet. The room brightened, and I looked around. Daymar had a distant look on his face, and Cawti seemed flushed and tired. I wanted to order wine from someone upstairs, but even the energy required for psionic contact seemed too much.

"Well," I announced to the room in general, "I guess he didn't have any protections against witchcraft."

Daymar said, "That was very interesting, Vlad. Thanks for letting me come along."

I suddenly realized that he had no idea that he'd almost destroyed me with his "help." I tried to think of some way to tell him, but gave up. I'd just remember it in the future, if he was ever around when I did more witchcraft. I held out the crystal to him; he accepted it. He studied it carefully for a few seconds, then nodded slowly.

"Well," I asked, "can you pin down where he is from that?"

"I think so. I'll try, anyway. How soon do you need it?"

"As soon as you can get it to me."

"Okay," he said. Then, casually, "By the way, why are you looking for him, anyway?"

"Why do you want to know?"

"Oh, just curious."

That figured. "I'd rather not say, if you don't mind," I told him.

"Have it your way," he said, miffed. "Going to kill him, eh?"

"Daymar—"

"Sorry. I'll let you know when I've found him. It shouldn't take more than a day or so."

"Good. I'll see you then. Or," I added as an after-thought, "you can just give it to Kragar."

"Fine," he said, nodding, and vanished.

I forced my legs to work and pushed away from the wall. I killed the lamps and helped Cawti out the door; locked it.

"We'd better get some food," I said.

"Sounds good. Then a bath, then about twenty years of sleep."

"I wish I could take the time for the last two, but I'm going to have to get back to work."

"Okay," she said cheerfully, "I'll sleep for you, too."

"Damned helpful of you."

Leaning on each other, we took the stairs, one at a time. I felt Loiosh, still lying against the side of my neck, sleeping.

6.

"True heroics must be carefully planned—and strenuously avoided."

Cawti and I shared a lunch at one of the restaurants that I had an interest in. We ate slowly and allowed our strength to return. The sense of physical exhaustion that accompanies witchcraft is usually very short-lived; the psionic drain is longer. By halfway through the meal I felt comfortable again and well rested. On the other hand, I still felt that it would be something of an effort even to achieve psionic contact. I hoped no one would need to reach me during lunch.

We ate the meal in silence, enjoying each other's company, feeling no need to talk. As we were finishing, Cawti said, "So, you get work, while I stay home and wither away from boredom."

"You don't look withered to me," I said, checking. "And I don't remember your asking me for help with that little matter last month."

"Hmmmmph," she said. "I didn't need any help with that, but this looks like something big. I recognized the target. I hope you're getting a reasonable price for him."

I told her what I was getting for him.

She raised her eyebrows. "Nice! Who wants him?"

I looked around the restaurant, which was almost deserted. I didn't like taking chances, but Cawti deserved an answer. "The whole bloody Jhereg wants him, or will if and when they find out."

"What did he do?" she asked. "He didn't start talking, did he?"

I shuddered. "No, not that, thank Verra. He ran off with nine million gold in council operating funds."

She looked stunned and was silent for a moment, as she realized that I wasn't kidding. "When did this happen?"

"Three days ago, now." I thought for a second, then, "I was approached by the Demon, personally."

"Whew! Battle of the giant jhereg," she said. "Are you sure you aren't getting involved in more than you can handle?"

"No," I answered, cheerfully.

"My husband, the optimist," she remarked. "I suppose you've already accepted."

"That's right. Would I have gone to all of that trouble to locate him if I hadn't?"

"I suppose not. I was just hoping."

Loiosh woke up with a start, looked around, and jumped down from my shoulder. He began working on the remains of my tsalmoth ribs.

"Do you have any idea why you got the job?" she asked, suddenly worried. I could see her mind making the same jumps as mine had.

"Yes, and it makes sense." I explained the Demon's reasoning to her and she seemed satisfied.

"What do you think about subcontracting this one?"

"Nope," I said, "I'm too greedy. If I subcontract it, I won't be able to build you that castle."

She chuckled a little.

"Why?" I continued. "Do you and Norathar want to do it?"

"Not likely," she answered drily. "It sounds too dangerous. And she's retired in any case. Besides," she added, rather nastily, "you couldn't afford us."

I laughed and lifted my glass to her. Loiosh moved over to her plate and began working on it. "I guess you're right," I admitted, "I'll just have to stumble along on my own."

She grinned for a moment, then turned serious. "Actually, Vlad, it is something of an honor to be given a job like this."

I nodded. "I guess it is, to a degree. But the Demon is convinced that Mellar is out East somewhere; he figures that I can operate better than a Dragaeran out there. Since you went into pseudo-retirement, there aren't many humans who do 'work.'"

Cawti looked thoughtful for a moment. "What makes him think that Mellar is in the East?"

I explained his thinking on the matter, and Cawti nodded. "That makes sense, in a way. But, as you yourself said, he'd stand out in the East like a lightning bolt. I can't believe that Mellar is so naive that he'd think the House wouldn't go after him."

I thought this over. "You may be right. I do have a few friends in the East I can check with. In fact, I was planning on trying to get hold of them if Daymar can't find out where he is. I don't really see what else we can do but check out the Demon's theory, at this point."

"There isn't anything, I suppose," she said. "But it makes me a little nervous. Do you have any idea how long Mellar's been planning this move? If there was some way to figure that, it would give us an idea of how hard he's going to be to track down."

"I'm not sure. It seems to me that it doesn't make sense unless it was a sudden, spur of the moment kind of thing, but Kragar has an idea that he's been planning it all along, from the minute he joined the Jhereg, in fact."

"If Kragar is right, he must have something planned for this," she said. "In fact, if it was that long, he should have realized that someone would, or at least, *could* try to trace him using witchcraft. If that were the case, he would have some way to set up a block against it."

"On the other hand," she continued, "if he *did* plan it for that long and somehow couldn't block witchcraft, or didn't think of it, it may mean the Demon underestimated his defenses."

"What do you mean?" I asked.

"Well, don't you think that, in years, you could come up with a sorcery block that even the Left Hand couldn't break down in the time they've had?"

I thought that over for a long time. "He couldn't do it, Cawti. It's always easier to break down a block than it is to set one up. There is no way he could get the resources to put up a strong enough trace-block to keep out the Left Hand. The impression I got was that the Demon had the best there is working on it. I'd defy Sethra Lavode to put up a block that would hold them out for more than a day."

"Then why haven't they found him?" she asked, pointedly.

"Distance. Before they can break down the block, they have to find the right general area. That takes time. Even a standard teleport trace spell can be difficult if the person teleports far enough away. That's why the Demon is figuring the East. Using just standard tracing spells, it could take years to find him, if that's where he went."

"I suppose you're right," she conceded. "But I'm nervous about the thing."

"Me too," I said. "And that isn't all I'm nervous about."

"What else?"

"Time. The Demon wants this done a lot faster than I like to work. What it boils down to is that I have to make sure Mellar is taken out before everyone in the Jhereg finds out what he did. And that could happen any day."

Cawti shook her head. "That's bad, Vlad. Why, by the Demon Goddess, did you accept the job with a time limit? I've never heard of one even being offered that way."

"Neither have I. I took it that way because those were the terms. And it isn't really a time limit, as such, although he implied it could come to that later. It's just that I have to move as fast as I can."

"That's bad enough," she said. "You work fast, you make mistakes. And you can't afford to make a mistake."

I had to agree. "But you understand my position, don't you? If we don't get him, we've just shot the reputation of the Jhereg council. There won't be any way to keep House funds secure, once people get the idea that it can be done. Hell, I just put sixty-five thousand gold into a room in the office and forgot about it. I know it's safe, because there isn't anyone who would dare touch it. But, once this gets started. . . ." I shrugged.

"And the other thing," I went on, "is that he told me straight out that if one of his people finds Mellar before I do, they aren't going to wait for me."

"Why should that bother you?" she asked. "You'll still have the payment."

"Sure. That isn't the problem. But think about it: some clod goes up to Mellar to take him out. Who is it going to be? It's not going to be a professional, because the Demon is going to want to say, 'Hey, you, go nail this guy here and now,' and no professional will agree to work that way. So it's going to be some two-silverpiece muscle, or maybe a button-man who thinks he can handle it himself. Then what? Then the guy bungles it, that's what. And I'm left trying to take Mellar out after he's been alerted. Oh, sure, the guy might succeed, but he might not. I don't trust amateurs.''

Cawti nodded. "I see the problem. And I'm beginning to understand the reason for the price he's paying.''

I stood up, after making sure that Loiosh had finished his meal. "Let's get going. I may as well try to get something done with the rest of the day.''

Loiosh found a napkin, carefully rubbed his face in it, and joined us. I didn't pay, of course, since I was a part owner, but I did leave a rather healthy tip.

Out of habit, Cawti stepped out of the door an instant before me and scanned the street. She nodded, and I came out. There had been a time, not too long before, when that had saved my life. Loiosh, after all, can't be *everywhere*. We walked back to the office.

I kissed her goodbye at the door and went up, while she headed back to our apartment. Then I sat down and began going over the day's business. I noted with some satisfaction that Kragar had found the punk who'd mugged the Teckla the other day, at a cost of only four hundred gold or so, and had carried out my instructions. I destroyed the note and picked up a proposal that a new gambling establishment be opened by one of my button-men who wanted to better himself. I felt somewhat sympathetic. I'd gotten started that way, too.

"Don't do it, Vlad.''

"Wha—? Kragar, would you cut it out?''

"Give the guy at least another year to prove himself. He's too new for that kind of trust.''

"I swear, Kragar, one of these days I'm going to—''

"Daymar reported in.''

"What?'' I switched modes. "Good!''

Kragar shook his head.

"Not good?'' I asked. "He shouldn't have been able to tell this quickly that he couldn't find the guy. Did he change his mind about helping us?''

"No. He found Mellar, all right."

"Excellent. Then what's the problem?"

"You aren't going to like this, Vlad. . . ."

"Come on, Kragar, out with it."

"The Demon was wrong; he didn't go out East after all."

"Really? Then where?"

Kragar slumped in his chair a little bit. He put his head on his hand and shook his head.

"He's at Castle Black," he said.

Slowly, a piece at a time, it sunk in.

"That bastard," I said softly. "That clever, clever bastard."

The Dragaeran memory is long.

The Empire has existed—I don't know—somewhere between two and two-and-a-half *hundred thousand* years. Since the creation of the Imperial Orb, back at the very beginning, each of the Seventeen Houses has kept its records, and the House of the Lyorn has kept records of them all.

At my father's insistence, I knew at least as much about the history of House Jhereg as any Dragaeran born into the House. Jhereg records do, I will admit, tend to be somewhat more scanty than those of other Houses, since anyone with enough pull, or even enough gold, can arrange to have what he wants deleted, or even inserted. Nevertheless, they are worth studying.

About ten thousand years ago, nearly a full turn of the cycle before the Interregnum, the House of the Athyra held the throne and the Orb. At this time, for a reason which is lost to us, a certain Jhereg decided that another Jhereg had to be removed. He hired an assassin, who traced the fellow to the keep of a noble of the House of the Dragon. Now, by Jhereg tradition (with good, solid reasons behind it that I may go into later), the target would have been quite safe if he'd stayed in his own home. No assassin will kill anyone in his house. Of course, no one can stay in his house forever, and if this Jhereg tried to hide that way, he would have found it impossible to leave, either by teleporting or by walking, without being followed. It could be, of course, that he didn't know he'd been marked for extinction—usually one doesn't know until it's too late.

But, for whatever reason, he was in the home of a

Dragonlord. The assassin knew that he couldn't put up a
trace spell around the home of a neutral party. The person
would find out and almost certainly take offense, which
wouldn't be good for anyone.

There is, however, no Jhereg custom that says that you
have to leave someone alone just because he's over at a
friend's house. The assassin waited long enough to be sure
that the fellow wasn't planning to leave right away; then he
got in past the Dragonlord's defenses and took care of his
target.

And then the jaws of Deathsgate swung open.

The Dragons, it seemed, didn't approve of assassins
plying their trade on guests. They demanded an apology
from House Jhereg and got one. Then they demanded the
assassin's head, and instead got the head of their messenger returned to them in a basket.

The insult, reasoned the Jhereg, wasn't *that* great. After
all, they hadn't destroyed the poor fellow's brain, or done
anything else to make him unrevivifiable. They were just
sending the Dragons a message.

The Dragons got the message and sent back one of their
own. Somehow, they found out who had issued the contract. The day after the messenger was returned to them,
they raided the home of this fellow. They killed him and his
family, and burned down his house. Two days later, the
Dragon heir to the throne was found just outside the Imperial Palace with a six-inch spike driven through his head.

Four bars along Lower Kieron Road, all owned by the
Jhereg, and all housing some illegal activity upstairs or in
back, were raided and burned, and many of the patrons
were killed. All Jhereg in all of them were killed. Morganti
weapons were used on several.

The next day, the Warlord of the Empire disappeared.
Pieces of her were found over the next few days at the
homes of various Dragon nobles.

The House of the Dragon declared that it intended to
wipe House Jhereg out of the cycle. The Dragons said that
they fully intended to kill each and every Jhereg in
existence.

House Jhereg responded by sending assassins after each
Dragon general who commanded more than a thousand
troops and then began working its way down.

The e'Kieron line of the Dragons was almost wiped out, and for a while it seemed that the e'Baritt line had been.

Have you heard enough?

All in all, it was a disaster. The "Dragon-Jhereg War" lasted about six months. At the end, when the Athyra Emperor forced a meeting between the surviving Dragon leaders and the Jhereg council and forced a peace treaty down both of their throats, there had been some changes. The best brains, the best generals, and the best warriors in the House of the Dragon were dead, and House Jhereg was damn near out of business.

It is admitted by the Jhereg that they came out pretty much the losers. This should be expected, since they were at the bottom of the cycle, and the Dragons were near the top. But still, the Dragons don't boast of the outcome.

It was fortunate that the Athyra reign was long, and the Phoenix reign even longer after that, or there would have been real trouble having a House of the Dragon strong enough to take the throne and the Orb when their turn came, following the Phoenix. It took the Jhereg the entire time until their turn at the throne, nearly half the cycle away, which worked out to several thousand years, to achieve a stable business.

I summed it up, as I went over the whole affair in my mind. Since that time, no Dragon has given sanctuary to a Jhereg, and no Jhereg has attempted to assassinate anyone in the home of a Dragonlord.

Castle Black was the home of Lord Morrolan e'Drien, of the House of the Dragon.

"How do you think he did it?" asked Kragar.

"How the hell should I know?" I said. "He found some way of tricking Morrolan into it, that's for sure. Morrolan would be the last person on Dragaera to deliberately let his home be used by a Jhereg on the run."

"Do you think Morrolan will kick him out, once he finds out that he's been used?"

"That depends on exactly how Mellar tricked him. But if Morrolan actually invited him there, he'll never agree to allowing him to be harmed, and he won't deny him sanctuary, not unless Mellar sneaked in without an invitation."

Kragar nodded and sat quietly for a while, thinking.

"Well, Vlad," he said at last, "he can't stay there forever."

"No. He can stay there long enough, though. All he has to do is to set up a new identity and figure out a good place to run. We can't keep up a vigilance on him for hundreds of years, and he can afford to wait that long if he has to.

"And what's more," I continued, "we can't even wait more than a few days. Once the information gets out, we've blown it."

"Do you think we can put up a tracer net around Castle Black, so we can at least find him if he leaves?"

I shrugged. "I suspect Morrolan wouldn't mind that. He might even do it himself, if he's as upset about being used this way as I expect him to be. But we still have the time problem."

"I don't suppose," said Kragar slowly, "that, since Morrolan is a friend of yours, he might, just this once . . ."

"I don't even want to ask him. Oh, I will, if we get desperate enough, but I don't think we have much of a chance of his agreeing. He was a Dragonlord long before he was a friend of mine."

"Do you think we might be able to make it look like an accident?"

I thought about that for a long time. "No. For one thing, the Demon wants it known that the Jhereg killed him—that's sort of the point of doing it in the first place. For another, I'm not sure it's possible. Remember: this has to be permanent. By Morrolan's rules, we can kill him as many times as we want, as long as we make sure he can be, and *is*, revivified after. People are killed every day at Castle Black, but he hasn't had one permanent death there since he had the place built. There's no point in having an accident that isn't permanent; and do you have any idea how hard it would be to set up an 'accident' so he's killed unrevivifiably? What am I supposed to do, have him trip and fall on a Morganti dagger?

"And another thing," I went on, "if we were to kill him that way, you can be damn sure that Morrolan would throw everything he had into an investigation. He takes a lot of pride in his record and would probably feel 'dishonored' if someone were to die, even accidentally, at Castle Black."

I shook my head. "It's really a strange place. You know

how many duels are fought there every day? And not one
of them on any terms other than no cuts to the head, and
revivification afterwards. He'd check everything himself,
twenty times, if Mellar had an 'accident,' and chances are
good that he'd find out what happened."

"All right," said Kragar. "I'm convinced."

"There's one more thing. Just to put this away, or anything like it, I'd better make it clear that I consider
Morrolan a friend, and I'm not going to let him get hurt like
that if there's any way I can prevent it. I owe him too
much."

"*You're rambling, boss.*"

"*Shut up, Loiosh. I was done anyway.*"

Kragar shrugged. "Okay, you've convinced me. So what
can we do?"

"I don't know yet. Let me think about it. And if you get
any more ideas, let me know."

"Oh, I will. Someone has to do your thinking for you.
Which reminds me—"

"Yes?"

"One piece of good news out of this whole thing."

"Oh, really? What is it?"

"Well, now we have an excuse to talk to the Lady Aliera.
After all, she is Morrolan's cousin, and she is staying with
him, last I heard. From what I know about her, by the way,
she isn't going to be at all pleased that her cousin is being
used by a Jhereg. In fact, she'll probably end up an ally, if
we work it right."

I took out a dagger and absently started flipping it as I
thought that over. "Not bad," I agreed. "Okay, then I'll
make seeing her and Morrolan my first priority."

Kragar shook his head, in mock sorrow. "I don't know,
boss. First the witchcraft thing, and now this business with
Aliera. I've been coming up with all the ideas around here.
I think you're slipping. What the hell would you do without
me, anyway?"

"I'd have been dead a long time ago," I said. "Want to
make something of it?"

He laughed and got up. "Nope, not a thing. What now?"

"Tell Morrolan that I'm coming to see him."

"When?"

"Right away. And get a sorcerer up here to do a teleport.

The way I'm feeling right now, I don't trust my own spells."

Kragar walked out the door, shaking his head sadly. I put my dagger away and held out an arm to Loiosh. He flew over and landed on my shoulder. I stood by the window and looked out over the streets below. It was quiet and only moderately busy. There were few street vendors in this part of town and not really a lot of traffic until nightfall. By then I'd be at Castle Black, some two hundred miles to the Northeast.

Morrolan, I knew, was going to be mighty angry at someone. Unlike a Dzur, however, an angry Dragon is unpredictable.

"This could get really ugly, boss," said Loiosh.

"Yeah," I told him. *"I know."*

7

"Always speak politely to an enraged Dragon."

My first reaction, years before, upon hearing about the Castle Black, had been contempt. For one thing, black has been considered the color of sorcery for hundreds of thousands of years on Dragaera, and it takes a bit of gall to name one's home that. Also, of course, is the fact that the Castle floats. It hangs there, about a mile off the ground, looking real impressive from a distance. It was the only floating castle then in existence.

I should mention that there had been many floating castles before the Interregnum. I guess the spell isn't all that difficult, if you care to put enough work into it in the first place. The reason that they are currently out of vogue is the Interregnum itself. One day, over four hundred years ago now, sorcery stopped working . . . just like that. If you look around in the right places in the countryside you will still find broken husks and shattered remnants of what were once floating castles.

Lord Morrolan e'Drien was born during the Interregnum, which he spent mostly in the East, studying witchcraft. This is very rare for a Dragaeran. While the Easterners were using the failure of Dragaeran sorcery to turn the tables and invade *them* for a change, Morrolan was quietly building up skill and power.

Then, when Zerika, of the House of the Phoenix, came strolling out of the Paths of the Dead with the Orb clutched in her greedy little hands, Morrolan was right there, helping her stomp her way to the throne. After that, he was instrumental in driving back the Easterners, and he helped cure the plagues they left behind them as remembrances of their visit.

All this conspired to make him more tolerant of Easterners than is normal for a Dragaeran, particularly a Dragonlord. That is partly how I ended up working for him on a permanent basis, after we almost killed each other the first time we met. Little misunderstandings, and all.

I slowly came to realize that the Lord Morrolan was actually worthy of having a home called Castle Black—not that he would have cared a teckla's squeal what I thought of it in any case. I also came to understand part of the reason behind the name.

You must understand that Dragonlords, particularly when they are young (if you've been paying attention, you'll note that Morrolan was under five hundred), tend to be—how shall I put this—excitable. Morrolan knew quite well that naming his keep what he did was somewhat pretentious, and he also knew that, from time to time, people would mock him for it. When that happened, he would challenge them to duel and then take great delight in killing them.

Lord Morrolan, of the House of the Dragon, was one of damn few nobles who deserved the title. I have seen him show most of the attributes one expects of a noble: courtesy, kindness, honor. I would also say that he is one of the most bloodthirsty bastards I have ever met.

I was welcomed to Castle Black, as always, by Lady Teldra, of the House of the Issola. I don't know what Morrolan paid her for her services as reception committee and welcoming service. Lady Teldra was tall, beautiful, and graceful as a dzur. Her eyes were as soft as an iorich's wing, and her walk was smooth, flowing, and delicate as a court dancer's. She held herself with the relaxed, confident poise of, well, of an issola.

I bowed low to her, and she returned my bow along with a stream of meaningless pleasantries that made me very glad I had come and almost made me forget my mission.

She showed me to the library, where Morrolan was

seated, going over some kind of large tome or ledger, making notes as he went.

"Enter," said Morrolan.

I did, and bowed deeply to him; he acknowledged.

"What is it, Vlad?"

"Problems," I told him, as Lady Teldra swished back to her position near the castle entrance. "What else do you think I'd be doing here? You don't think I'd deign to visit you socially, do you?"

He permitted himself a smile and held out his right arm to Loiosh, who flew over to it and accepted some head-scratching. "Of course not," he responded. "That was only an illusion of you at the party the other day."

"Exactly. How clever of you to notice. Is Aliera around?"

"Somewhere. Why?"

"The problem also involves her. And, for that matter, Sethra should be in on it too, if she's available. It would be easier if I could explain to all of you at once."

Morrolan's brows came together for a moment; then he nodded to me. "Okay, Aliera is on her way, and she'll mention it to Sethra."

Aliera arrived almost immediately, and Morrolan and I stood for her. She gave us each a small bow. Morrolan was a bit tall for a Dragaeran. His cousin Aliera, however, was the shortest Dragaeran I have ever known; she could have been mistaken for a tall human. Bothered by this, it was her habit to wear gowns that were too long, and then make up the difference by levitating rather than walking. There have been those who made disparaging remarks about this. Aliera, however, was never one to hold a grudge. She almost always revivified them afterwards.

Both Morrolan and Aliera had something of the typical Dragon facial features—the high cheekbones, rather thin faces and sharp brows of the House; but there was little else in common. Morrolan's hair was as black as mine, whereas Aliera had golden hair—rare in a Dragaeran and almost unheard of in a Dragonlord. Her eyes were normally green, another oddity, but I've seen them change from green to gray, and occasionally to ice blue. When Aliera's eyes turn blue, I'm very, very careful around her.

Sethra arrived just after her. What can I tell you about Sethra Lavode? Those who believe in her say she has lived ten thousand years (some say twenty). Others say she is a myth. Call her life unnatural, feel her undead breath. Color her black for sorcery, color her gray for death.

She smiled at me. We were all friends here. Morrolan carried Blackwand, which slew a thousand at the Wall of Baritt's Tomb. Aliera carried Pathfinder, which they say served a power higher than the Empire. Sethra carried Iceflame, which embodied within it the power of Dzur Mountain. I carried myself rather well, thank you.

We all sat down, making us equals.

"And so, Vlad," said Morrolan, "what's up?"

"My ire," I told him.

His eyebrows arched. "Not at anyone I know, I hope."

"As a matter of fact, at one of your guests."

"Indeed? How dreadfully unfortunate for you both. Which one, if I may ask?"

"Do you know a certain Lord Mellar? Jhereg?"

"Why, yes. It happens that I do."

"Might I inquire as to the circumstances?"

(*Giggle.*) *"You're starting to sound like him, boss."*

"Shut up, Loiosh."

Morrolan shrugged. "He sent word to me a few weeks ago that he'd acquired a certain book I've been interested in, and made an appointment to bring it by. He arrived with it . . . let me see . . . three days ago now. He has remained as my guest since that time."

"I presume he actually had the book?"

"You presume correctly." Morrolan indicated the tome he'd been reading as I entered. I looked at the cover, which bore a symbol I didn't recognize.

"What is it?" I asked him.

He looked at me for a moment, as if wondering whether I was trustworthy, or perhaps whether he should allow himself to be questioned; then he shrugged.

"Pre-Empire sorcery," he said.

I whistled in appreciation, as well as surprise. I glanced around the room quickly, but none of the others seemed astonished by this revelation. They had probably known all along. I keep finding things out about people, just when I think I know them. "Does the Empress know about this little hobby of yours?" I asked him.

He smiled a little. "Somehow I keep forgetting to mention it to her."

"How unlike you," I remarked.

When he didn't say anything, I asked, "How long have you been studying it?"

"Pre-Empire sorcery? It's been rather an interest of mine for a hundred years or so. In fact, the Empress undoubtedly knows; it isn't all that much of a secret. Naturally, I've never acknowledged it officially, but it's a bit like owning a Morganti blade: if they need an excuse to harass a fellow, they have one. Other than that they won't bother one about it. Unless, of course, one starts using it."

"Or unless one happens to be a Jhereg," I muttered.

"There is that, isn't there?"

I turned back to the main subject. "How did Mellar end up staying here, after he delivered the book?"

Morrolan looked thoughtful. "Would you mind terribly if I asked what this is all about?"

I glanced around the room again and saw that Sethra and Aliera also seemed interested. Aliera was sitting on the couch, an arm thrown casually across it, a wineglass in her other hand (Where had she gotten it?) held so that the light from the large ceiling lamp reflected off it and made pretty patterns on her cheek. She surveyed me coolly from under her eyelids, her head tilted slightly.

Sethra was looking at me steadily, intently. She had chosen a black upholstered chair which blended with her gown, and her pale white, undead skin shone out. I felt a tension in her, as if she had a feeling that something unpleasant was going on. Knowing Sethra, she probably did.

Morrolan sat at the other end of the couch from Aliera—relaxed, and yet looking as if he were posing for a painting. I shook my head.

"I'll tell you if you insist," I said, "but I'd rather find out a little more first, so I have a better idea of what I'm talking about."

"Or how much you feel like telling us?" asked Aliera, sweetly.

I couldn't repress a smile.

"I might point out," said Morrolan, "that if you want our help with anything, you're going to have to give us essentially the whole story."

"I'm aware of that," I said.

Morrolan gathered in the others' opinions with a glance. Aliera shrugged with her wineglass, as if it made no difference in the world to her. Sethra nodded, once.

Morrolan turned back to me. "Very well, then, Vlad. What exactly did you wish to know?"

"How was it that Mellar happened to stay here after delivering the book? You aren't in the habit of inviting Jhereg into your home."

Morrolan permitted himself another smile. "With a few exceptions," he said.

"Some of us are special."

"Shut up, Loiosh."

"Count Mellar," said Morrolan, "contacted me some four days ago. He informed me that he had a volume that he thought I'd want and politely suggested that he drop by and deliver it."

I interrupted. "Didn't it seem a bit odd that he'd hand it over himself, rather than have a flunky deliver it?"

"Yes, it did occur to me as odd. But after all, such a book *is* illegal and I made the assumption that he didn't want anyone to know that he had it. His employees, after all, were Jhereg. How could he trust them?" He paused for a moment, to see if I'd respond to the cut, but I let it go by. "In any case," he continued, "the Count appeared to be a very polite fellow. I did a bit of checking around on him, and found him to be a trustworthy sort, for a Jhereg. After deciding that he probably wouldn't make any trouble, I invited him to dine with me and a few other guests, and he accepted."

I glanced quickly at Aliera and Sethra. Sethra shook her head, indicating that she hadn't been there. Aliera was looking moderately interested. She nodded.

"I remember him," she said. "He was dull."

With that ultimate condemnation, I turned back to Morrolan, who continued. "The dinner went well enough that I felt no compunctions about inviting him to the general party. I will admit that a few of my coarser guests, who don't think well of Jhereg, tried to give him trouble in one fashion or another, but he was quite friendly and went out of his way to avoid problems.

"So I gave him an invitation to stay here for seventeen days, if he cared to. I will admit to being somewhat startled when he accepted, but I assumed he wanted a short vacation or something. What else did you wish to know?"

I held up my hand, asking for a moment's grace while I sorted out this new information. Could he . . .? What were the chances? How sure could Mellar be?

"Do you have any idea," I asked, "how he might have gotten his hands on the book in the first place?"

Morrolan shook his head. "The one stipulation that he had for returning it was that I make no effort to find out how he got it. You see, at one time it held a place in my library. It was, as you would say, 'lifted.' I might add this occurred before I started making improvements in my security system."

I nodded. Unfortunately, it was all fitting in rather well.

"Didn't that make you suspicious?" I asked.

"I assumed that it was a Jhereg who stole it, of course. But, as you should be aware of more than I, there are endless possibilities as to how this fellow could have received it, 'legitimately,' if you will. For example, the fellow who had taken it could have found that he couldn't sell it safely, and Count Mellar might have done him a favor by making sure that I never found out the details of the crime. Jhereg do tend to operate that way, you know."

I knew. "How long ago was this book stolen?"

"How long? Let me think . . . it would be . . . about ten years ago now, I believe."

"Damn," I muttered to myself, "so Kragar was right."

"What is it, Vlad?" asked Aliera. She was genuinely interested, now.

I looked at the three of them. How should I go about this? I had a sudden urge to answer, "Oh, nothing," get up, and see how close I could get to the door before they stopped me. I didn't really like the idea of having the three of them fly into a sudden rage—with me being the bearer of bad tidings and all. Of course, I didn't really think any of them would hurt me, but. . . .

I tried to think of an indirect approach and got nowhere.
"Suggestions, Loiosh?"
"Tell 'em straight out, boss. Then teleport."
"I can't teleport fast enough. Serious suggestions, Loiosh?"

Nothing. I had found a way to shut him up. Somehow my joy at this discovery was somewhat dimmed, under the circumstances.

"He's using you, Morrolan," I said, flatly.

" 'Using' me? How, pray?"

"Mellar is on the run from the Jhereg. He's staying here for one reason only: he knows that no Jhereg can touch him while he's a guest in a Dragonlord's home."

Morrolan's brows came together. I felt a storm brewing over the horizon. "Are you quite certain of this?" he asked, mildly.

I nodded. "I think," I said slowly, "that if you were to do some checking, you'd find that it was Mellar himself who took the book, or else hired someone to take it. It all fits in. Yes, I'm sure."

I glanced over at Aliera. She was staring at Morrolan, with a look of shock on her face. The cute dilettante who'd been sitting there seconds ago was gone.

"Of all the nerve!" she burst out.

"Oh, he's nervy all right," I told her.

Sethra cut in. "Vlad, how could Mellar have known that he'd be invited to stay at Castle Black?"

I sighed inwardly. I had hoped that no one would ask me that. "That's no trick. He must have done a study on Morrolan and found out what he'd have to do to receive an invitation. I hate to say this, Morrolan, but you are rather predictable in certain matters."

Morrolan shot me a look of disgust, but, fortunately, was not otherwise affected. I noticed that Sethra was gently stroking the hilt of Iceflame. I shuddered. Aliera's eyes had turned gray. Morrolan was looking grim. He stood up and began pacing in front of us. Aliera, Sethra, and I held our peace. After a couple of trips, he said. "Are you certain he knows that the Jhereg is after him?"

"He knows."

"And," Morrolan continued, "you are convinced that he

would have been aware of this when he first contacted me?"

"Morrolan, he planned it that way. I'll go even further; according to all the evidence we have, he's been planning this whole thing for at least ten years."

"I see." He shook his head, slowly. His hand came to rest on the hilt of Blackwand, and I shuddered again. After a time, he said, "You know how I feel concerning treatment and safety of my guests, do you not?"

I nodded.

"Then you are no doubt aware that we cannot harm him in any way—at least, not until his seventeen days are up."

I nodded again. "Unless he leaves of his own free will," I put in.

He looked at me, suspiciously.

Aliera spoke, then. "You aren't going to just let him get away with this, are you?" she asked. There was just the hint of an edge to her voice. I suddenly wished that I had Kragar's ability to be unnoticeable.

"For today, my dear cousin, and thirteen more days after, he is perfectly safe here. After that," his voice suddenly turned cold and hard, "he's dead."

"I can't give you the details," I said, "but in thirteen days he will have irreparably damaged the Jhereg."

Morrolan shrugged, and Aliera gave me a brushing-off motion. So what? Who cared about the Jhereg, anyway? But I noticed Sethra nodding, as if she understood.

"And in thirteen days," she put in, "he'll be long gone."

Aliera gave a toss of her head and stood, flinging her cloak to the side and bringing her hand down to Pathfinder's hilt. "Let him try to hide," she said.

"You are missing the point," said Sethra. "I'm not doubting that you and Pathfinder will be able to track him down. What I'm saying is that with all the time he's had, he'll be able to, at least, make it difficult for you. It could take you days to find him if, for example, he goes out East. And in the meantime," her voice took on a cutting edge, "he'll have succeeded in using a Dragon to hide from the Jhereg."

This hit the two of them, and they didn't like it. But there was something else that was bothering me.

"Aliera," I said, "are you *sure* that there isn't anything he could do to prevent you from finding him with Pathfinder? It doesn't make sense that he'd work for this long on such an intricate scheme, only to let you and Morrolan track him down and kill him."

"As you may recall," she said, "I've only had Pathfinder for a few months, and it's hardly common knowledge that I have a Great Weapon at all. It's something that he couldn't have counted on. If I didn't have it, he could have figured on escaping us."

I accepted that. Yes, it was possible. No matter how carefully you plan things, there is always the chance that you could miss something important. This is a risky business we're in.

Aliera turned to Morrolan. "I don't think," she said, "that we should wait the rest of those seventeen days."

Morrolan turned away.

"Here it comes, boss."

"I know, Loiosh. Let's hope Sethra can handle it—and wants to."

"Don't you see," continued Aliera, "that this, this *Jhereg* is trying to make you nothing more than a bodyguard from his own House?"

"I'm quite aware of this, I assure you, Aliera," he answered softly.

"And that doesn't bother you? He's dishonoring the entire House of the Dragon! How *dare* he use a Dragonlord?"

"Ha!" said Morrolan. "How dare he use *me*? But it's rather obvious that he *does* dare, and equally obvious that he's gotten away with it." Morrolan's gaze was fixed on her. He was either challenging her or waiting to see if she would challenge him. Either way, I decided, it didn't much matter.

"He hasn't gotten away with it yet," said Aliera, grimly.

"And what exactly does that mean?" asked Morrolan.

"Just what it sounds like. He hasn't gotten away with anything. He's assuming that, just because he's a guest, he can insult you as much as he wants, and no one will touch him."

"And he is correct," said Morrolan.

"Is he?" asked Aliera. "Is he really? Are you sure?"

"Quite sure," said Morrolan.

Aliera matched stares with him for a while, then she said, "If you choose to ignore the insult to your honor, that's your business. But when an insult is given to the entire House of the Dragon, it's my business, too."

"Nevertheless," said Morrolan, "since the insult was delivered through me, it is my right, and my duty, to avenge it, don't you think?"

Aliera smiled. She sat back, relaxed, the very picture of one who's just had her worries removed. "Oh, good!" she said. "So you'll kill him after all!"

"Why certainly I shall," said Morrolan, showing his teeth, "thirteen days from now."

I glanced at Sethra to see how this was affecting her. She hadn't yet said anything, but the look on her face was far from pleasant. I was hoping that she'd be willing and able to mediate between the two of them if things started to get pushed too far. Looking at her, however, made me wonder if she had any such inclination.

Aliera wasn't smiling any more. Her hand gripped the hilt of Pathfinder, and her knuckles were white. "That," she explained, "is doing nothing. I will not permit a Jhereg to —"

"You will not touch him, Aliera," said Morrolan. "So long as I live, no guest in my house need fear for his life. I don't care who he is, why he's here; so long as I have extended him my welcome, he may consider himself safe.

"I have entertained my own blood enemies at my table, and arranged Morganti duels with them. I have seen the Necromancer speaking quietly to one who had been an enemy of hers for six incarnations. I have seen Sethra," he gestured toward her, "sitting across from a Dzurlord who had sworn to destroy her. I will not allow you, my own cousin, to cast my name in the mud; to make me an oathbreaker. Is that how you would preserve the honor of the House of the Dragon?"

"Oh, speak on, great protector of honor," she said. "Why not go all the way? Put up a poster outside the Jhereg barracks, saying that you are always willing to protect anyone who wants to run from their hired killers?"

He ignored the sarcasm. "And can you explain to me," he said, "how it is that we can defend our honor as a House if each member does not honor even his own words?"

Aliera shook her head and continued in a softer voice. "Don't you see, Morrolan, that there is a difference between the codes of honor, and of practice, that have come down from the traditions of the House of the Dragon, and your own custom? I'm not objecting to your having your little customs; I think it's a fine thing. But it isn't on the same level as the traditions of the House."

He nodded. "I understand that, Aliera," he said. "But it isn't just a 'custom' I'm talking about; it's an oath that I've sworn to make Castle Black a place of refuge. It would be different if we were at, say, Dzur Mountain."

She shook her head. "I just don't understand you. Of course you want to live by your oath, but does that mean that you have to allow yourself, and the House, to be used by it? He isn't just living under your oath, he's abusing it."

"That's true," agreed Morrolan. "But I'm afraid he's correct. There simply isn't any chance of my breaking it, and he realizes that. I'm rather surprised that you can't understand that."

I decided the time was right to intervene. "It seems to me that—"

"Silence, Jhereg," snapped Aliera. "This doesn't concern you."

I reconsidered.

"It isn't that I can't understand it," she went on to Morrolan, "it's just that I think your priorities are wrong."

He shrugged. "I'm sorry you feel that way."

It was the wrong thing to say. Aliera rose, and her eyes, I saw, had turned ice blue. "As it happens," she said, "it wasn't my oath, it was yours. If you were no longer master of Castle Black, we wouldn't have this problem, would we? And I don't recall anything in your oath that prevents a guest from attacking you!"

Morrolan's hand was white where he gripped the hilt of Blackwand. Loiosh dived under my cloak. I would have liked to do the same.

"That's true," said Morrolan, evenly. "Attack away."

Sethra spoke for the first time, gently. "Need I point out the guest laws, Aliera?"

She didn't answer. She stood, gripping her blade, and staring hard at Morrolan. It occurred to me then that she didn't want to attack Morrolan at all; she wanted him to attack her. I wasn't surprised at her next statement.

"And guest laws," Aliera said, "apply to all hosts. Even if they claim to be Dragons, but don't have the courage to avenge an insult done to all of us."

It almost worked, but Morrolan stopped himself. His tone matched the color of her eyes. "You may consider it fortunate that I have the rule I do, and that you are as much a guest as this Jhereg, although it is clear that he knows far more than you about the courtesy a guest owes a host."

"Ha!" cried Aliera, drawing Pathfinder.

"Oh, shit," I said.

"All right, Morrolan, then I release you from your oath, as regards me. It doesn't matter anyway, since I'd much rather be a dead dragon than a live teckla!" Pathfinder stood out like a short green rod of light, pulsating gently.

"You don't seem to realize, cousin," he said, "that you don't have power over my oath."

Now Sethra stood up. Thank the Lords of Judgment, she hadn't drawn Iceflame. She calmly stepped between them. "You both lose," she said. "Neither of you has any intention of attacking the other, and you both know it. Aliera wants Morrolan to kill her, which preserves her honor and breaks his oath, so that he may as well go ahead and kill Mellar. Morrolan wants Aliera to kill him, being the one to break guest-laws, so she can then go ahead and kill Mellar herself. I, however, have no intention of allowing either of you to be killed or dishonored, so you may as well forget the provocations."

They stood that way for a moment, then Morrolan allowed the ghost of a smile to pass over his lips. Aliera did the same. Loiosh peeked out from under my cloak, then resumed his position on my right shoulder.

Sethra turned to me. "Vlad," she said, "isn't it true that you are—" she stopped, reconsidered, and tried again, "—that you know the person who is supposed to kill Mellar?"

I rubbed my neck, which I discovered had become rather tense, and said drily, "I expect I could put a hand on him."

"Good. Maybe we should all start trying to think of ways to help out this fellow, instead of ways to goad ourselves into murdering each other."

Morrolan and Aliera both scowled at the idea of helping a Jhereg, then shrugged.

I gave a short prayer of thanks to Verra that I'd thought of asking Sethra to show up.

"How much time is there that the assassin can wait?" asked Sethra.

How the hell did she find out so much? I asked myself, for the millionth time since I'd known her. "Maybe a few days," I said.

"All right, what can we do to help?"

I shrugged. "The only thing I can think of is just what Aliera thought of earlier—tracing him with Pathfinder. The problem is that we need some way of getting him to leave soon enough, without, of course, forcing him to."

Aliera took her seat again, but Morrolan turned and headed for the door. "All things considered," he said, "I don't think it quite proper that I include myself in this. I trust you all," he looked significantly at Aliera, "not to violate my oath, but I don't think it would be right for me to conspire against my own guest. Excuse me." Bowing, he left.

Aliera picked up the threads of the conversation. "You mean, trick him into leaving?"

"Something like that. I don't know, maybe put a spell on him, so he thinks he's safe. Can that be done?"

Sethra looked thoughtful, but Aliera cut in before she could speak. "No, that won't do," she said. "I expect it could be done, but, in the first place, Morrolan would detect it. And, in the second place, we can't use any form of magic against him without violating Morrolan's oath."

"By Adron's Disaster!" I said, "you mean we can't trick him, either?"

"No, no," said Aliera. "We're free to convince him to leave on his own, even if we have to lie to do it. But we can't use magic against him. Morrolan doesn't see any difference between, for instance, using an energy bolt to blast him, or using a mind implant to make him leave."

"Oh, that's just charming," I said. "I don't suppose either of you has any idea of how we're going to accomplish this?"

They both shook their heads.

I stood up. "All right, I'll be heading back to my office. Please keep thinking about it, and let me know if you get anywhere."

They nodded and settled back, deep in discussion. I didn't think much of the chances of their actually coming up with something. I mean, they were both damn good at what they did, but what they did wasn't assassination. On the other hand, I could be surprised. In any case, it was certainly better having them work with me than against me.

I bowed, and left.

**"There is no such thing as
sufficient preparation."**

I returned to my office and allowed my stomach to recover
from the aftereffects of the teleport. After about ten
minutes, I contacted my secretary. *"Please ask Kragar to
step in here,"* I communicated.

"But, boss—he went in five minutes ago."

I looked up and found him seated in his usual place and
looking innocent.

"Never mind."

I shook my head. "I really wish you'd stop doing that."

"Doing what?"

I sighed. "Kragar, Aliera is willing to help us."

"Good. Do you have a plan yet?"

"No, only the start of one. But Aliera, and, by the way,
Sethra Lavode, are trying to come up with the rest of it."

He looked impressed. "Sethra? Not bad. What
happened?"

"Nothing—but just barely."

"Eh?"

I gave him a report on what had occurred. "So," I con-
cluded, "now we need to figure out how we're going to get
Mellar to leave early."

"Well," he said thoughtfully, "you could ask the
Demon."

"Oh, sure. And if he doesn't have any ideas, I'll ask the
Empress. And—"

"What's wrong with asking the Demon? Since you're going to be talking to him anyway, why not take the op—"

"I'm going to what?"

"The Demon wants to meet with you, right away. A message came in just before you did."

"What does he want to meet with me about?"

"He didn't say. Maybe he's come across some information."

"Information he could just send over. Dammit, he'd better not be jogging my sword-arm. He knows better than that."

"Sure he does," snorted Kragar. "But what the hell are you going to do about it if he decides to do it anyway?"

"There is that, isn't there?"

He nodded.

"When, and where? No, let me guess, same time and place, right?"

"Half-right. Same place, but noon."

"Noon? But isn't it already—" I stopped, concentrated a moment, and got the time. By the Great Sea of Chaos, it was barely half an hour before noon! That whole conversation had taken less than an hour. Verra!

"That means he's buying me lunch, doesn't it?"

"Right."

"And it also means that we don't really have time to set up something, in case *he's* set up something."

"Right again. You know, Vlad, we'd be within our rights to just refuse to meet with him. You aren't bound by something like this."

"Do you think that's a good idea?"

He thought for a minute, then shook his head.

"Neither do I," I said.

"Well, would you like me to put someone in there as a guest? We could arrange for one or two people—"

"No. He's pick up on it, and we can't let that happen at this point. It would indicate that we don't trust him. Which we don't, of course, but . . ."

"Yeah, I know."

He shrugged and changed the subject. "About this business with Aliera and Sethra, do you have any ideas on how we're going to convince Mellar to leave Castle Black?"

"Well," I said, "we could invite him to a business meeting."

Kragar chuckled. "Next idea," he said.

"I don't know. That's been the problem from the beginning, hasn't it?"

"Uh-huh."

I shrugged. "Maybe something will come up. By the way, if there's anything more we can do in terms of digging into Mellar's background, let's do it. I'd dearly love to find a weak spot in him just about now."

He nodded. "It would be nice, wouldn't it?"

"Dammit, he came from somewhere. The information we got from the Demon doesn't start until he joined the Jhereg. We don't know a damn thing before then."

"I know, but how are we supposed to dig up more than the Demon could?"

"I don't know . . . Yes! I do! Aliera! That was what I'd wanted her help with in the first place, and then when things got hot over there I never thought about asking her."

"Asking her what?"

"Well, among other things, she specializes in genetic research."

"So?"

"So tell me—what House was Mellar born into?"

"I assume Jhereg. What makes you think differently?"

"I don't, but we have no reason to be sure. If it is Jhereg, there's a chance that Aliera could lead us to his parents, and we could start digging there. If not, that would tell us something worthwhile in itself and might lead us in other directions."

"Okay. I guess that isn't something the Demon would have been able to check out. Are you going to contact her yourself, or do you want me to set up another appointment?"

I thought it over before answering. "You set it up," I decided. "As long as this mess continues, we do everything formally. Make it for this evening, early, if possible. If I'm still alive. Ask her to check him over."

"Okay, I'll take care of it. If you're dead, I'll apologize to her for you."

"Oh, good. That's a great load off my mind."

Once again, I had my back to the door. My right arm was

next to my wineglass; I could get a dagger from my left arm-sheath and throw it well enough to hit a moving wine cork from fifteen feet away in less than half a second. Loiosh kept his eyes fixed on the door. I was keenly aware that, if I were, indeed, about to be removed, none of these things would really give me enough of an edge.

My palms, however, were dry. There were three reasons for this: first, I had been in many situations before where I might suddenly have to move at top speed to save my life. Second, I really didn't think it very likely that the Demon was going to take me out. There are simpler ways to do it, and I was pretty sure by this time that everything was legitimate. And third, I continually wiped my hands on the legs of my breeches.

"Here he comes, boss."

"Alone?"

"Two bodyguards, but they're waiting by the door."

The Demon slid smoothly into the seat across from me. "Good afternoon," he said. "How are things coming?"

"They're coming. I recommend the tsalmoth in garlic butter."

"As you say." He signaled over a waiter, who took our orders with enough respect to show that he knew who I, at least, was. The Demon picked out a light *Nyroth* wine to go along with it, showing that he also knew something about eating.

"Things are looking a little more urgent now, Vlad. May I call you Vlad?" he added.

"Tell him, 'no,' boss."

"Of course." I chuckled. "I'll call you 'Demon.'"

He smiled, without showing how bored he must have been at the remark. "As I was saying—things *are* starting to look serious. It seems that a few too many people know already. The best sorceresses in the Left Hand have figured out that someone big is interested in finding Mellar, but there wasn't any way to avoid that. On the other hand, there are a few others who are wondering about some cutbacks we've had to make in our operations. All it's going to take is for someone to start putting the two things together, and then things get unpleasant real fast."

"So, are you—" I stopped, as the soup came. Out of reflex, I passed my left hand over it briefly, but there wasn't any poison, of course. Poison is clumsy and unpredictable, and few Dragaerans knew enough about the metabolism of an Easterner to leave me seriously worried about it.

I continued when the waiter left. "Are you saying you want me to push it a bit?" I held down my annoyance; the last thing this side of Deathsgate I wanted just then was for the Demon to get the idea that I was upset.

"As much as you can without risking mistakes. But that wasn't really what I wanted—I know you're moving as fast as you can."

Sure, he did. The soup was flat, I decided.

"We've learned something that may interest you," he continued.

I waited.

"Mellar is holed up in Castle Black."

He looked for a reaction from me, and, when he didn't get one, continued.

"Our sorcerers broke through about two hours ago, and I got in touch with your people right away. So, you can forget checking out East. The reason we couldn't find him for so long was because Castle Black is close to two hundred miles from Adrilankha—but, of course, you know that. You work for Morrolan, right?"

"Work for him? No. I'm on his payroll as a security consultant, nothing more."

He nodded. He worked on his soup for a while, then, "You didn't seem surprised when I told you where he was."

"Thank you very much," I said.

The Demon let me know that he had teeth and raised his glass in salute. Smiling, say the sages, comes from an early form of baring the teeth. While jhereg don't bare their teeth, Jhereg do. "Did you know?" asked the Demon, bluntly.

I nodded.

"I'm impressed," he said. "You move quickly."

I continued to wait, while finishing up my soup. I still didn't know why he was here, but I was quite sure that it wasn't in order to compliment me on my information sources, or to give me information he could have had sent over by a courier.

He picked up his wineglass and looked into it, swirled it

around a little, and sipped it. Crazily, he suddenly reminded me of the Necromancer. "Vlad," he said, "I think
we may have a possible conflict of interest developing
here."

"Indeed?"

"Well, it is known that you are a friend of Morrolan.
Now, Morrolan is harboring Mellar. It would seem that our
goals, and his goals, might not run along the same paths."

I still didn't say anything. The waiter showed up with the
main course, and I checked it, and started in. The Demon
pretended not to notice my gesture. I pretended not to notice when he did the same thing.

He continued, after swallowing and making the obligato-
ry murmur of satisfaction. "Things could get very unpleasant for Morrolan."

"I can't imagine how," I said, "unless you plan to start
another Dragon-Jhereg war. And Mellar, no matter what
he did, can't be worth that much."

Now it was the Demon who said nothing. I got a sinking
feeling in the pit of my stomach.

I said slowly, "He *can't* be worth another Dragon-Jhereg
war."

He still said nothing.

I shook my head. Would he really go ahead and try to
nail Mellar right in Morrolan's castle? Gods! He was saying
that he would! He'd bring every Dragon on Dragaera down
on our heads. This could be worse than the last one. It was
the reign of the Phoenix, which made the Dragons corre-
spondingly higher on the Cycle. The higher a House is, the
more fate tends to favor it. I don't know the why or how of
that, but it works that way. The Demon knew it, too.

"Why?" I asked him.

"At this point," he said slowly, "I don't think that there
is any need to start such a war. I think that it can be worked
around, which is why I'm talking to you. But, I will say this:
if I'm wrong, and the only options I can see are letting
Mellar get away with this or starting another war, I'll start
the war. Why? Because if we have a war, things will get
bad, yes, very bad, but then it will be over. We know what
to expect this time, and we'll be ready for it. Oh, sure,
they'll hurt us. Perhaps badly. But we will recover,
eventually—in a few thousand years.

"On the other hand, if Mellar gets away with this, there won't be an end to it. Ever. As long as House Jhereg lasts, we'll have to contend with thieves plotting after our funds. We'll be crippled forever."

His eyes became thin lines, and I saw his teeth clench for a moment. "*I* built us up after Adron's Disaster. *I* made a dispirited, broken House into a viable business again. I'm willing to see my work set back a thousand years, or ten thousand years if I have to, but I'm not willing to see us weakened forever."

He sat back. I let his remarks sink in. The worst thing was, he was right. If I were in his position, I would probably find myself making the same decision. I shook my head.

"You're right," I told him. "We have a conflict of interest. If you give me enough time, I'll finish my work. But I'm not going to let you nail someone in Castle Black. I'm sorry, but that's how it is."

He nodded, thoughtfully. "How much time do you need?"

"I don't know. As soon as he leaves Castle Black, I can get him. But I haven't come up with a way to get him to leave yet."

"Will two days do it?"

I thought that over. "Maybe," I said finally. "Probably not."

He nodded and was silent.

I used a piece of only slightly stale bread to get the rest of the garlic butter (I never said it was a good restaurant for *eating* in), and asked him, "What is your idea for avoiding the Dragon-Jhereg war?"

He shook his head, slowly. He wasn't going to give me any more information about that. Instead, he signaled the waiter over and paid him. "I'm sorry," he told me as the waiter walked away. "We'll have to do it without your cooperation. You could have been very helpful." He left the table and walked toward the door.

The waiter, I noticed, was returning with the change. I absently waved him away. That's when it hit me. The Demon would have realized that this outcome was possible, but wanted to give me a chance to save myself. Oh, shit. I felt the waves of panic start up, but forced them down. I wouldn't leave this place, I decided, until help arrived. I started to reach out for contact with Kragar.

The waiter hadn't caught my signal and was still approaching. I started to gesture him away again when Loiosh screamed a warning into my mind. I caught the flicker of motion almost at the same time. I pushed the table away from me and reached for a dagger at the same moment that Loiosh left my shoulder to attack. But I also knew, in that instant, that both of us would be too late. The timing had been perfect, the setup professional. I turned, hoping to at least get the assassin.

There was a gurgling sound as I turned and stood up. Instead of lunging at me, the "waiter" fell against me, then continued on to the floor. There was a large kitchen cleaver in his hand, and the point of a dagger sticking out of his throat.

I looked around the room as the screams started. It took me a while, but I finally located Kragar, seated at a table a few feet from mine. He stood up and walked over to me. I felt myself start trembling, but I didn't allow myself to fall back into my chair until I was sure the Demon had left.

He had. His bodyguards were gone, probably having been out the door before the assassin's body had fallen. Wise, of course. Any of his people left here were dead. Loiosh returned to my shoulder, and I felt him glancing around the room, as if to make any guilty party cower in shame. There would be none of them left now. He'd taken his best shot, and it had almost worked.

I sat down and trembled for a while.

"Thanks, Kragar. Were you there the whole time?"

"Yeah. As a matter of fact, you looked right through me a couple of times. So did the Demon. So did the waiters," he added sourly.

"Kragar, the next time you feel like ignoring my orders, do it."

He gave me his Kragar smile. "Vlad," he said, "never trust anyone who calls himself a demon."

"I'll remember that."

The Imperial guards would be showing up in a few minutes, and there were a few things I had to get done before they arrived. I was still trembling with unused adrenalin as I walked over to the kitchen, through it, and into the back office. The owner, a Dragaeran named Nethrond, was sitting behind his desk. He had been my partner in this place since I'd taken half-ownership of it in exchange for canceling out a rather impressive sum he owed me. I suppose he had no real reason to love me, but still. . . .

I walked in, and he looked at me as if he were seeing Death personified. Which, of course, he was. Kragar was behind me and stopped at the door to make sure no one came in to ask Nethrond to sign for an order of parsley or something.

I noticed he was trembling. Good. I no longer was.

"How much did he pay you, dead man?"

(Gulp) "Pay me? Who—?"

"You know," I said conversationally, "you've been a rotten gambler for as long as I've known you. That's what got you into this in the first place. Now, how much did he pay you?"

"B-b-b-but no one—"

I reached forward suddenly and grabbed his throat with my left hand. I felt my lips drawing up into a classic Jhereg sneer. "You are the only one, besides me, authorized to hire anyone in this place. There was a new waiter here today. I didn't hire him, therefore you did. It happened that he was an assassin. As a waiter, he was even worse than the fools you usually hire to drive customers away. Now, I think his main qualifications as a waiter were the gold Imperials you got for hiring him. I want to know how much."

He tried to shake his head in denial, but I was holding it too tightly. He started to speak the denial, but I squeezed that option shut. He tried to swallow; I relaxed enough to let him. He opened his mouth, closed it again, and then opened it and said, "I don't know what you—"

I discovered, with some surprise, that I had never resheathed the dagger that I'd drawn when first attacked. It was a nice tool; mostly point, and about seven inches long. It fitted well into my right hand, which is moderately rare for a Dragaeran weapon. I used it to poke him in the sternum. A small spot of blood appeared, soaking through the white chef's garment. He gave a small scream and seemed about to pass out. I was strongly reminded of our first conversation, when I'd let him know that I was his new partner and carefully outlined what would happen if the partnership didn't work out. His House was Jhegaala, but he was doing a good Teckla imitation.

He nodded, then, and managed to hand me a purse from next to him. I didn't touch it.

"How much is in it?" I asked.

He gurgled and said, "A th-thousand gold, M-milord."

I laughed shortly. "That isn't even enough to buy me out," I said. "Who approached you? Was it the assassin, the Demon, or a flunky?"

He closed his eyes as if he wanted me to disappear. I'd oblige him momentarily.

"It was the Demon," he said in a whisper.

"Really!" I said. "Well, I'm flattered that he takes such an interest in me."

He started whimpering.

"And he guaranteed that I'd be dead, right?"

He nodded miserably.

"And he guaranteed protection?"

He nodded again.

I shook my head sadly.

I called Kragar in to teleport us back to the office. He glanced at the body, his face expressionless.

"Shame about that fellow killing himself, isn't it?" he said.

I had to agree.

"Any sign of guards?"

"No. They'll get here eventually, but no one is in any hurry to call them, and this isn't their favorite neighborhood to patrol."

"Good. Let's get back home."

He started working the teleport. I turned back to the body.

"Never," I told it, "trust anyone who calls himself a demon."

The walls vanished around us.

9.

"You can't put it together again unless you've torn it apart first."

Over the years, I have developed a ritual that I go through after an attempt has been made to assassinate me. First, I return to my office by the fastest available means. Then I sit at my desk and stare off into space for a little while. After that I get very, very sick. Then I return to my desk and shake for a long time.

Sometime in there, while I'm alone and shaking, Cawti shows up, and she takes me home. If I haven't eaten, she feeds me. If it is practical, she puts me to bed.

This was the fourth time that I had almost had my tale of years snipped at the buttocks. It wasn't possible for me to sleep this time, since Aliera was expecting me. When I had recovered sufficiently to actually move, I went into the back room to do the teleport. I am a good enough sorcerer to do it myself when I have to, although generally I don't bother. This time I didn't feel like calling in anyone else. It wasn't that I didn't trust them. . . . Well, maybe it was.

I took out my enchanted dagger (a cheap, over-the-counter enchanted dagger, but better than plain steel), and began carefully drawing the diagrams and symbols that aren't at all necessary for a teleport, but *do* help settle one's mind down when one is feeling that one's magic might not be all it ought to be.

Cawti kissed me before I left and seemed to hang onto me a bit more than she had to. Or maybe not. I was feeling extraordinarily sensitive, just at the moment.

The teleport worked smoothly and left me in the court-yard. I spun quickly as I arrived, almost losing lunch in the process. No, there wasn't anyone behind me.

I walked toward the great double doors of the castle, looking carefully around. The doors swung open before me, and I had to repress an urge to dive away from them.

"Boss, would you settle down?"

"No."

"No one is going to attack you at Castle Black."

"So what?"

"So what's the point in being so jumpy?"

"It makes me feel better."

"Well, it bothers hell out of me."

"Tough."

"Take it easy, all right? I'll take care of you."

"I'm not doubting you, it's just that I feel like being jumpy, all right?"

"Not really."

"Then lump it."

He was right, however. I resolved to relax just a bit as I nodded to Lady Teldra. She pretended that there was nothing odd in my having her walk in front of me by five paces. I trusted Lady Teldra, of course, but this could be an impostor, after all. Well, it could, couldn't it?

I found myself in front of Aliera's chambers. Lady Teldra bowed to me and left. I clapped, and Aliera called to me to come in. I opened the door, letting it swing fully open, while stepping to the side. Nothing came out at me, so I risked a look inside.

Aliera was sitting by the back of the bed, staring off into space. I noted that, curled up as she was, she could still draw Pathfinder. I scanned the room carefully.

Entering, I moved a chair so my back was against the wall. Aliera's eyes focused on me, and she looked puzzled.

"Is something wrong, Vlad?"

"No."

She looked bemused, then quizzical. "You're quite sure," she said.

I nodded. If I were going to take someone out from that position, I thought, how would I go about it? Let's see. . . .

Aliera raised her hand suddenly, and I recognized the gesture as the casting of a spell.

Loiosh hissed with indignation as I hit the floor rolling, and Spellbreaker snapped out.

I didn't feel any of the tingling that normally accompanies Spellbreaker's intercepting magic aimed at me, however. I lay there, looking at Aliera, who was watching me carefully.

"What's gotten into you, anyway?" asked Aliera.

"What was that spell?"

"I wanted to check your genetic background," she said drily. "I thought I'd look for some latent Teckla genes."

I cracked up. This just broke me up completely. I sat on the floor, my body shaking with laughter, and felt tears stream down my face. Aliera, I'm sure, was trying to figure out whether to join me, or to cure me.

I settled down, finally, feeling much better. I got back into the chair and caught my breath. I wiped the tears from my face, still chuckling. Loiosh flew quickly over to Aliera, licked her right ear, and returned to my shoulder.

"Thanks," I said, "that helped."

"What was the problem, anyway?"

I shook my head, then shrugged. "Someone just tried to kill me," I explained.

She looked more puzzled than ever. "So?"

That almost broke me up again, but I contained it, with great effort.

"It's my latent Teckla genes," I said.

"I see."

Gods! What a nightmare! I was pulling out of it, though. I started to think about business again. I had to make sure that Mellar didn't go through what I'd just gone through. "Were you able to do whatever it is you do on Mellar?" I asked.

She nodded.

"Did he detect it?"

"No chance," she said.

"Good. And did you learn anything of interest?"

She looked strange again, just as she had when I first walked in. "Vlad," she asked me, "what made you ask about his genes? I mean, it is a little specialty of mine, but everyone has his little specialties. Why did you happen to ask about this?"

I shrugged. "I haven't been able to learn anything about

his background, and I thought you might be able to learn something about his parents that would help. It isn't something that's easily found out, you know. Normally, I don't have any trouble finding everything I need to about a person, but this guy isn't normal."

"I'll agree with you there!" she said fervently.

"What does that mean? You found something?"

She nodded significantly in the direction of the wine cabinet. I rose and fetched a bottle of Ailour dessert wine, and presented it to her. She held it for a moment, did a quick spell to chill it down, and returned it to me. I opened it and poured. She sipped hers.

"I found out something, all right."

"You're sure he didn't detect it?"

"He had no protection spells up, and it's really quite easy to do."

"Good! So, what is it?"

She shook her head. "Gods, but it's weird!"

"What is? Will you tell me already? You're as bad as Loiosh."

"Remember that crack next time you roll over in bed and find a dead teckla on your pillow."

I ignored him. Aliera didn't rise to the bait. She just shook her head in puzzlement. "Vlad," she said slowly, "he has Dragon genes."

I digested that. "You're sure? No possible doubt?"

"None. If I'd wanted to take more time, I could have told you which line of the Dragons. But that isn't all—he's a cross-breed."

"Indeed?" was all I said. Cross-breeds were rare, and almost never accepted by any House except the Jhereg. On the other hand, they had an easier time of it than Easterners, so I wasn't about to get all teary-eyed for the fellow.

She nodded. "He's clearly got three Houses in his genes. Dragon and Dzur on one side, and Jhereg on the other."

"Hmmm. I see. I wasn't aware that you could identify Jhereg genes as such. I'd thought that they were just a mish-mash of all the other Houses."

She smiled. "If you get a mish-mash, as you put it, together for enough generations, it becomes identifiable as something in and of itself."

I shook my head. "This is all beyond me, anyway. I don't

even know how you can pick out a gene, much less recognize it as being associated with a particular House."

She shrugged. "It's something like a mind-probe," she said, "except that you aren't looking for the mind. And, of course, you have to go much deeper. That's why it's so hard to detect, in fact. Anyone can tell when his mind is being examined, unless the examiner is an expert, but having your finger mind-probed is a bit trickier to spot."

This image came to mind of the Empress, with the Orb circling her head, holding up a severed finger and saying, "Now talk! What till have you been in?" I chuckled, and missed Aliera's next statement.

"I'm sorry, Aliera, what was that?"

"I said that determining a person's House isn't hard at all if you know what you're looking for. Surely you realize that each animal is different, and—"

"Wait a minute! 'Each animal is different,' sure. But we aren't talking about animals, we're talking about Dragaerans." I repressed a nasty remark at that point, since Aliera didn't seem to be in the right mood for it.

"Oh, come on, Vlad," she answered. "The names of the Houses aren't accidents."

"What do you mean?"

"Okay, for instance, how do you suppose the House of the Dragon got its name?"

"I guess I've always assumed it was because you have characters similar to that of dragons. You're bad-tempered, reptilian, used to getting your own way—"

"Hmmmph! I guess I asked for that, eater of carrion. But you're wrong. Since I'm of the House of the Dragon, it means that if you go back a few hundred thousand generations, you'll find actual dragons in my lineage."

And you're proud of this? I thought, but didn't say. I must have looked as shocked as I felt, though, because she said, "I'd thought you realized this."

"It's the first I've heard of it, I assure you. Do you mean, for example, that Chreothas are descended from actual chreothas?"

She looked puzzled. "Not 'descended' exactly. It's a bit more complicated than that. All Dragaerans are initially of the same stock. But things changed when—How shall I put this? All right: Certain, uh, beings once ruled on Dragaera.

They were a race called Jenoine. They used the Dragaeran race (and, I might add, the Easterners) as stock to practice genetic experimentation. When they left, the Dragaerans divided into tribes based on natural kinship, and the Houses were formed from this after the formation of the Empire by Kieron the Conqueror."

She didn't add "my ancestor," but I felt it anyway.

"The experiments they did on Dragaerans involved using some of the wildlife of the area as a gene pool."

I interrupted. "But Dragaerans can't actually cross-breed with these various animals, can they?"

"No."

"Well, then how—"

"We don't really know how they went about it. That's one thing I've been researching myself, and I haven't solved it yet."

"What did these—Jenine?"

"Jen-o-ine."

"Jenoine. What did these Jenoine do to Easterners?"

"We aren't really sure, to tell you the truth. One popular theory is that they bred in psionic ability."

"Hmmm. Fascinating. Aliera, has it ever occurred to you that Dragaerans and Easterners could be of the same stock originally?"

"Don't be absurd," she said sharply. "Dragaerans and Easterners can't interbreed. In fact, there are some theories which claim that Easterners aren't native to Dragaera at all, but were brought in by the Jenoine from somewhere else to use as controls for their tests."

" 'Controls?' "

"Yes. They gave the Easterners psionic abilities equal to, or almost equal to, that of Dragaerans. Then they started messing around with Dragaerans, and sat back to see what the two races would do to each other."

I shuddered. "Do you mean that these Jenoine might still be around, watching us—"

"No," she said flatly. "They're gone. Not all of them are destroyed, but they rarely come to Dragaera anymore— and when they do, they can't dominate us as they did long ago. In fact, Sethra Lavode fought with and destroyed one only a few years ago."

My mind flashed back to my first meeting with Sethra.

She had looked a bit worried, and said, "I can't leave Dzur Mountain just now." And later, she had looked exhausted, as if she'd been in a fight. One more old mystery cleared up.

"How were they destroyed? Did the Dragaerans turn on them?"

She shook her head. "They had other interests besides genetics. One of them was the study of Chaos. We'll probably never know exactly what happened, but, in essence, an experiment got out of control, or else an argument came up between some of them, or something, and boom! We have a Great Sea of Chaos, a few new gods, and no more Jenoine."

So much, I decided, for my history lesson for today. I couldn't deny being interested, however. It wasn't really my history, but it had some kind of fascination for me, nevertheless. "That sounds remarkably like what happened to Adron on a smaller scale, a few years back. You know, the thing that made the Sea of Chaos up north, the Interregnum. . . . Aliera?"

She was looking at me strangely and not saying anything.

A light broke through. "Say!" I said, "That's what pre-Empire sorcery is! The sorcery of the Jenoine." I stopped long enough to shudder, as I realized the implications. "No wonder the Empire doesn't like people studying it."

Aliera nodded. "To be more precise, pre-Empire sorcery is direct manipulation of raw chaos—bending it to one's will."

I found myself shuddering again. "It sounds rather dangerous."

She shrugged, but didn't say more. Of course, she would see it a little differently. Aliera's father, I had learned, was none other than Adron himself, who had accidentally blown up the old city of Dragaera and created a sea of chaos on its site.

"I hope," I said, "that Morrolan isn't planning on doing another number like your father did."

"He couldn't."

"Why not? If he's using pre-Empire sorcery. . . ."

She grimaced prettily. "I'll correct what I said before. Pre-Empire sorcery is not *exactly* direct manipulation of chaos; it's one step removed. Direct manipulation is something else again—and that's what Adron was doing. He had the ability to use, in fact, the ability to *create* chaos. If you combine that with the skills of pre-Empire sorcery. . . ."

"And Morrolan doesn't have the skill to create chaos? Poor fellow. How can he live without it?"

Aliera chuckled. "It isn't a skill one can learn. It goes back to genes again. So far as I know, it is only the e'Kieron line of the House of the Dragon that holds the ability— although it is said that Kieron himself never used it."

"I wonder," I said, "how genetic heritage interacts with reincarnation of the soul."

"Oddly," said Aliera e'Kieron.

"Oh. So, anyway, that explains where the Dragaeran Houses come from. I'm surprised that the Jenoine wasted their time breeding an animal like the Jhereg into some Dragaerans," I said.

"That's another one I owe you, boss."

"Shut up, Loiosh."

"Oh," said Aliera, "but they didn't."

"Eh?"

"They played around with jheregs and found a way to put human-level intelligence into a brain the size of a rednut, but they never put any jhereg genes into Dragaerans."

"There, Loiosh. You should feel grateful to the Jenoine, for—"

"Shut up, boss."

"But I thought you said—"

"The Jhereg is the exception. They didn't start out as a tribe the way the others did."

"Then how?"

"Okay, we have to go back to the days when the Empire was first being formed. In fact, we have to go back even further. As far as we know, there were originally about thirty distinct tribes of Dragaerans. We don't know the exact number, since there were no records being kept back then.

"Eventually, many of them died off. Finally, there were sixteen tribes left. Well, fifteen, plus a tribe of the Teckla, which really didn't do much of anything."

"They invented agriculture," I cut in. "That's something."

She brushed it aside. "The tribes were called together, or parts of each tribe, by Kieron the Conqueror and a union of some of the best Shamans of the time, and they got together to drive the Easterners out of some of the better lands."

"For farming," I said.

"Now, in addition to the tribes, there were a lot of outcasts. Many of them came from the tribe of the Dragon—probably because the Dragons had higher standards than the others—" She tossed her head as she said this; I let it go by.

"Anyway," she continued, "there were a lot of outcasts, mostly living in small groups. While the other tribes were coming together under Kieron, a certain ex-Dragon named Dolivar managed to unite most of these independent groups—primarily by killing any of the leaders who didn't agree with the idea.

"So they got together, and, I guess more sarcastically than anything else, they began calling themselves 'the tribe of the Jhereg.' They lived mostly off the other tribes—stealing, looting, and then running off. They even had a few Shamans."

"Why didn't the other tribes get together to wipe them out?" I asked.

She shrugged. "A lot of the tribes wanted to, but Kieron needed scouts and spies for the war against the Easterners, and the Jheregs were obviously the only ones who could manage it properly."

"Why did the Jheregs agree to help?"

"I guess," she remarked drily, "Dolivar decided it was preferable to being wiped out. He met with Kieron before the Great March started, and got an agreement that, if his 'tribe' helped out, they would be included in the Empire when it was over."

"I see. So that's how the Jhereg became part of the Cycle. Interesting."

"Yes. It also ended up killing Kieron."

"What did?"

"The bargain; the strain of forcing the tribes to adhere to the bargain after the fighting was over and the other tribes no longer saw that the Jhereg could be of any value to them. He was eventually killed by a group of Lyorn warriors and Shamans who decided that he was responsible for some of the problems the Jheregs brought to the Empire."

"So," I said, "we owe it all to Kieron the Conqueror, eh?"

"Kieron," she agreed, "and this Jhereg chieftain named Dolivar who forced the deal in the first place, and then forced the others in his tribe to agree to it."

"Why is it, I wonder, that I've never heard of this Jhereg chieftain? I don't know of any House records on him, and you'd think he'd be considered some kind of hero."

"Oh, you can find him if you dig enough. As you know better than I, The Jhereg isn't too concerned with heroes. The Lyorns have records of him."

"Is that how you found out all this?"

She shook her head, "No. I learned a lot of it talking to Sethra. And some I remembered, of course."

"What!?"

Aliera nodded. "Sethra was there, as Sethra. I've heard her age given at ten thousand years. Well, that's wrong. It's off by a factor of twenty. She is, quite literally, older than the Empire."

"Aliera, that's impossible! Two hundred thousand years? That's ridiculous!"

"Tell it to Dzur Mountain."

"But . . . and you! How could *you* remember?"

"Don't be a fool, Vlad. Regression, of course. In my case, it's a memory of past lives. Did you think reincarnation was just a myth, or a religious belief, like you Easterners have?"

Her eyes were glowing strangely, as I fought to digest this new information.

"I've seen it through my own eyes—lived it again.

"I was there, Vlad, when Kieron was backed into a corner by an ex-Dragon named Dolivar, who had been Kieron's brother before he shamed himself and the whole tribe. Dolivar was tortured and expelled.

"I share the guilt there, too, as does Sethra. Sethra was supposed to hamstring the yendi, but she missed—deliberately. I saw, but I didn't say anything. Perhaps that makes me responsible for my brother's death, later. I don't know . . ."

"Your brother!" This was too much.

"My brother," she repeated. "We started out as one family. Kieron, Dolivar, and I."

She turned fully toward me, and I felt a rushing in my ears as I listened to her spin tales that I couldn't quite dismiss as mad ravings or myths.

"I," she said, "was a Shaman in that life, and I think I was a good one, too. I was a Shaman, and Kieron was a warrior. He is still there, Vlad, in the Paths of the Dead. I've spoken to him. He recognized me.

"Three of us. The Shaman, the warrior—and the traitor. By the time Dolivar betrayed us, we no longer considered him a brother. He was a Jhereg, down to his soul.

"His soul . . ." she repeated, trailing off.

"Yes," she continued, " 'Odd' is the right way to describe the way heredity of the body interacts with reincarnation of the soul. Kieron was never reincarnated. I have been born into a body descended from the brother of my soul. And you—" she gave me a look that I couldn't interpret, but I suddenly knew what was coming. I wanted to scream at her not to say it, but, throughout the millennia, Aliera has always been just a little faster than me. "—You became an Easterner, brother."

10-

"One man's mistake is another man's opportunity."

One damn thing after another.

I returned to my office and looked at nothing in particular for a while. I needed time, probably days, to get adjusted to this information. Instead, I had about ten minutes.

"Vlad?" said Kragar. "Hey, Vlad!"

I looked up. After a moment, I focused in on Kragar, who was sitting opposite me and looking worried.

"What is it?" I asked him.

"That's what I was wondering."

"Huh?"

"Is something wrong?"

"Yes. No. Hell, Kragar, I don't know."

"It sounds serious," he said.

"It is. My whole world has just been flipped around, and I haven't sorted it out yet."

I leaned toward him, then, and grabbed his jerkin. "Just one thing, old friend: If you value your sanity, never, but *never* have a deep, heart-to-heart talk with Aliera."

"Sounds *really* serious."

"Yeah."

We sat in silence for a moment. Then I said, "Kragar?"

"Yeah, boss?"

I bit my lip. I'd never broached this subject before, but . . .

"How did you feel when you were kicked out of the House of the Dragon?"

"Relieved," he said, with no hesitation. "Why?"

I sighed. "Never mind."

I tried to force the mood and the contemplation from me and almost succeeded. "What's on your mind, Kragar?"

"I was wondering if you found out anything," he said, in all innocence.

Did I find out anything? I asked myself. The question began to reverberate in my head, and I heard myself laughing. I saw Kragar giving me a funny look; worried. I kept laughing. I tried to stop, but couldn't. Ha! Did I learn anything?

Kragar leaned across the desk and slapped me once—hard.

"Hey boss," said Loiosh, *"cut it out."*

I sobered up. *"Easy for you to say,"* I told him. *"You haven't just learned that you once were everything you hate—the very kind of person you despise."*

"So? You haven't just learned that you were supposed to be a blithering idiot, except that some pseudo-god decided to have a little fun with your ancestors," Loiosh barked back.

I realized that he had a point. I turned to Kragar. "I'm all right now. Thanks."

He still looked worried. "Are you sure?"

"No."

He rolled his eyes. "Great. So, if you can avoid having hysterics again, what *did* you learn?"

I almost did have hysterics again, but controlled myself before Kragar could slap me again. What had I learned? Well, I wasn't going to tell him that, or that, uh, or that either. What did that leave? Oh, of course.

"I learned that Mellar is the product of three Houses," I said. I gave him a report on that part of the discussion.

He pondered the information.

"Now that," he said, "is interesting. A Dzur, eh? And a Dragon. Hmmm. Okay, why don't you see what you can dig up about the Dzur side, and I'll work on the Dragons."

"I think it would make more sense to do it the other way around, since I have some connections in the Dragons."

He looked at me closely. "Are you quite sure," he said, "that you want to use those connections just at the moment?"

Oh. I thought about that, and nodded. "Okay, I'll check

the Dzur records. What do you think we should look for?"

"I'm not sure," he said. Then he cocked his head for a minute and seemed to be thinking about something, or else he was in psionic contact. I waited.

"Vlad," he said, "do you have any idea what it's like to be a cross-breed?"

"I know it isn't as bad as being an Easterner!"

"Isn't it?"

"What are you getting at? You know damn well what I've had to put up with."

"Oh, sure, Mellar isn't going to have all the problems you have, or had. But suppose he inherited the true spirit of each House. Do you have any idea how frustrating it would be for a Dzur to be denied his place in the lists of heroes of the House, if he was good enough to earn it? Or a Dragon, denied the right to command all the troops he was competent to lead? The only House that would take him is us, and Hell, Vlad, there are even some Jhereg that would make him eat Dragon-dung. Sure, Vlad; you have it worse in fact, but he can't help but feel that he's entitled to better."

"And I'm not?"

"You know what I mean."

"I suppose," I conceded. "I see your point. Where are you going with it?"

Kragar got a puzzled look on his face. "I don't know, exactly, but it's bound to have an effect on his character."

I nodded. "I'll keep that in mind."

"Okay, I'll get started right away."

"Fine. Oh, could you try to get that crystal with Mellar's face in it back from Daymar? I may want to use it."

"Sure. When do you need it?"

"Tomorrow morning will be fine. I'm taking the evening off. I'll start on it tomorrow."

Kragar's eyes were sympathetic, which was rare. "Sure, boss. I'll cover for you here. See you tomorrow."

I ate mechanically and thanked the Lords of Judgment that it was Cawti's night to cook and clean. I didn't think I'd be up to it.

After eating, I rose and went into the living room. I sat down and started trying to sort out some things. I didn't get anywhere. Presently, Cawti came in and sat down next to me. We sat in silence for a while.

I tried to deny what Aliera had told me, or pass it off as a combination of myth, misplaced superstition, and delusion. Unfortunately, it made too much sense for that to work. Why, after all, had Sethra Lavode been so friendly to me, a Jhereg and an Easterner? And Aliera obviously believed all of this, or why had she treated me as almost an equal on occasion?

But, more than that was the undeniable fact that it *felt* true. That was the really frightening thing—somewhere, deep within me, doubtless in my "soul," I knew that what Aliera had said was true.

And that meant—what? That the thing that had driven me into the Jhereg—my hatred of Dragaerans—was in fact a fraud. That my contempt for Dragons wasn't a feeling of superiority for my system of values over theirs, but was in fact a feeling of inadequacy going back, how long? Two hundred thousand years? Two hundred and fifty thousand years? By the multi-jointed fingers of Verra!

I became conscious of Cawti holding my hand. I smiled at her, a bit wanly perhaps.

"Want to talk about it?" she asked, quietly.

That was another good question. I wasn't sure if I wanted to talk about it or not. But I did, haltingly, over the course of about two hours. Cawti was quietly sympathetic, but didn't seem really upset.

"Really, Vlad, what's the difference?"

I started to answer, but she stopped me with a shake of her head. "I know. You've thought that it was being an Easterner that made you what you are, and now you're wondering. But being human is only one aspect, isn't it? The fact that you had an earlier life as a Dragaeran—maybe several, in fact—doesn't change what you've gone through in this life."

"No," I admitted. "I suppose not. But—"

"I know. Tell you what, Vlad. After this is all over and forgotten, maybe a year from now, we'll go talk to Sethra. We'll find out more about what happened and maybe, if you want to, she'll take you back to that time, and you can experience it again. *If* you want to. But in the meantime, forget it. You are who you are, and whatever went into making that is all to the good, as far as I'm concerned."

I squeezed her hand, glad that I'd discussed it with her. I felt a bit more relaxed and started to feel tired. I kissed Cawti's hand. "Thanks for the meal," I said.

She raised her eyebrow. "I'll bet you don't even know what it was," she said.

I thought for a minute. Jhegaala eggs? No, she'd made that yesterday.

"Hey!" I said. "It was *my* night to do the cooking, wasn't it?"

She grinned broadly. "Sure was, comrade. I've tricked you into owing me still another one. Clever, aren't I?"

"Damn," I said.

She shook her head in mock sadness. "That makes it, let me see now, about two hundred and forty-seven favors you owe me."

"But who's counting, right?"

"Right."

I stood up then, still holding her hand. She followed me into the bedroom, where I paid back her favor, or she did me another one, or we did one for each other, depending on exactly how one counts these things.

The servants of Lord Keleth admitted me to his castle with obvious distaste. I ignored them.

"The Duke will see you in his study," said the butler, looking down at me.

He held out his hand for my cloak; I gave him my sword instead. He seemed surprised, but took it. The trick to surviving a fight with a Dzur hero is not to have one. The trick to not having one is to seem as helpless as possible. Dzur heroes are reluctant to fight when the odds aren't against them.

I'd been proud of the scheme that had led me here. It was nothing unusual, of course, but it was good, solid, low-risk, and had a high probability of gain. Most important, it was very—well—*me*. I'd been worried that my encounter with Aliera had dulled my edge, somehow changed me, made me less able to conceive and execute an elegant plan. The execution of this one was still unresolved, but I was no longer worried about the conception.

I was escorted to the study. I noted signs of disrepair

along the way: chipping grate on the floor, cracks in the ceiling, places along the wall that had probably once held expensive tapestries.

The butler ushered me into the study. The Duke of Keletharan was old and what passes for "squat" in a Dragaeran, meaning that his shoulders were a bit broader than usual, and you could actually see the muscles in his arms. His face was smooth (Dzurlords don't go in for wrinkles, I guess), and his eyes had that bit of upward slant associated with the House. His eyebrows were remarkably bushy, and he would have had a wispy white beard, if Dragaerans had beards. He was seated in a straight-backed chair with no arms. A broadsword hung at his side, and a wizard's staff was leaning against the desk. He didn't invite me to sit down; I did anyway. It is best to get certain things established at the beginning of a conversation. I saw his lips tighten, but that was all. Good. Score one for our side.

"Well, Jhereg, what is it?" he asked.

"My lord, I hope I didn't disturb you!"

"You did."

"A small matter has come to my attention which requires that I speak with you."

Keleth looked up at the butler, who bowed to us and left. The door snicked shut behind him. Then the Duke allowed himself to look disgusted. "The 'small matter,' no doubt, being four thousand gold Imperials."

I tried to look like I was trying to look apologetic. "Yes, my lord. According to our records, it was due over a month ago. Now, we have tried to be patient, but—"

"Patient, hell!" he snapped. "At the interest rates you charge, I'd think you could stand to hold off a little while with a man who's having a few minor financial troubles."

That was a laugh. As far as I could tell, his troubles were anything but "minor," and it was doubtful that they would end any time in the near future. I decided, however, that it wouldn't be politic to mention this, or to suggest that he wouldn't be having these problems at all if he could control his fondness for s'yang-stones. Instead, I said, "With all respect, my lord, it seems that a month is a reasonable length of time to hold off. And, again with all respect, you knew the interest rates when you came to us for help."

"I came to you for 'help,' as you put it, because—never

mind." He had come to us for "help," as I'd put it, because
we had made it clear to him that if he didn't, we would
make sure that the whole Empire, particularly the House
of the Dzur, knew that he couldn't control his urge to gam-
ble, or pay off his debts when he lost. Perhaps having a reputation as a rotten gambler would have been the worst
thing about it, to him.

I shrugged. "As you wish," I said. "Nevertheless, I must
insist—"

"I tell you I just don't have it," he exploded. "What else
can I say? If I had the gold, I'd give it to you. If you keep
this up, I swear by the Imperial Phoenix that I'll go to the
Empire and let them know about a few untaxed gambling
games I'm aware of, and certain untaxed moneylenders."

Here is where it is helpful to know whom you are dealing
with. In most such cases, I would have carefully let him
know that if he did that, his body would be found within a
week, probably behind a lower-class brothel, and looking
as if he were killed in a fight with a drunken tavern brawler.
I've used this technique before on Dzur heroes, and with
good effect. It isn't the idea of being killed which scares
them, it is the thought of people thinking that they'd been
killed in a tavern brawl by some nameless Teckla.

I knew this would frighten Keleth, but it would also send
him into a murderous rage, and the fact that I was "un-
armed and helpless" might not stop him. Also, if he didn't
kill me on the spot, it would certainly guarantee that he'd
carry out his threat of going to the Empire. Clearly, a different approach was called for.

"Oh, come now, Lord Keleth," I said. "What would *that*
do to your reputation?"

"No more than it would do to it to have you expose my
personal finances anyway, for not paying off your blood
money."

Dzur tend to be careless with terms, but I didn't correct
him. I gave him my patient-man-trying-to-be-helpful-but-
almost-exasperated sigh. "How much time do you need?"

"Another month, maybe two."

I shook my head, sadly. "I'm afraid that's quite impossible. I guess you'll just have to go to the Empire. It means
that one or two of our games will have to find new locations, and a certain moneylender will have to take a short

vacation, but I assure you that it won't hurt us nearly as much as it will hurt you."

I stood up, bowed low, and turned to leave. He didn't rise to see me out, which I thought was rude, but understandable, under the circumstances. Just before my hand touched the doorknob, I stopped, and turned around. "Unless—"

"Unless what?" he asked, suspiciously.

"Well," I lied, "it just occurred to me that there may be something you could help me out with."

He stared at me, long and hard, trying to guess what kind of game I was playing. I kept my face expressionless. If I'd wanted him to know the rules, I'd have written them out.

"And what is that?" he asked.

"I'm looking for a little information that involves the history of your House. I could find out myself, I suppose, but it would take a little work that I don't feel like doing. It is possible, I'm sure, for you to find out. In fact, you might even know already. If you could help me, I'd appreciate it."

He was still suspicious, but he was beginning to sound eager, too. "And what form," he asked, "will this 'appreciation' take?"

I pretended to think it over. "I think I could arrange for a two-month extension for you. In fact, I'd even go so far as to freeze the interest—if you can find this information for me quickly enough."

He chewed on his lower lip for a while, thinking it over, but I knew I had him. This was too good a chance for him to pass up. I'd planned it that way.

"What is it you want to know?" he said at last.

I reached into an inner pocket of my cloak and removed the small crystal I'd gotten back from Daymar. I concentrated on it, and Mellar's face appeared. I showed it to him.

"This person," I said. "Do you know him, or could you find out who he is, what connection he has with the House of the Dzur, or who his parents were? Anything you can find out would be helpful. We know that he has some connection with your House. You can see it in his face, if you look closely."

Keleth's face went white as soon as he saw Mellar. I was surprised by the reaction. Keleth knew him. His lips became a thin line and he turned away.

"Who is he?" I asked.

"I'm afraid," said Keleth, "that I can't help you."

The question at that point wasn't "Should I press?" or even, "How much should I press?" It was, rather, "How should I press?" I decided to continue the game I'd started.

I shrugged and put the crystal away. "I'm sorry to hear that," I said. "As you wish. I've no doubt that you have good reasons for not wishing to share your information. Still, it is a shame that your good name must be befouled." I turned away again.

"Wait, I—"

I turned back to him. I was beginning to get dizzy. He seemed to be struggling with himself. I stopped worrying; I could see which side would win.

His face was a mask of twisted rage, as he said, "Damn you, Jhereg! You can't do this to me!"

There was, of course, nothing to say to this blatantly incorrect statement of our positions. I waited patiently.

He sank back into his chair, and covered his face with his hands. "His name," he said at last, "is Leareth. I don't know where he came from, or who his parents are. He appeared twelve years ago and joined our House."

"Joined your House? How can one join the House of the Dzur?" That was startling. I'd thought only the Jhereg allowed one to buy a title.

Lord Keleth looked at me as if he were about to snarl. I suddenly recalled Aliera's contention that the Dzurlords were descended, in part, from actual dzur. I could believe it.

"To join the House of the Dzur," he explained in the most vicious monotone I've ever heard, "you must defeat, in equal combat, seventeen champions chosen by the House." His eyes suddenly turned bleak. "I was the fourteenth. He is the only man I can remember hearing of who has succeeded since the Interregnum."

I shrugged. "So, he became a Dzurlord. I don't see what is so secret about that."

"We later learned," said Keleth, "something of his origins. He was a cross-breed. A mongrel."

"Well, yes," I said slowly, "I can see where that could be a touch annoying, but—"

"And then," he interrupted, "after he'd only been a Dzur for two years, he just gave up all his titles and joined House Jhereg. Can't you see what that means? He made fools of us! A mongrel can defeat the best the House of the Dzur has, and then chooses to throw it all away—" He stopped and shrugged.

I thought it over. This Leareth must be one hell of a swordsman.

"It's funny," I said, "that I've never heard of this incident. I've been investigating this fellow pretty thoroughly."

"It was kept secret by the House," said Keleth. "Leareth promised us that he'd have the whole Empire told of the story if he was killed or if any Dzur attempted to harm him. We'd never be able to live it down."

I felt a sudden desire to laugh out loud, but I controlled it for health reasons. I was starting to like this guy Mellar, or Leareth, or whatever. I mean, for the past twelve years, he'd had the entire House of Heroes by the balls. The two most important things to the House of the Dzur, as to an individual Dzurlord, are honor and reputation. And this Mellar had managed to play one off against the other.

"What happens if someone else kills him?" I asked.

"We have to hope it looks like an accident," he said.

I shook my head, and stood up. "Okay, thanks. You've given me what I needed. You can forget about paying the loan for two months, and the interest. I'll handle the details. And if you ever need my help for something, just let me know. I'm in your debt."

He nodded, still downcast.

I left him and picked up my blade from the servant.

I walked out of the castle, thinking. Mellar was not going to be easy. He had outfought the best warriors in the House of the Dzur, outmaneuvered the best brains in House Jhereg, and caught the House of the Dragon out on a point of honor.

I shook my head sadly. No, this wasn't going to be easy. And then something else hit me. If I did succeed in this, I was going to make a lot of Dzurlords mighty unhappy. If they ever found out who had killed him, they wouldn't wait for evidence, as the Empire would. This didn't exactly make my day, either.

* * *

Loiosh gave me an Imperial chewing out for not having brought him along, most of which I ignored. Kragar filled me in on what he'd learned: nothing.

"I found a few servants who used to work in the Dragon records," he said. "They didn't know anything."

"What about some that still do?" I asked.

"They wouldn't talk."

"Hmmmm. Too bad."

"Yeah. I put my Dragon outfit on and found a Lady of the House who was willing to do some looking for me, though."

"But you didn't get anything there, either?"

"Well, I wouldn't say that, exactly."

"Oh? Oh."

"How about you?"

I took great relish in delivering the information I'd gotten, since it was rare that I was able to one-up him on a point like this.

He dutifully noted everything, then said, "You know, Vlad, no one wakes up one morning and discovers that he is good enough to fight his way into the Dzur. He must have worked on that for quite a while."

"That makes sense," I said.

"Okay, that will give me something to work with. I'll start checking it through from that angle."

"Do you think it'll help?"

"Who can say? If he was good enough to get into the Dzur, he's got to have been trained somewhere. I'll see what I can find."

"Okay," I said. "And there's something else that bothers me, by the way."

"Yes?"

"Why?"

Kragar was silent for a moment, then he said, "There are two possibilities I can think of. First, he could have wanted to become part of the House because he felt it his right, and then discovered that it didn't help—that he was treated the same after as before, or that he didn't like it."

"That makes sense. And the other?"

"The other possibility is that there was something he wanted, and he had to be a Dzur to get it. And there was no need to stay in the House after he had it."

That made sense, too, I decided. "What kind of thing could it be?" I asked.

"I don't know," he said. "But if that's what it is, then I think we'd damn well better find out."

Kragar leaned back in his chair for a moment, watching me closely. Probably, still worried about yesterday. I didn't say anything; best to let him discover in his own way that I was all right. I *was* all right, wasn't I? I watched myself for a moment. I *seemed* all right. It was strange.

I shook the mood off. "Okay," I said, "start checking it. Let me know as soon as you have something."

He nodded, then said, "I heard something interesting today."

"Oh, what did you hear?"

"One of my button-men was talking, and I overheard him say that his girl friend thinks something is wrong with the council."

I felt suddenly sick. "Wrong how?"

"She didn't know, but she thought it was something pretty big. And she mentioned Mellar's name."

I knew what that meant, of course. We didn't have much time left. Maybe a day, perhaps two. Three at the most. Then it would be too late. The Demon was certainly hearing rumors by now, too. What would he do? Try to get to Mellar, of course. Me? Would he make another try for me? What about Kragar? Or, for that matter, Cawti? Normally, no one would be interested in them, since it was I who was at the top. But would the Demon be trying for them now, in order to get to me?

"Shit," I said.

He agreed with my sentiments.

"Kragar, do you know who this fellow's girl friend is?"

He nodded. "A sorceress. Left Hand. Competent."

"Good," I said. "Kill her."

He nodded again.

I stood up and took off my cloak. Laying it across my desk, I began removing things from it, and from various places around my person. "Would you mind heading down to the arsenal and picking up the standard assortment for me? I may as well do something useful while we're talking."

He nodded and departed. I found an empty box in the

corner and began putting discarded weapons in it.

"Still ready to protect me, Loiosh?"

"Somebody has to, boss."

He flew over from his windowsill and landed on my right shoulder. I scratched him under the chin with my right hand, which brought my wrist up to eye level. Spell-breaker, wrapped tightly around my forearm, gleamed golden in the light. I had hopes of that chain being able to defend me against any magic I might encounter; and the rest of my weapons, if used properly, gave me a chance of taking out anyone using a normal blade. But it all depended on getting sufficient warning.

And, as an assassin, one thing kept revolving around in my head: Given time and skill, anyone can be assassinated. *Anyone.* My great hope, and my great fear, all rolled into one.

I took a dagger out of the box in front of me and checked its edge—Box? I looked up and saw that Kragar had returned.

"Would you mind telling me how you keep doing that?" I asked.

He smiled and shook his head in mock sadness. I looked at him, but learned nothing new. Kragar was about as average a Dragaeran as it is possible to get. He stood just about seven feet tall. His hair was light brown over a thin, angular face over a thin, angular body. His ears were just a bit pointed. No facial hair (which was why I grew a mustache), but other than that it was hard to tell a Dragaeran from a human by looking only at his face.

"How?" I repeated.

He raised his eyebrows. "You really want to know?" he asked.

"Are you really willing to tell me?"

He shrugged. "I don't know, to be honest. It isn't anything I do deliberately. It's just that people don't notice me. That's why I never made it as a Dragonlord. I'd give an order in the middle of a battle and no one would pay any attention. They gave me so much trouble over it that I finally told 'em all to jump off Deathgate Falls."

I nodded and let it pass. The last part, I knew, was a lie. He hadn't left the House of the Dragon on his own; he'd been expelled. I knew it, and he knew I knew it. But that was the story he wanted to give, so I accepted it.

Hell, I had my own scars that I didn't let Kragar scratch at; I could hardly begrudge him the right to keep me away from his.

I looked at the dagger that was still in my hand, made sure of the edge and balance, and slipped it into the upside-down spring-sheath under my left arm.

"I'm thinking," said Kragar, changing the subject, "that you don't want Mellar to know you're involved in this any sooner than you have to."

"Do you think he'll come after me?"

"Probably. He's going to have something of an organization left, even now. Most of it will have scattered, or be in the middle of scattering, but he's bound to have a few personal friends willing to do things for him."

I nodded. "I hadn't planned to advertise it."

"I suppose not. Do you have any thoughts yet on how to approach the problem of getting him to leave Castle Black?"

I added another dagger to the pile of weapons in the "used" box. I picked out a replacement, tested it, and slipped it into the cloak's lining sheath outside of where my left arm would be. I checked the draw and added a little more oil to the blade. I worked it back and forth in the sheath and continued.

"No," I told him, "I don't have the hint of an idea yet, to tell you the truth. I'm still working on it. I don't suppose you have anything?"

"No. That's your job."

"Thanks heaps."

I tested the balance on each of the throwing darts, and filled the quills with my own combination of blood, muscle, and nerve poison. I set them aside to dry, discarded the used ones, and looked at the shuriken.

"My original idea," I said, "was to convince him that we'd stopped looking for him and then maybe set up something attractive-looking in terms of escape. Unfortunately, I don't think I'll be able to do that in three days. Damn, but I hate working under a time limit."

"I'm sure Mellar would be awfully sorry to hear that."

I thought that over for a minute. "Maybe he would, come to think of it. I think I'll ask him."

"What?"

"I'd like to see him myself, talk to him, get a feel for what he's like. I still don't really know enough about him."

"You're nuts! We just agreed that you don't want to go anywhere near him. You'll let him know that you're after him and put him on the alert!"

"Will he figure that out? Think about it. He must know that I'm working for Morrolan. By now, he is aware that Morrolan is onto him, so he's probably expecting a visit from Morrolan's security people. And if he does suspect that I'm after him, so what? Sure, we lose an edge, but he isn't going to leave Castle Black until he's ready to, or until Morrolan kicks him out. So what is he going to do about it?"

"He can't kill me at Castle Black for the same reason that I can't kill him there. If he guesses that I'm the one who's going to take him, he'll guess that I'm revealing it to him so that he'll bolt, and he'll just hole up tighter than ever."

"Which," pointed out Kragar, "is exactly what we *don't* want."

I shrugged. "If we're going to get him to leave, we'll have to come up with something weird and tricky enough to force him out no matter how badly he wants to stay. This isn't going to matter one way or the other."

Kragar pondered this for a while, then nodded. "Okay, it sounds workable. Want me to come along?"

"No thanks. Keep things running here, and keep working on Mellar's background. Loiosh will protect me. He promised."

11.

"When the blameless
And the righteous die,
The very gods
For vengeance cry."

They say that the banquet hall of Castle Black has never
been empty since it was built, over three hundred years
ago. They also say that more duels have been fought there
than in Kieron Square outside the Imperial Palace.

You teleport in at approximately the center of the court-
yard of the Castle Black. The great double doors of the
keep open as you approach, and your first sight of the inte-
rior of the castle shows you a dimly lit hallway in which
Lady Teldra is framed, like the Guardian, that figure that
stands motionless atop Deathgate Falls, overlooking the
Paths of the Dead, where the real becomes the fanciful—
but only by degrees.

Lady Teldra bows to you. She bows exactly the right
amount for your House and Rank, and greets you by name
whether she knows you or not. She says such words as will
make you to feel welcome, whether your mission be of
friendship or hostility. Then, if it be your desire, you are escorted up to the banquet hall. You ascend a long, black-
marble stairway. The stairs are comfortable if you are human, a bit shallow (hence, elegant) if you are Dragaeran.
They are long, winding, sweeping things, these stairs.
There are lamps along the wall that highlight paintings
from the long, violent, sometimes strangely moving history
of the Dragaeran Empire.

Here is one done by the Necromancer (you didn't know
she was an artist, did you?), which shows a wounded drag-

133

on, reptilian head and neck curled around its young, as its eyes stare through you and pierce your soul. Here is one by a nameless Lyorn showing Kieron the Conqueror debating with the Shamans—with his broadsword. Cute, eh?

At the top, you may look to the right and see the doors of the actual dining hall. But if you turn to the left, you soon come to a large set of double doors, standing open. There is always a guard here, sometimes two. As you look through, the room makes itself felt only a little at a time. First, you notice the picture that fills the entire ceiling; it is a depiction of the Third Seige of Dzur Mountain, done by none other than Katana e'M'archala. Looking at it, and tracing the details from wall to wall, gives you an idea of just how massive the room really is. The walls are done in black marble, thinly veined with silver. The room is dark, but somehow there is never any problem seeing.

Only then do you become aware of people. The place is always packed. The tables around the edges, where food and drink are served, are focal points for an endless migration of humanity, if I may use the word. At the far end there are double doors again, these letting out onto a terrace. At other sides are smaller doors which lead to private rooms where you can bring some innocent fool to tell your life story to, if you so choose, or ask a Dragon general if he really had that last counterattack planned all along.

Aliera uses these rooms often. Morrolan, seldom. Myself, never.

"You know, boss—this place is a friggin' menagerie."
"Very true, my fine jhereg."
"Oh, we're a wit, today; yes, indeed."

I shouldered my way through the crowd, nodding to acquaintances and sneering at enemies as I went. Sethra Lavode spotted me, and we chatted for a few minutes about nothing. I didn't really know how to deal with her any more, so I cut the conversation short. She gave me a warm-despite-the-cold kiss on the cheek; she either knew or suspected, but wasn't talking.

I exchanged pleasant smiles with the Necromancer, who then turned her attention back to the Orca noble she was baiting.

"By the Orb, boss; I swear there are more undead than living in this damn place."

I gave a cold stare to the Sorceress in Green, which she returned. I nodded noncommitally at Sethra the Younger, and took a good look around.

In one corner of the room, the crowd had cleared for a Dzur and a Dragon, who were shouting insults at each other in preparation for carving each other up. One of Morrolan's wizard-guards stood by, casting the spells that would prevent any serious damage to the head, and laying down the Law of the Castle with regard to duels.

I continued searching until I spotted one of Morrolan's security people. I caught his eye, nodded to him, and he nodded back. He slowly drifted toward me. I noted that he did a fair-to-good job of moving through the crowd without disturbing anyone or giving the impression that he was heading anywhere in particular. Good. I made a mental note about him.

"Have you seen Lord Mellar?" I asked him when he reached me.

He nodded. "I've been keeping an eye on him. He should be over in the corner near the wine-tasting."

We continued to smile and nod as we talked—just a chance meeting of casual acquaintances.

"Good. Thanks."

"Should I be ready for trouble?" he asked.

"Always. But not in particular at the moment. Just stay alert."

"Always," he agreed.

"Is Morrolan here at the moment? I haven't seen him."

"Neither have I. I think he's in the library."

"Okay."

I began walking toward the wine-tasting.

I scanned in one direction, Loiosh in the other. He rode on my right shoulder, as if daring anyone to make a remark about his presence. He spotted Mellar first.

"There he is, boss."

"Eh? Where?"

"Against the wall—see?"

"Oh, yes. Thanks."

I approached slowly, sizing him up. He had been hard to spot because there was nothing particularly distinctive about him. He stood just under seven feet tall. His hair was dark brown and somewhat wavy, falling to just above his shoulders. I suppose a Dragaeran would have considered him handsome, but not remarkably so. He had an air about him, like a jhereg. Watchful, quiet, and controlled; very dangerous. I could read "Do Not Mess With Me" signs on him.

He was speaking to a noble of the House of the Hawk that I didn't know, and who was almost certainly unaware that, as he spoke, Mellar was constantly scanning the crowd, perhaps even unconsciously, alert, looking. . . . He spotted me.

We looked at each other for a moment as I approached, and I felt myself come under expert scrutiny. I wondered how many of my weapons and devices he was spotting. A good number, of course. And, naturally, not all of them. I walked up to him.

"Count Mellar," I said. "How do you do? I am Vladimir Taltos."

He nodded to me. I bowed from the neck. The Hawklord turned at the sound of my voice, noted that I was an Easterner, and scowled. He addressed Mellar. "It seems that Morrolan will let anyone in these days."

Mellar shrugged, and smiled a little.

The Hawklord bowed to him then, and turned away. "Perhaps later, my lord."

"Yes. A pleasure meeting you, my lord."

Mellar turned back to me. "Baronet, isn't it?"

I nodded. "I hope I didn't interrupt anything important."

"Not at all."

This was going to be different than my dealing with the Dzurlord, Keleth. Unlike him, Mellar knew all the rules. He'd used my title to let me know that he knew who I was—implying that it might be safe to tell him more. I knew how the game was played as well.

This was a strange conversation in other ways, however. For one thing, it simply isn't my custom to speak to people that I'm going to nail. Before I'm ready, I don't want to go anywhere near them. I have no desire to give the target any idea who I am or what I'm like, even if he doesn't realize that I'm going to become his executioner.

But this was different. I was going to have to get him to set himself up. That meant that I needed to know the bastard better than I'd ever known any other target in my career. And, just to put the honey in the klava, I knew less about him that I did about anyone else I'd ever set out after.

So, I had to find out a few things about him, and he, no doubt, would like to find out a few things about me; or at least what I was doing here. I thought up and rejected a dozen or so opening gambits before I settled on one.

"I understand from Lord Morrolan that you acquired a book he was interested in."

"Yes. Did he tell you what it was?"

"Not in detail. I hope he was satisfied with it."

"He seemed to be."

"Good. It's always nice to help people."

"Isn't it, though?"

"How did you happen to get hold of the volume? I understand that it's quite rare and hard to come by."

He smiled a little. "I'm surprised Morrolan asked," he said, which told me something. Not much perhaps, but it confirmed that he knew that I worked for Morrolan. File that away.

"He didn't," I said. "I was just curious myself."

He nodded, and the smile came on again briefly.

We made small talk for a while longer, each letting the other be the first to commit himself to revealing how much he knew in a gambit to learn what the other knew. I decided, after a while, that he was not going to be first. He was the one with only a little to gain, so—

"I understand Aliera introduced herself to you."

He seemed startled by the turn of the conversation. "Why, yes, she did."

"Quite remarkable, isn't she?"

"Is she? In what way?"

I shrugged. "She's got a good brain, for a Dragonlord."

"I hadn't noticed. She seemed rather vague, to me."

Good! Unless he was a lot sharper than he had any right to be, and a damn good liar (which was possible), he hadn't realized that she'd been casting a spell as she was speaking to him. That gave me a clue as to his level of sorcery—not up to hers.

"Indeed?" I said. "What did you talk about?"

"Oh, nothing, really. Pleasantries."

"Well, that's something, isn't it? How many Dragons do

you know who will exchange pleasantries with a Jhereg?"

"Perhaps. On the other hand, of course, she may have been trying to find something out about me."

"What makes you think so?"

"I didn't say I thought so, just that she may have been. I've wondered myself as to her reasons for seeking me out."

"I can imagine. I haven't noticed that Dragons tend toward subtlety, however. Did she seem irritated with you?"

I could see his mind working. How much, he was thinking, should I tell this guy, hoping to pull information out of him? He couldn't risk a lie that I would recognize, or I wouldn't be of any further use to him, and he couldn't really know how much I knew. We were both playing the same game, and either one of us could put the limit on it. How much did he want to know? How badly did he want to know it? How worried was he?

"Not on the surface," he said at last, "but I did get the impression that she might not have liked me. It ruined my whole day, I'm telling you."

I chuckled a little. "Any idea why?"

This time I'd gone too far. I could see him clam up.

"None at all," he said.

Okay, so I'd gotten a little, and he'd gotten a little. Which one of us had gotten more would be determined by which one of us was alive after this was over.

"Well, Loiosh, did you find out anything?"

"More than you did, boss."

"Oh? What in specific?"

Mental images of two faces appeared to my mind's eye.

"These two. They were watching you the entire time from a few feet away."

"Oh, really? So he has bodyguards, eh?"

"At least two of them. Are you surprised?"

"Not really. I'm just surprised that I didn't pick up on them."

"I guess they're pretty good."

"Yeah. Thanks, by the way."

"No problem. It's a good thing that one of us stays awake."

I made my way out of the banquet hall and considered

my next move. Let's see. I really should check in with Morrolan. First, however, I wanted to talk to one of the security people and arrange for some surveillance on those two bodyguards. I wanted to learn a bit about them before I found myself confronting them on any important issue.

Morrolan's security officer on duty had an office just a few doors down from the Library. I walked in without knocking—the nature of my job putting me a step above this fellow.

The person who looked up at me as I stepped in was called Uliron, and he should have been working the next shift, not this one. "What are you doing here?" I asked. "Where is Fentor?"

He shrugged. "He wanted me to take his shift this time, and he'd take mine. I guess he had some kind of business."

I was bothered by this. "Do you do this often?" I asked.

"Well," he said, looking puzzled, "both you and Morrolan said it was all right for us to switch from time to time, and we logged it last shift."

"But do you do it often?"

"No, not really very often. Does it matter?"

"I don't know. Shut up for a minute; I want to think."

Fentor was a Tsalmoth, and he'd been with Morrolan's security forces for over fifty years. It was hard to imagine him suddenly being on the take, but it is possible to bring pressures down on anyone. Why? What did they want?

The other thing I couldn't figure out was why I had such a strong reaction to the switch. Sure, it was coming at a bad time, but they'd done it before. I almost dismissed it, but I've learned something about my own hunches: the only time they turn out to be meaningful is when I ignore them.

I sat on the edge of the desk and tried to sort it out. There was something significant about this; there had to be. I drew a dagger and started flipping it.

"What do you make of this, Loiosh?"

"I don't make anything of it, boss. Why do you think there's something wrong?"

"I don't know. Just that there's a break in routine, right now, when we know that the Demon wants to get at Mellar, and he isn't going to let the fact that Mellar is in Castle Black stop him."

"You think this could be a shot at Mellar?"

"Or the setup for it. I don't know. I'm worried."

"But didn't the Demon say that there wouldn't be any need to start a war? He said it could be 'worked around.'"

"Yes, he did. I hadn't forgotten that. I just don't see how he can do it—"

I stopped. At that moment, I saw very clearly how he could do it. That, of course, was why the Demon had tried to get my cooperation and then tried to kill me when I wouldn't give it. Oh, shit.

I didn't want to take the time to run down the hall. I reached out for contact with Morrolan. There was a good chance that I was already too late, of course, but perhaps not. If I could reach him, I would have to try to convince him not to leave Castle Black, under any circumstances. I'd have to . . . I became aware that I wasn't reaching him.

I felt myself slipping into automatic—where my brain takes off on its own, and lets me know what I'm supposed to do next. I concentrated on Aliera, and got contact.

"Yes, Vlad? What is it?"

"Morrolan. I can't reach him, and it's urgent. Can you find him with Pathfinder?"

"What's wrong, Vlad?"

"If we hurry, we might be able to get him before they make him unrevivifiable."

The echo of the thoughts hadn't died out in my head before she was standing next to me, Pathfinder naked in her hand. I heard a gasp from behind me, and remembered Uliron.

"Hold the keep for us," I told him. "And pray."

I sheathed my dagger; I wanted to have both hands free. If I don't know what I'm going to run into, I consider hands to be more versatile than any given weapon. I longed to unwrap Spellbreaker and be holding it ready, but I didn't. I was better off this way.

Aliera was deep in concentration, and I saw Pathfinder begin to emit a soft green glow. This was something I despised—having to sit there, ready to do something, but waiting for someone else to finish before I could. I studied Pathfinder. It shimmered green along its hard, black length. Pathfinder was a short weapon, compared to most swords that Dragaerans use. It was both shorter and heavier than the rapiers I liked to use, but in Aliera's hands it was light and capable. And, of course, it was a Great Weapon.

What is a Great Weapon? That's a good question. I wondered the same thing myself as I watched Aliera concentrating, her eyes narrowed to slits, and her hand steadily holding the pulsating blade.

As far as my knowledge goes, however, there is this: a Morganti weapon, made by one of the small, strange race called Serioli that dwell in the jungles and mountains of Dragaera, is capable of destroying the soul of the person it kills. They are, all of them, strange and frightening things, endowed with a kind of sentience. They come in differing degrees of power, and some are enchanted in other ways.

But there are a few—legend says seventeen—that go beyond "a kind of sentience." These are the Great Weapons. They are, all of them, powerful. They all have enough sentience to actually *decide* whether or not to destroy the soul of the victim. Each has its own abilities, skills, and powers. And each one, it is said, is linked to the soul of the one who bears it. It can, and will, do anything necessary to preserve its bearer, if he is the One chosen for it. And the things those weapons can do. . . .

Aliera tugged at my sleeve and nodded when I looked up. There was a twist down in my bowels, the walls vanished, and I felt sick, as usual. We were standing in what appeared to be an unused warehouse. Aliera gave a gasp, and I followed her glance.

Morrolan's body was lying on the floor a few feet from us. There was a dark red spot on his chest. I approached him, feeling sicker than ever. I dropped to my knee next to him and saw that he wasn't breathing.

Aliera sheathed Pathfinder and dropped down beside me. She ran her hands over Morrolan's body once, her face closed with concentration. Then she sat back and shook her head.

"Unrevivifiable?" I asked.

She nodded. Her eyes were cold and gray. Mourning, if there was to be any, would come later.

12-

"Tread lightly near thine own traps."

"Is there anything we can do, Aliera?"

"I'm not sure," she said. "Bide." She carefully ran her hands once more over Morrolan's body, while I made a cursory survey of the warehouse. I didn't find anything, but there were several areas that I couldn't see.

"I can't break it," she said at last.

"Break what?"

"The spell preventing revivification."

"Oh."

"However, the sorcerer who put it on could, if it's done soon enough. We'll have to find him quickly."

"Her," I corrected automatically.

She was up in an instant, staring at me. *"You know who did it?"*

"Not exactly," I said. "But I think we're safe in limiting it to the Left Hand of the Jhereg, and most of them are female."

She looked puzzled. "Why would the Jhereg want to kill Morrolan?"

I shook my head. "I'll explain later. Right now, we have to find that sorceress."

"Any suggestions as to how we do this?"

"Pathfinder?"

"Has nothing to work with. I need a psionic image, or at least a face or a name. I've checked around the room, but I'm not able to pick up anything."

143

"You generally don't with Jhereg. If she's competent, she wouldn't have had to feel any strong emotions in order to do what she did."

She nodded. I began looking around the room, hoping to find some kind of clue. Loiosh was faster, however. He flew around the perimeter and quickly spotted something.

"Over here, boss!"

Aliera and I rushed over there, and almost tripped over another body, lying face down on the floor. I turned it over and saw Fentor's face staring up at me. His throat had been cut by a wide-bladed knife, used skillfully and with precision. The jugular had been neatly slit.

I turned to Aliera, to ask if he was revivifiable, but she was already checking. I stepped back to give her room.

She nodded, once, then laid her left hand on his throat. She held it there for a moment and removed it. The wound was closed, and from where I stood I could only barely make out a faint scar.

She continued checking over his body and turned it over to make sure that there was nothing on his back. She turned it over again and laid both of her hands on his chest. She closed her eyes, and I could see the lines of tension on her face.

Fentor started breathing.

I let the air out of my lungs, realizing that I'd been holding it in.

His eyes fluttered open. Fear, recognition, relief, puzzlement, understanding.

I wondered what my own face had looked like, that time Aliera had brought me back to life.

He reached up with his right hand and touched his throat; he shivered. He saw me, but had no reaction that indicated guilt. Good; he hadn't been bought off, at least. I'd have liked to have given him time to recover, but we couldn't afford it. Every second we waited made it that much less likely that we could find the sorceress who had finished off Morrolan. And we had to find her and make her—

I reached out for contact with Kragar. After a long time, or so it seemed, I reached him.

"What is it, boss?"

"Can you get a fix on me?"

"It'll take a while. Problems?"

"You guessed it. I need a Morganti blade. Don't bother making it untraceable this time, just make it strong."

"Check. Sword, or dagger?"

"Dagger, if possible, but a sword will do."

"Okay. And you want it sent to where you are?"

"Right. And hurry."

"All right. Leave our link open, so I can trace down it."

"Right."

I turned back to Fentor. "What happened? Briefly."

He closed his eyes for a moment, collecting his thoughts. "I was sitting at the security office, when—"

"No," I interrupted. "We don't have time for the whole thing right now. Just what happened after you got here."

He nodded. "Okay. I showed up, was slugged. When I woke up I was blindfolded. I heard some talking, but I couldn't make out anything anyone said. I tried to reach you, and then Morrolan, but they had some kind of block up. I sat there for about fifteen minutes and tried to get out. Someone touched me on the throat with a knife to let me know I was being watched, so I stopped. I felt someone teleport in, around then, and then someone cut my throat." He winced and turned away. When he turned back, his face was composed again. "That's all I know."

"So we still don't have anything," I said.

"Not necessarily," said Aliera. She turned to Fentor. "You say you heard voices?"

He nodded.

"Were any of them female?"

He squinted for a moment, trying to remember, then nodded.

"Yes. There was definitely a woman there."

She reached forward again and placed her hand on his forehead.

"Now," she instructed, "think about that voice. Concentrate on it. Try to hear it in your mind."

He realized what was going on and looked over at me, his eyes wide. No one, no matter how innocent, enjoys being mind-probed.

"Do it," I said. "Cooperate."

He dropped his head back and closed his eyes.

After about a minute, Aliera opened her eyes and

looked up. "I think I've got it," she said. She drew Pathfinder, and Fentor gasped and tried to draw away.

At about that moment, there was a small popping sound, and I heard Kragar's pseudo-voice say, *"Okay, here it is."*

I saw a sheathed dagger at my feet.

"Good work," I told him, and cut the link before he could get around to asking any questions.

I drew the dagger and studied it. The instant it was out of the sheath, I recognized it as Morganti. I felt the blade's sentience ringing within my mind, and I shuddered.

It was a large knife, with a point and an edge. Two edges, in fact, as it was sharpened a few inches along the back. The blade was about sixteen inches long, and had a wicked curve along the back where it was sharpened. A knife-fighter's weapon. The hilt was large, and quite plain. The handle was a trifle uncomfortable in my hand; it had been made for Dragaerans, of course.

I sheathed it, and hung it on my belt, on the left side. It was next to the sword, in front of it, and set up for a cross-body draw. I tested it a few times, to make sure that its placement didn't interfere with getting to my sword. I looked over at Aliera and nodded that I was ready. "Fentor," I said, "when you're feeling strong enough, contact Uliron; he'll arrange to get you back. Consider yourself temporarily suspended from duties."

He managed a nod, as I felt the gut-wrenching twist of a teleport take effect.

Some general pointers on assassination and similar activities: Do not have yourself teleported so that when you arrive at the scene, you are feeling sick to your stomach. Particularly avoid it when you have no idea whatsoever as to where you're going to end up. Failing these, at least make sure that it isn't a crowded tavern at the height of the rush hour, when you don't know exactly where your victim is. If you do, the people around you will have time to react to you before you can begin to move. And, of course, don't do it in a place where your victim is sitting at a table surrounded by sorceresses.

If, for some reason, you have to violate all of the above rules, try to have next to you an enraged Dragonlord with a Great Weapon. Fortunately, I wasn't here to do an assassination. Well, not exactly.

Aliera faced one direction; I faced the other. I spotted them first, but not before I heard a shout and saw several people go into various types of frenzied actions. If this was a typical Jhereg-owned establishment, there could be up to a half-dozen people here who regularly brought body-guards with them. At least some of the bodyguards would recognize me, and hence be aware that an assassin was now among them.

"Duck, boss!"

I dropped to one knee, as I spotted the table, and so avoided a knife that came whistling at my head. I saw someone, female, point her finger at me. Spellbreaker fell into my hand, and I swung it out. It must have intercepted whatever it was that she was trying to do to me; I wasn't blasted, or paralyzed, or . . . whatever.

A problem occurred to me just then: I had recognized the table because there were a lot of people at it that I knew to be with the Left Hand, and because they had reacted to my suddenly showing up. One of them, therefore, must have understood what I was doing there (which was con-firmed by Aliera's presence), and acted accordingly. I could safely kill all but her. But which one was it? I couldn't tell by looking at them. By this time, they were all standing up and ready to destroy us. I was paralyzed as surely as if a spell had hit me.

Aliera wasn't, however. She must have asked Pathfinder which one it was as soon as she had seen the table—just a fraction of a second after I did. As it happened, she didn't feel like stopping long enough to let me in on the secret. She jumped past me, Pathfinder arcing wildly. I saw what must have been another spell aimed at me, and I swung Spellbreaker again—caught it.

Aliera had her left hand in front of her. I could see multi-colored light striking it. Pathfinder connected with the head of a sorceress with light brown, curly hair, who would have been quite pretty if it weren't for the look on her face and the dent in her forehead.

I shouted over the screams as I rolled along the floor, hoping to present a difficult target. "Dammit, Aliera, which one?"

She cut again, and another fell, her head departing her shoulders and coming to rest next to me. But Aliera had heard me. Her left hand stopped blocking spells and she pointed directly at one of the sorceresses for a moment. It was someone I didn't know. Something seemed to strike Aliera at that moment, but Pathfinder emitted a bright green flash for an instant and she continued with the mayhem.

My left hand found three shuriken, and I flipped them at one of the sorceresses who was trying to do something or other to Aliera.

You know, that's what I hate most about fighting against magic: you never know what they're trying to do to you until it hits. The sorceress knew what hit her, however. Two of the shuriken got past whatever defenses she had. One caught her just below the throat, the other in the middle of her chest. It wouldn't kill her, but she wouldn't be fighting anyone for a while.

I noticed Loiosh, about then, flying into people's faces and forcing them to fend him off, or else heal the poison. I began to work my way toward our target. Grab her, then have Aliera teleport us out and put up trace blocks.

The sorceress beat us to it.

I was on my feet and moving toward her. I was perhaps five steps away when she vanished. At the same moment something hit me. I discovered that I couldn't move. I'd been running and I wasn't especially in balance, so I hit the floor rather hard. I ended up on my back, in a position where I could see Aliera, torn between helping me and trying to trace and follow the vanished sorceress.

"I'm fine!" I lied to her psionically. *"Just get that bitch and stuff her somewhere!"*

Aliera promptly vanished, leaving me all alone. Paralyzed. What the hell had I done that for? I asked myself.

At the edge of my line of sight (the paralysis was complete enough that I couldn't even move my eyeballs, which is remarkably frustrating) I saw one of the sorceresses pointing her finger at me. I would, I suppose, have prepared to die if I had known how.

She didn't get a chance to complete the spell, however.

At that moment, a winged shape hit her face from the side, and I heard her scream and she fell out of my line of sight.

"Loiosh, back off and get out of here!"

"Go to Deathsgate, boss."

So where did he think I *was* going?

The sorceress was back in my line of sight, now, and I saw a look of rage on her face. She held out her hand again, but it wasn't pointed at me this time. She tried to follow Loiosh with her hand, but was having problems. I couldn't see the jhereg, but I knew what he must be doing.

I couldn't move to activate Spellbreaker, much less do something meaningful. I could have tried to summon Kragar, but it would all be over before I could even contact him. Witchcraft also just took too damn long.

I would have screamed if I could have. It wasn't so much that they were going to kill me; but, lying there, utterly helpless, while Loiosh was going to be burned to a crisp, I almost exploded with frustration. My mind hammered at the invisible bonds that held me, as I recklessly drew on my link to the Orb for power, but there was not a chance that I could break the bindings. I just wasn't a sorcerer of the same class as they were. If only Aliera were here.

That was a laugh! They wouldn't have been able to bind her like this. If they had the nerve to try, she'd dissolve them all in chaos. . . .

Dissolve them in chaos.

The phrase rang through my mind, and echoed through the warehouse of my memory. "I wonder how genetic heritage interacts with reincarnation of the soul."

"Oddly."

I was Aliera's brother.

The thoughts took no time whatsoever. I knew what I had to do then, although I had no idea how to do it. But at that point I didn't care. Let the whole world blow up. Let the entire planet be dissolved in chaos. The sorceress, who was still within my range of vision, became my whole world for a moment.

I envisioned her dissolving, dissipating, vanishing. All of the sorcerous energy I had summoned and been unable to use, I threw, then, and my rage and frustration guided it.

I have heard, since, that those who were looking on saw a stream of something like formless, colorless fire shoot from me toward the tall sorceress with the finger pointing off into the air, who never saw it coming.

As for me, I suddenly felt myself drained of energy, of hate, of everything. I saw her fall in upon herself and dissolve into a swirling mass of all the colors I could conceive of, and several that I couldn't.

Screams reached my ears. They meant nothing. I found that I could move again when my head suddenly hit the floor, and I realized that it had been up at an angle. I tried to look around, but couldn't raise my head. I think someone yelled, "It's spreading!" which struck me as odd.

"Boss, get up!"

"Wha—? Oh. Later, Loiosh."

"Boss, now! Hurry! It's moving toward you!"

"What is?"

"Whatever it was that you threw at her. Hurry, boss! It's almost reached you!"

That was odd enough that I forced my head up a little bit. He was right. There seemed to be almost a pool of—something—that more or less centered where the sorceress had been standing. Now that was strange, I thought.

Several things occurred to me at once. First, that this must be what happened when something dissolved into chaos—it spread. Second, that I really should control it. Third, that I had no idea at all of how one went about controlling chaos—it seemed rather a contradiction in terms, if you see my point. Fourth, I became aware that the outermost tendrils were damn close to me. Finally, I realized that I just plain didn't have the strength to move.

And then there was another cry, from off to my side, and I became aware that someone had teleported in. That almost set me off laughing. No, no, I wanted to say. You don't teleport *in* to a situation like this, you teleport *out*.

There was a bright green glow off to my right, and I saw Aliera, striding directly up to the edge of the formless mass that filled that part of the room. Loiosh landed next to me, and began licking my ear.

"C'mon boss. Get up now!"

That was out of the question, of course. Much too much work. But I did succeed in holding my head up enough to watch Aliera. That was very interesting, in a hazy, unimportant sort of way. She stopped at the edge of the formless mass and held out Pathfinder with her right hand. Her left hand was raised up, palm out, in a gesture of warding.

And, so help me Verra, it stopped spreading! I thought I

was imagining things at first, but no, it had certainly stopped spreading. Then, slowly, it assumed a single, uniform color: green. It was very interesting, watching it change. It started at the edges and then worked in until the entire mass was a sort of emerald shade.

She began gesturing with her left hand, then, and the green mass began to shimmer, and slowly it turned blue. I thought it was very pretty. I looked closely. Was it my imagination, or did the blue mass seem a bit smaller than it had been? I looked around the edges of where it had been and confirmed it. There was nothing there, now. The wooden floor of the restaurant was gone, and it pulled back to reveal the edge of what appeared to be a pit. I looked up, and discovered that part of the ceiling was missing as well.

Gradually, I began to see the blue mass shrinking. It took on the form, slowly, of a circle, or rather a sphere, about ten feet in diameter. Aliera was moving forward, levitating over the hole in the floor. The ten feet became five feet, then a foot, then Aliera's body obscured it completely.

I felt strength returning to me. Loiosh was still next to me, licking my ear. I heaved myself up to a sitting position as Aliera turned and came toward me, appearing to walk over the nothingness below her. When she reached me, she grasped my shoulder and forced me to stand up. I couldn't read the expression on her face. She held out her hand to me when I was stable on my feet again. In her hand was a small, blue crystal. I took it, and felt a warmth from it, pulsating gently. I shuddered.

She spoke for the first time. "A bauble for your wife," she said. "Tell her how you got it if you wish; she'll never believe you, anyway."

I looked around. The room was empty. Hardly surprising. No one with any brains feels like rubbing shoulders with an uncontrolled mass of raw chaos.

"How—How did you do it?" I asked.

She shook her head.

"Spend fifty or a hundred years studying it," she said. "Then walk into the Great Sea of Chaos and make friends with it—after assuring yourself that you have the e'Kieron genes. After you do all that, maybe, if you absolutely have to, you can risk doing something like what you did."

She stopped for a minute, and said, "That was really incredibly stupid, you know."

I shrugged, not feeling a whole lot like answering just then. I was, however, beginning to feel a bit more like myself. I stretched, and said, "We'd better get going, before the Imperial Guards show up."

Aliera shrugged, made a brushing-off motion, and started to say something when Loiosh suddenly said, *"Guards, boss!"* and I heard the sound of feet tromping. Right on cue.

There were three of them, pulling their grim, official faces, and holding greatswords. Their eyes focused on me, not seeming to notice Aliera at all. I could hardly blame them, of course. They hear about a big mess in a Jhereg-owned bar, come in, and see an Easterner in the colors of House Jhereg. What are they supposed to think?

I had three weapons pointing at me, then. I didn't move. Looking at them, I gave myself even odds of fighting my way out, given that Loiosh was there and these fools generally don't know much about dealing with poison or thrown weapons of any kind. I didn't do anything about it, of course. Even if I'd felt in top shape and there was only one of them, I wouldn't have touched him. You do *not* kill Imperial Guards. Ever. You can bribe them, plead with them, reason with them; you don't fight them. If you do, there are only two possible outcomes: either you lose, in which case you are dead; or you win, in which case you are dead.

But this time, it turned out, I had no reason to worry. I heard Aliera's voice, over my shoulder. "Leave us," she said.

The guard turned his attention to her, seemingly for the first time. He raised his eyebrows, recognizing her for a Dragonlord, and not quite knowing how to take all this. I felt tremendous amounts of sympathy for the fellow.

"Who are you?" he asked, approaching her, but keeping his blade politely out of line.

Aliera flung back her cloak, and placed her hand on the hilt of Pathfinder. They must have sensed what it was immediately, for I saw them all recoil somewhat. And they knew, as I knew, that there was all the difference in the world between an Imperial Guard killed by a Jhereg and a fight between Dragons.

"I," she announced, "am Aliera e'Kieron. This Jhereg is mine. You may go."

He looked nervous for a moment, licked his lips, and turned back to the others. As far as I could tell, they didn't express an opinion one way or the other. He turned back to Aliera and looked at her for a moment. Then he bowed and, without a word, turned and left, his fellows falling in behind. I would be very interested in hearing what they put in their reports, I decided.

Aliera turned back to me. "What hit you?" she asked.

"A complete external binding, as far as I can tell. They didn't get my ears, or for that matter, my heart or lungs, but they got just about everything else."

She nodded. I suddenly remembered what we'd been doing there.

"The sorceress! Did you get her?"

She smiled, nodded, and patted the hilt of Pathfinder.

I shuddered again. "You had to destroy her?"

She shook her head. "You forget, Vlad—this is a Great Weapon. Her body is back in Castle Black, and her soul is here, where we can get at it whenever we want it." She chuckled.

I shuddered still another time. I'm sorry, but some things bother me. "And Morrolan's body?"

"He's at Castle Black, too. The Necromancer is looking after him, seeing if she can find a way to break the spell. It doesn't look hopeful unless we can convince our friend to help."

I nodded. "Okay, then let's get going."

At this point I suddenly remembered that, when those Imperial Guards were here, I'd been carrying a high potency Morganti weapon on my person. If I'd remembered that at the time, I don't know what I would have done, but I'd have been a lot more worried. This was the first time I'd come close to actually getting caught with one, and I was suddenly very happy that Aliera was along.

By the time we returned to Castle Black, my stomach was more than just a little irritated with me. If I'd eaten recently, I would probably have lost the meal. I resolved to be extra kind to my innards the rest of the day.

Morrolan has a tower, high up in his castle. It is the center of much of his power, I'm told. Besides himself, very few people are allowed up there. I'm one, Aliera is another. Still another is the Necromancer. The tower is the center of Morrolan's worship of Verra, the Demon Goddess he serves. And I do mean "serves." He has been known to sacrifice entire villages to her.

The tower is always dark, lit only by a few black candles. There is a single window in it, which does not look down on the courtyard below. If you're lucky, it doesn't look upon anything at all. If you aren't, it will look upon things which may destroy your sanity.

We laid Morrolan's body on the floor beneath the window. On the altar in the center of the room was the sorceress. Her head was propped up, so that she could see the window. This was at my suggestion. I had no intention of actually using the window for anything, but having her see it would help with what we were trying to do.

The Necromancer aided Aliera, who revivified the sorceress. It could, conceivably, have been the other way around, too. There are few who know more about the transfer of souls, and the mysteries of death, than the Necromancer. But it was Aliera's Great Weapon, so she did the necessary spells.

The sorceress's eyes fluttered open, and her face went through the same patterns that Fentor's had, earlier, except that it ended with fear.

This part was my job. I had no desire to give her time to take in her surroundings more than casually, or to orient herself. The fact that she had been picked by whoever had killed Morrolan guaranteed that she was good, which guaranteed that she was tough. I didn't figure to have an easy time of this, by any means.

And so the first thing she saw when she opened her eyes was the window. It was politely empty at the moment, but nonetheless effective. And before she had time to adjust to that, she saw my face. I was standing over her and doing my best to look unfriendly.

"Well," I said, "did you enjoy the experience?"

She didn't answer. I wondered what it was like, having your soul eaten, so I asked her. She still didn't answer.

By this time, she would be cognizant of several things—including the chains that held her tied to the altar and the spells in the room which kept her from using sorcery.

I waited for a moment, to make sure it all sank in properly. "You know," I said conversationally, "Aliera enjoyed killing you that way. She wanted to do it again."

Fear. Controlled.

"I wouldn't let her," I said. "I wanted to do it."

No reaction.

"You okay, boss?"

"Damn! Is it showing that much?"

"Only to me."

"Good. No, I'm not okay, but there isn't anything I can do about it, either."

"Perhaps," I went on to her, "it is a flaw in my character, but I truly enjoy using Morganti weapons on you bitches."

Still nothing.

"That's why we brought you back, you know." As I said it, I drew the dagger Kragar had supplied me with and held it before her eyes. They widened with recognition. She shook her head in denial.

I'd never had to do anything like this before, and I wasn't liking it now. It wasn't as if she'd done something wrong— she'd just accepted a standard contract, much as I would have done. Unfortunately, she'd gotten involved with the wrong people. And, unfortunately, we needed her cooperation because she'd done a good job. I couldn't stop myself from identifying closely with her.

I touched her throat with the back of the blade, above the edge. I felt it fighting me—trying to turn around, to get at the skin, to cut, to drink.

She felt it too.

I held onto control. "However, being an honorable sort, I have to inform you that if you cooperate with us, I won't be allowed to use this on you. A pity, if that were to happen."

Her face showed the gleam of hope she felt, and she hated herself for it. Well, after all, I didn't feel real good about myself just then either, but that's the game.

I grabbed her hair, and lifted her head a bit more. Her eyes landed on Morrolan's figure, lying directly under the window, which still showed only black. "You know what we want," I said. "I, personally, don't give a teckla's squawk if you do it or not. But some others here do. We arrived at a compromise. I have to ask you, just once, to remove the spell you put on. If you don't agree, I can have you. If you do, Morrolan gets to decide what to do with you."

She was openly trembling, now.

To a Jhereg professional, a contract is an almost sacred bond. Most of us would rather lose our souls than break a contract—in the abstract. However, when it comes right down to the moment, well . . . we'd soon see. I'd never been in the kind of situation she was in, and I prayed to Verra that I never would be, feeling very much the hypocrite. I think I would have broken about there, myself. Well, maybe not. It's so hard to say.

"Well, what is it?" I asked, harshly. I saw her face torn with indecision. Sometimes I truly loathe the things I do. Maybe I should have been a thief after all.

I grabbed hold of her dress and raised it up, exposing her legs. I pulled at one knee. Loiosh hissed, right on cue, and I said, aloud, "No! Not until I'm done with her!"

I licked the forefinger of my left hand and wetted down a spot on the inside of her thigh. She was close to tears, now, which meant she was also close to breaking. Well, now or never.

"Too late," I said with relish, and lowered the Morganti blade, slowly and deliberately, toward her thigh. The point touched.

"No! My god, stop! I'll do it!"

I dropped the knife onto the floor and grabbed her head again and supported her shoulders. She was facing Morrolan's body; her own was shaking with sobs. I nodded to Aliera, who dropped the protection spells which had cut off her sorcery. If she'd been faking, she was now in a position to put up a fight. But she knew damn well that she wouldn't be able to win against both Aliera and me, not to mention the Necromancer.

"Then do it now!" I snapped. "Before I change my mind."

She nodded, weakly, still sobbing quietly. I saw her concentrate for a moment.

The Necromancer spoke for the first time. "It is done," she said.

I let the sorceress fall back. I felt sick again.

The Necromancer stepped up to Morrolan's body and began working on it. I didn't watch. The only sounds were the sobbing of the sorceress and, very faintly, our breathing.

After a few minutes, the Necromancer stood up. Her dull, undead eyes looked almost happy for a moment. I looked over at Morrolan, who was breathing now, evenly and deeply. His eyes opened.

Unlike the others, his first reaction was anger. I saw a scowl form on his lips, then confusion. He looked around.

"What happened?" he asked.

"You were set up," I said.

He looked puzzled and shook his head. He held a hand up, and assisted him to his feet. He looked at all of us, his eyes coming to rest on the sorceress, who was still sobbing quietly.

He looked back and forth at Aliera and me for a moment, then asked, "Who is this one?"

"Left Hand," I explained. "She was retained, I expect, by whoever did the job on you. She was to make sure you couldn't be revivified. She did it, too. But of course, whoever put the spell on can take it off again, and we convinced her to remove it."

He looked thoughtfully at her. "She's pretty good then, eh?"

"Good enough," said Aliera.

"Then," said Morrolan, "I suspect she did more than that. Someone hit me as soon as I arrived at that—place."

"Warehouse," I said.

"That warehouse. Someone succeeded in stripping away all of my defensive spells. Could that have been you, my lady?"

She looked over at him bleakly, but didn't respond.

"It must have been," I said. "Why hire two sorceresses when you only need one?"

He nodded.

I retrieved the dagger from the floor, sheathed it, and handed it to Morrolan. He collects Morganti weapons, and I didn't ever want to see this one again. He looked at it and nodded. The knife disappeared into his cloak.

"Let's get out of here," I said.

We headed for the exit. Aliera caught my eye, and she

couldn't quite keep the disgust from her face. I looked away.

"What about *her*?" I asked Morrolan. "We guaranteed her her soul if she'd help us, but made no promises other than that."

He nodded, looked back at her, and drew a plain-steel dagger from his belt.

The rest of us went out the door, none of us really desirous of seeing the end of the affair.

13-

"The bite of the yendi can never be fully healed."

Morrolan had caught up to us by the time we reached the library, and his dagger was sheathed. I tried to put the whole incident out of mind. I failed, of course.

In fact—and here's a funny thing, if you're in the mood for a laugh—I had done forty-one assassinations at this point, and I had never been bothered by one. I mean, not a bit. But this time, when I actually hadn't even hurt the bitch, it bothered me so much that for years afterward I'd wake up seeing her face. It could be that she laid some kind of curse on me, but I doubt it. It's just that, oh, Hell. I don't want to talk about it.

Fentor was in the library when we arrived. When he saw Morrolan, he almost broke down. He rushed up and fell to his knees, casting his head down. I thought I was going to get sick all over again, but Morrolan was more understanding.

"Get up," he said gruffly. "Then sit down and tell us about it."

Fentor nodded and stood. Morrolan guided him to a seat and poured him a glass of wine. He drank it thirstily, failing to appreciate the vintage, while we found seats and poured wine for ourselves. Presently, he was able to speak.

"It was this morning, my lord, that I received a message."

"How?" Morrolan interrupted.

"Psionic."

"All right, proceed."

"He identified himself as a Jhereg and he said he had some information to sell me."

"Indeed? What kind of 'information?' "

"A name, my lord. He said that there was going to be an attempt made on Mellar, who was one of our guests, and that the assassin didn't care that he was here." Fentor gave an apologetic shrug, as if to apologize for his contact's lack of judgment. "He said the assassin was good enough to beat our security system."

Morrolan looked at me and raised his eyebrow. I was in charge of security, he was saying, in his eloquent way. *Could* it be beaten?

"Anyone can be assassinated," I told Morrolan, drily.

He allowed his lips to smile a bit, nodded, and returned his attention to Fentor.

"Did you really think," Morrolan asked him, "that they were prepared to start another Dragon-Jhereg war?"

I opened my mouth to speak, but thought better of it. Let him finish his tale.

"I was afraid he might," said Fentor. "In any case, I thought it would be a good idea to get the name, just to be safe."

"He was willing to give you the name of the assassin?" I found myself asking.

He nodded. "He said that he was desperate for money, and had come across it, and knew Morrolan would be interested."

"I don't suppose," said Morrolan, "that it occurred to you to bring this information to me before you tried to do anything yourself?"

Fentor was silent for a moment, then he asked, "Would you have done it, my lord?"

"Most assuredly not," said Morrolan. "I would hardly submit to anyone's extortion." He lifted his chin slightly.

(Be still, my beating stomach.)

Fentor nodded. "I assumed that you would have that re-action, my lord. On the other hand, it's my job to make sure nothing happens to your guests, and I thought I'd need any advantage I could get, if there really was an assassin who was going to try for Mellar."

"How much did he want?" I asked.

"Three thousand gold Imperials."

"Cheap," I remarked, "given what he was risking."

"Where did the gold come from?" Morrolan asked.

Fentor shrugged. "I'm not really poor," he said. "And since I was doing it on my own—"

"I suspected as much," said Morrolan. "You will be reimbursed."

Fentor shook his head. "Oh, I still have the gold," he said. "They never took it."

I could have told him that. After all, we were dealing with professionals.

Fentor continued. "I arrived at the teleport coordinates they gave me and was hit as soon as I got there. I was blindfolded and then killed. I had no idea what had happened, or why, until I got up, after Aliera revivified me, and saw—" he choked for a minute, and looked away "—and saw your body, my lord. That was when I arranged to have us teleported back."

I felt a momentary twinge of sympathy for him. We probably should have let him know about Morrolan's corpse a few feet away, but then, I hadn't exactly been in the mood for polite chit-chat, nor had the time for it.

Morrolan nodded sagely as he finished.

"I've temporarily relieved him from duty," I put in.

Morrolan stood up, and went over to him. He looked down on Fentor for a moment, then he said, "All right. I approve of the motivations behind your actions. I understand and sympathize with your reasoning. But there is not to be a repetition of this action in the future. Is this understood?"

"Yes, my lord. And thank you."

Morrolan clapped him on the shoulder. "Very well," he said. "You are restored to full duty. Get back to work."

Fentor bowed and left. Morrolan shut the door behind him after seeing him out, sat down, and sipped his wine.

"No doubt," he said, "you are all hoping to hear what happened to me."

"You guessed it," I said.

He shrugged. "I received a message, from the same individual who contacted Fentor, most likely. Fentor, he claimed, was being held. I was *instructed*," he said the word as if it tasted bad, "to withdraw my protection of the Lord

Mellar and remove him from my home. They told me that if I didn't, they would kill Fentor. They threatened to use a Morganti blade on him if I made any attempt to rescue him."

"So naturally," I said, "you went charging right in there."

"Naturally," he agreed, ignoring my sarcasm. "I kept him talking long enough to trace where he was, put up my standard protection spells, and teleported in."

"Was Fentor alive then?" I asked.

He nodded. "Yes. While I was trying the trace, I made them put me in contact with him, to verify that he was alive. He was unconscious, but living.

"In any case," he continued, "I arrived. That, uh, lady we just left threw some kind of spell. I assume it was preset. I didn't realize that it was her until just now, of course, but whatever it was removed my protections against physical attack." He shook his head. "I'm forced to admire their timing. You would have appreciated it, Vlad. Before I was really aware of what had happened, something hit me in the back of the head and I saw a knife coming toward me. Most unpleasant. I had no time to counterattack in any way. As they intended, of course."

I nodded. "They knew what they were doing. I should have figured it out sooner."

"How did you catch on at all?" asked Aliera.

"Certain parties had mentioned that they had found a way to kill Mellar without bringing the whole House of the Dragon down on their heads. It took me way too long, but it finally occurred to me that the one way to do that, without getting Mellar to leave Castle Black, would be if Morrolan were to turn up conveniently dead. Then, of course, there wouldn't be a problem, since he'd no longer be Morrolan's guest, as it were."

Morrolan shook his head, sadly.

I continued. "As soon as I found out that Fentor and Uliron had changed shifts, I knew something was up. I figured out what it had to be, contacted Aliera, and, well, you know the rest."

He didn't, of course, but I wasn't really in the mood to tell him how I almost managed to dissolve myself—and half of Adrilankha—in raw chaos.

Morrolan looked at me hard. "And who," he asked, "is this person, who came up with this marvelous scheme?"

I matched his stare, and shook my head. "No," I said. "That information I can't give even you."

He looked at me a moment longer, then shrugged. "Well, my thanks, in any case."

"You know what the real irony is?" I said.

"What?"

"I've been trying to come up with some way to prevent another Dragon-Jhereg war myself, and when one drops right into my lap, I chuck it out."

Morrolan allowed himself a small smile. "I don't really think they'd go that far, do you?" he asked.

I started to nod, stopped. Damn right they'd go that far! And, knowing the Demon, he wouldn't waste a lot of time being about it!

"What's wrong, Vlad?" asked Aliera.

I shook my head and contacted Fentor.

"Yes, my lord?"

"Are you back on duty?"

"Yes, my lord."

"Run a full check on all our secure areas. Now. Make sure nothing's been breached. I want it done an hour ago. Move!"

I held the contact while he gave the necessary orders. If I were going to take out Mellar, how would I get past Morrolan's security system? I ran it through my mind. I'd set the damn thing up myself, however, so of course *I* couldn't see any flaws in it. Ask Kiera? Later, if there was time. If it wasn't already too late.

"Everything checks, my lord."

"Okay. Bide a moment."

Morrolan and Aliera were looking at me, puzzled. I ignored them. Now . . . forget the windows—no one gets in that way. Tunnel? Ha! From a mile in the air? When Morrolan can detect any sorcery done around the castle? No way. A hole in the wall? If they weren't going to use sorcery, which they shouldn't be able to, it would take too long. Doors? The main door had witchcraft, sorcery, and Lady Teldra. Forget that. Rear doors? Servants' entrances? No, we had guards.

Guards. Could the guards have been bribed? It would

take, how many? Damn! Only two. How long did he have to set this up? Not more than two days. No, he couldn't find two guards who would take in only two days, without finding one who would talk first. Kill all the ones who said no?

"Fentor, any deaths of guards within the last two days?"

"No, my lord."

Okay, good. No one was bribed. What else? Replace a guard? Oh, shit, *that's* what I'd do.

"Fentor, do we have any new guards working today? People who have been on the payroll less than three days? If not, check for servants. But check for guards first."

That's what I'd do, of course. Take a job as a guard, or a servant, and wait for the perfect moment. All I'd have to do is arrange for the right guard to be busy, or ill, or to need sudden days off, maybe bribe one person, maybe not even have to, if I could get access to the records and slip my name in.

"As a matter of fact, yes. We have someone new outside the banquet hall. The guard who normally has that duty—"

I broke the link. I was already running and half out the door before I heard Morrolan and Aliera shouting after me. The Necromancer, who hadn't said a word the entire time, remained behind. After all, what was another death, more or less, to her?

I charged down to the banquet hall at full tilt. Loiosh, however, was faster. He was flapping his way about ten paces ahead of me when I saw the two guards outside the door. I saw that they recognized me. They bowed slightly and came to alert as I started to get close. I noticed, from fifty feet away, that one of them had a dagger concealed under his uniform, which is very un-Dragonlike. Thank Barlen, we were in time.

Morrolan was close to my heels as I approached. The guard with the concealed dagger locked eyes with me for a moment; then he turned and bolted into the room, Loiosh close behind him. Morrolan and I raced after him. I took out a throwing knife; Morrolan drew Blackwand. I cringed involuntarily from the things that that unsheathed blade did to my mind, but I didn't let it slow me down.

There were shouts from inside the hall, doubtless in response to Morrolan's psionic orders. I ran past the door.

For a moment, I couldn't see him, obscured as he was by the crowd. Then I saw Loiosh strike. There was a scream, and I saw a sword flash.

We stopped. Mellar was now in plain view, looking not at all concerned. He favored Morrolan with a look of inquiry. At his very feet was the "guard." The latter's head was a few feet off to the side. A real guard stood over the body, his longsword bare and dripping. He looked up at Morrolan, who nodded to him.

Morrolan and I walked up to the body and removed a dagger from the outstretched hand. He took it and studied it for a moment. He said "good job," to the guard.

The guard shook his head. "Thank the jhereg," he said, looking at Loiosh with an expression of wonder on his face. "If he hadn't slowed him down, I'd never have made it in time."

"Finally, someone who appreciates me."

"Finally, you do a day's work."

"Two dead teckla on your pillow."

We ignored Mellar completely and walked back out of the room.

"All right," snapped Morrolan as we left. "Get this place cleaned up."

Aliera appeared beside us, and we headed back toward the library. Morrolan handed me the dagger. I touched it, and knew at once that it was Morganti. I shuddered and handed it back to him. There were just too damn many of those things floating around, lately.

"You realize what this means, don't you?" he said.

I nodded.

"And you knew this would happen?"

"I guessed it. When the attempt to nail you didn't work, they had to go ahead and get him anyway.

"We've been lucky," I added. "I've been too slow to pick up on most of this. If Mellar had happened to walk by the door any time in the last hour, it would be all over by now."

We entered the library. The Necromancer nodded a greeting to us and gestured with her wineglass, the strange, perpetual half-smile on her face. I've always liked her. Some day I hope to understand her. On the other hand, perhaps I'd better hope not to. As we seated ourselves, I said to Morrolan, "I've been meaning to get around to talking to you since I found out about the bodyguards."

"Bodyguards? Whose? Mellar's?"

"Right. As far as I can tell, he has two of them."

"As far as who can tell, boss?"

"Shut up, Loiosh."

"That is rather interesting," said Morrolan. "He most assuredly had no bodyguards when he arrived."

I shrugged. "So they aren't on your guest list. That makes them fair game, doesn't it?"

He nodded. "It appears that he doesn't especially trust my oath."

Something about that bothered me, but I couldn't quite put my finger on it.

"Possibly," I said. "But it's more likely that he doesn't trust the Jhereg not to start another war, just to get him."

"Well, he's correct in that, is he not, Vlad?"

I nodded, and looked away.

"Whoever this Mellar was in the Jhereg" said Morrolan, "he certainly must have hurt some pretty big people."

"Big enough," I said.

Morrolan shook his head. "I just can't believe that the Jhereg would be that stupid. Both Houses were very nearly destroyed the first time, and the last time—"

" 'Last time?' " I echoed. "It's only happened once, as far as I know."

He seemed surprised. "Didn't you know? But of course, it wouldn't be something the Jhereg would discuss excessively. I wouldn't know myself if Aliera hadn't told me about it."

"Told you what?" My voice sounded faint and hollow in my own ears.

Aliera cut in. "It happened once more. It started the same as before—with a Jhereg killed by an assassin while he was a guest in a Dragonlord's home. The Dragons retaliated, the Jhereg retaliated, and . . ." She shrugged.

"Why haven't I heard of this before?"

"Because things went to Hell after that, and it never got really well recorded. Briefly, the Jhereg who was killed was the friend of the Dragonlord, and he was helping him out on something. Someone found out what he was doing and put a stop to it.

"The Dragons demanded that the assassin be turned over to them, and, this time the Jhereg agreed. I guess House Jhereg felt that he should have known better, and also it may have been a private quarrel on some level. In any case, the assassin escaped from the Dragonlord's home before he was killed. He killed a couple of Dragons on the way out, then he killed a couple of the Jhereg bosses who had turned him in. He was killed himself, later, but by then it was too late to stop anyone."

"Why? If it was just the one individual—"

"This was during the reign of a decadent Phoenix, so nobody was trusting anybody. The Jhereg thought that it was the Dragons who had killed the bosses, and the Dragons thought it was the Jhereg who had arranged the escape."

"And then things went to hell, you say? Right then?"

She nodded. "The Jhereg killed enough of the right Dragonlords, including some wizards, so that a certain one, who'd been planning a coup, found himself forced to move too soon, and to rely too heavily on magic. And, without his best sorcerers, the spell got out of control, even after the Emperor was dead, and. . . ." Her voice trailed off. It started to sink in. I can subtract as well as anyone can, and if the first Dragon-Jhereg war was when it was, then the second one had to be . . . decadent Phoenix . . . Dragon coup . . . went to Hell . . . spell got out of control . . . dead Phoenix Emperor. . . .

"Adron," I said.

She nodded. "My father. The assassin had reasons of his own to hate the Emperor and was working with father to find a way to poison the Emperor when things fell apart. As you know, it was Mario who finally killed the Emperor, when he tried to use the Orb against the Jhereg. Another Phoenix tried to grab the throne, and father had to move too quickly. The next thing you know, we have a sea of chaos where the city of Dragaera used to be, no Emperor, no Orb, and no Empire. It was close to two hundred years before Zerika turned up with the Orb."

I shook my head. Just too damn many shocks in too damn few days. I couldn't handle it.

"And now," I said, "it's going to start up again."

Morrolan nodded at this. We were all silent for a time,

then Morrolan said quietly, "And if that happens, Vlad, which side will you be on?"

I looked away.

"You know," he continued, "that I'd be one of House Jhereg's first targets."

"I know," I said. "I also know that you'd be in the front lines trying to waste the organization. As would Aliera, for that matter. And, by the way, *I'd* be one of the first ones the Dragons went after."

He nodded. "Do you think you could convince the Jhereg to let this one go?"

I shook my head. "I'm not an Issola, Morrolan, and I don't have that sharp a tooth. And, to tell you the truth, I'm not all that sure that I'd do it if I could. I've heard all the reasons why Mellar has to go, and they're hard to argue with."

"I see. Perhaps you could convince them to wait. As you know, he'll only be staying here a few more days."

"No way, Morrolan. It can't be done."

He nodded. We sat there in silence for a time; then I said, "I don't suppose there is any way, just this once, that you could let us have him? All you have to do is kick him out, you know. I hadn't intended to even ask, but. . . ."

Aliera looked up, intent for a moment.

"Sorry, Vlad. No."

Aliera sighed.

"All right," I said. "I didn't really think you would."

We were all quiet again, for a few minutes; then Morrolan spoke once more. "I probably don't have to say this, but I will remind you that if anything, anything at all, happens to him in this house, I'm not going to rest until I find out the cause. I'm not going to hold back, even if it's you.

"And if it *is* you, or any other Jhereg, I will personally declare war on the House, and I'll have the backing of every Dragon in the Empire. We have been friends for a long time, and you have saved my life on more than one occasion, but I will not allow you, or anyone else, to get away with the murder of one of my guests. You understand that, don't you?"

"Morrolan," I said, "if I had intended to do anything

like that, I wouldn't have asked you about it, would I? I would have done it already. We've known each other for—how long? —four years? I'm surprised that you know me so little that you'd think I'd abuse your friendship."

He shook his head, sadly. "I never thought you would. I just had to make sure that the matter was stated clearly, and in the open, all right?"

"All right. I guess I had it coming to me for asking you what I did, anyway. I'll be heading off now. I'm going to have to think about this."

He stood as I did. I bowed to him, to Aliera, and to the Necromancer. Aliera bowed back; the Necromancer looked out at me from within her dark eyes, and she smiled. As I turned toward the door, Morrolan gripped my shoulder.

"Vlad, I'm sorry."

I nodded. "Me, too," I said.

14.

**"Oft 'tis startling to reveal
what the murky depths conceal."**

Cawti knew me better than any other being that I'm aware
of, with the possible exception of Loiosh. She suppressed
any desire she might have had for conversation and allowed me to brood in silence as we ate. She squelched the
suggestion that I take her turn at cooking since she'd taken
mine, and carefully cooked something bland and unin-
teresting so that I'd feel no compulsion to compliment
her on it. Clever lady, my wife.

Our apartment was a small, second-story number, which
had two virtues: it was well-lit and it had a large kitchen.
There is one way to tell an apartment owned by a member
of the Jhereg from any other kind of apartment: the lack of
spells to prevent or detect burglary. Why? Simple. No
common thief is going to lighten the apartment of a member of the organization except by mistake. If a mistake like
that happens, I will have everything back within two days,
guaranteed. Kragar may have to arrange for a few broken
bones to do it, but it will get done. The only other kind of
burglar there is, is someone like Kiera; someone specifical-
ly commissioned to get into my place and get something. If
this happens, there just isn't any kind of defense I could put
up that would matter a teckla's squawk. Keep Kiera out?
Ha!

So we sat, snug and secure, in our little kitchen, and I
said, "You know what the problem is?"

"What?"

171

"Every time I try to think of how to do it, all I can think of is what happens if I don't."

She nodded. "It's still hard for me to believe that the Demon would consciously and deliberately go out and start a Dragon-Jhereg war."

I shook my head. "What choice does he have, really?"

"Well, if you were in his position, would you?"

"That's just the thing," I said. "I think I would. Sure, they'd chew us up and spit us out again, but if Mellar gets away with this, it's slow death for the whole organization. If you get every punk on the street thinking that he can burn the council, one of them is bound to succeed, eventually. And then, even more will try, and it'll just keep getting worse."

It hit me, then, that I was parroting everything the Demon had told me. I shrugged. So what? It was true. If only there were some way to get rid of Mellar without a war—but, of course, there had been a way. The Demon had found one.

Sure, just kill Morrolan, he had thought. That was why he had given me that chance, back at the Blue Flame, to cooperate. Well, he was an honorable sort, after all, I couldn't deny that.

I wondered what his next move would be. He could take another try for me, or Morrolan, or skip it and go straight for Mellar. I guessed that he would try for Mellar, since time was becoming rather critical, with people already starting to talk. How much longer could this be held under our cloaks? Another day? Two, if we were lucky? Cawti was speaking, I realized.

"You're right," she was saying. "He has to be taken out."

"And I can't touch him while he's at Castle Black."

"And the Jhereg isn't about to wait until he leaves."

Not anymore, they wouldn't. How would the attack come this time? No matter, they couldn't set anything up in a day, and Morrolan had tightened his security again. It would wait until tomorrow. It had to. I wasn't good for much of anything today.

"Just as you said," I told her. "Caught between a dragon and a dzur."

"Wait a minute, Vlad! What about a Dzur? Couldn't you

maneuver a Dzur hero into taking him out for you? We could try to find one of the younger ones, who doesn't know the story about him, maybe a wizard. You know how easy it is to manipulate Dzur heroes."

I shook my head. "No good, beloved," I said, thinking of Morrolan's speech earlier. "Aside from the chance that Morrolan would figure out what happened, I'm just not willing to do that to him."

"But if he never found out—"

"No. I'd know that I was the one who had caused his oath to be broken. Remember, Mellar isn't just at the home of a Dragonlord, which would be bad enough; Morrolan in particular has made a point of having Castle Black be a kind of sanctuary for anyone and everyone he invites. It means too much to him for me to trifle with it."

"My, my, aren't we the honorable sort today?"

"Shut up, Loiosh. Clean your plate."

"It's your plate."

"Besides," I added to Cawti, "how would you feel if you had taken the job, and the target was holed up with Norathar?"

The mention of her old friend and partner stopped her "Hmmmm. Norathar would understand," she said after a while.

"Would she?"

"Yes . . . well, no, I suppose not."

"Right. And you wouldn't ask her to, would you?"

She was silent for a while longer, then, "No."

"I didn't think so."

She sighed. "Then I don't see any way out."

"Neither do I. The 'way out,' as you put it, is to convince Mellar to leave Castle Black of his own free will and then nail him when he does. We can trick him however we want, or set up any kind of fake message, but can't actually attack him, or use any form of magic against him while he's there."

"Wait a minute, Vlad. Morrolan won't let us attack him, or use magic, but if we, say, deliver a note that convinces him to leave, that's okay? Morrolan won't care?"

"Right."

A look of utter confusion passed over her features. "But . . . but that's ridiculous! What difference does it make to

Morrolan how we get him out, if we do? What does using magic have to do with it?"

I shook my head. "Have I ever claimed to understand Dragons?"

"But—"

"Oh, I can almost see it, in a way. We can't actually *do* anything to him, is the idea."

"But isn't tricking him 'doing something' to him?"

"Well, yes. Sort of. But it's different, at least to Morrolan. For one thing, it's a matter of free choice. Magic doesn't give the victim a choice; trickery does. I also suspect that part of it is that Morrolan doesn't think we'll be able to do it. And he has a point there. You know Mellar is going to be on his guard against anything like that. I don't really see how we're going to be able to do anything."

"I don't, either."

I nodded. "I've got Kragar digging into his background, and we're hoping we'll find some weak spot there, or something we can use. I'll have to admit I'm not real hopeful."

She was silent.

"I wonder," I said a little later, "what Mario would do."

"Mario?" she laughed. "He would hang around him, with no one seeing him, for years if he had to. When Mellar finally left Castle Black, however and whenever, Mario would be there, and take him."

"But the organization can't wait—"

"They'd wait for Mario."

"Remember, I took this on with time constraints."

"Yes," she said softly, "but Mario wouldn't have."

That stung a bit, but I had to admit that it was true, especially since I'd come to the same realization when the Demon had first proposed the job to me.

"In any case," she went on, "there's only one Mario."

I nodded sadly.

"And what," I asked her then, "would you and Norathar have done, if the thing had been given to you?"

She thought about that for a long time, then she said, "I'm not really sure, but remember that Morrolan isn't that close a friend of ours; or at least he wasn't when we were still working. Chances are we'd put some sort of spell on Mellar to get him to leave and make damn sure Morrolan never found out."

That didn't help, either.

"I wonder what Mellar would do? I understand he was a pretty fair assassin himself, on his way up. Maybe we'll invite him over some time and ask him."

Cawti laughed easily. "You'll have to ask him at Castle Black. I understand he isn't getting out much these days."

I idly watched Loiosh nibble at the scraps of our meal. I got up and wandered into the living room. I sat there for a while, thinking and looking at the light brown walls, but nothing came.

I still couldn't shake the nagging feeling that I'd gotten when I'd been talking to Morrolan. I tried to recall the part of the conversation that had triggered it. Something about bodyguards.

"Cawti," I called.

Her voice came back from the kitchen. "Yes, dear?"

"Did you know that Mellar has a couple of bodyguards?"

"No, but I'm not surprised."

"I'm not either. They must be pretty good, too, because they were watching me while I talked to Mellar, and I didn't notice them at all."

"Did you mention them to Morrolan?"

"Yes. He seemed a little surprised."

"I suppose. You know you're free to do them, don't you? Since they obviously sneaked in, they aren't guests."

"That's true," I agreed. "It also proves how good they are. Slipping into Castle Black isn't the work of an amateur, if our protections are half as good as I think they are. Of course, we hadn't increased the guards then, but still. . . ."

She finished up her cleaning, and sat down next to me. I rested my head on her shoulder. She moved away from me, then, and patted her lap. I stretched out and crossed my legs. Loiosh flew over and landed on my shoulder, nuzzling me with his head.

There was still something about those bodyguards that seemed funny. I couldn't quite put my finger on it, which was incredibly frustrating. In fact, there was something strange about this whole affair that I couldn't quite see.

"Do you think," said Cawti a little later, "that you might be able to buy off one of the bodyguards?"

"What do you think?" I said. "If you have a whole organization to choose from, don't you think you could find two people in it who were completely trustworthy? Especially if you had an extra nine million gold to pay them with?"

"I guess you're right," she admitted. "On the other hand, there are other kinds of pressures we could bring to bear."

"In two days, Cawti? I don't think so."

She nodded, and gently stroked my forehead. "And," she said, "even if we did, I don't suppose it would really help. If we can't take him anyway, it won't do any good to convince one of the bodyguards to step back at the right time."

Cling! I had it! Not much, perhaps, but I suddenly knew what had been bothering me. I sat up on the couch, startling Loiosh, who hissed his indignation at me.

I leaned over and kissed Cawti, long and hard.

"What was that for?" she asked, a little breathlessly. "Not, you understand, that I mind."

I gripped her hand, and locked eyes, and concentrated, letting her share my thoughts. She seemed a bit startled at first, but quickly settled into it. I brought up the memory of standing at the entranceway, and past it, running, and the sight of the dead assassin with a Morganti dagger in his hand. I played over the whole thing, remembering expressions, glimpses of the room, and things only an assassin would have noticed—as well as things an assassin should have noticed if they'd been there.

"Hey, boss, want to run by the part of me getting the guy one more time?"

"Shut up, Loiosh."

Cawti nodded as it unfolded, and shared it with me. We reached the point where Morrolan handed me the dagger, and I broke out of it.

"There," I said, "does anything strike you as odd?"

She thought it over. "Well, Mellar seemed pretty calm for someone who has almost been killed, and with a Morganti dagger. But other than that. . . ."

I brushed it aside. "Chances are, he never realized that it was Morganti. Yes, it was odd, but I don't mean that."

"Then I don't see what you're referring to."

"I'm referring to the strange action of the bodyguards at the assassination attempt."

"But the bodyguards did nothing at the assassination attempt."

"That was the strange action."

She nodded, slowly.

I continued. "If the Dragon guard had been just a little bit slower, Mellar would have been cut down. I can't reconcile that with our conclusion that they are competent. I suppose Mellar might have had time to get a weapon out, or something, but he sure didn't look like it. The bodyguards were just nowhere to be seen. If they're as good as we think they are, they should have been all over the assassin before Morrolan's guard had time to show steel."

"Ahem!"

"Or Loiosh had time to strike," I added.

"They couldn't be that fast."

Cawti looked thoughtful. "Could it be that they just weren't around? That Mellar sent them on some kind of errand?"

"That, my dear, is exactly what I'm thinking. And if so, I'd very much like to find out what it was that they were doing."

She nodded. "Of course," she said, "it could be that they were there, and were good enough to see that Morrolan's guard was going to stop him."

"That is also possible," I said. "But if they're that good, I'm really scared."

"Do you know if they are still with him?"

"Good point," I said. "Just a minute while I check."

I contacted one of Morrolan's people in the banquet hall, asked, and was answered. "They're still around," I said.

"Which means that they weren't bought off by the Demon, or the assassin. Whatever reason they had for their 'strange action,' it was good enough for Mellar."

I nodded. "And that, my dearest love, is a good place to start looking tomorrow. Come on, let's go to bed."

She gave me her wide-eyed-innocent look. "What did you have in mind, my lord?"

"What makes you think I have something in mind?"

"You always do. Are you trying to tell me that you don't

have everything planned out?" She walked into the bedroom.

"Nothing," I said, "has been planned out since I started this damned job. We'll just have to improvise."

I gave myself two days to complete the thing. I was aware that I was being unduly optimistic.

I arrived at the office somewhat early the next morning, hoping to spend the day looking for a solid plan, or at least the shade of a direction. I was congratulating myself on having beaten Kragar, who is normally an early riser, when I heard him coughing gently. He was seated opposite me, with his smug little, I've-been-sitting-here-for-ten-minutes-now look.

I gave him a moderate-to-dangerous Jhereg sneer and said, "What did you find out?"

"Well," he said, "why don't we start out with the bad news, before we get to the bad news, the bad news, or the other bad news."

"Damn. You're just full of high spirits today, aren't you?"

He shrugged.

"Okay," I said, "what's the bad news?"

"There have been rumors," he stated.

"Oh, joy. How accurate are they?"

"Not very. No one has quite put together the rumors of something unusual going on with Mellar, and the ones about the Jhereg's having financial trouble."

"Can it wait two days?"

He looked doubtful. "Maybe. Somebody's going to have to start answering questions soon, though. Tomorrow would be better, and today would be better still."

"Let me put it this way: will the day after tomorrow be too late?"

He looked thoughtful. "Probably," he said at last.

I shook my head. "Well, at any rate, it isn't me who's going to have to answer the questions."

"There is that," he agreed. "Oh, and one piece of good news."

"Really? Well, break out the kilinara, by Verra's hair! We'll have a bloody celebration."

"I'll bring the dead teckla."

"Don't drink yourself into a stupor yet. All it is, is that we've gotten that sorceress you wanted."

"The one who was spreading rumors? Already? Good! give the assassin a bonus."

"I already have. He said it was half luck—she just happened to be in the perfect place, and he took her right away."

"Good. You *make* luck like that, though. Remember the guy."

"I will."

"Okay, now for the rest. Did you find out anything about Mellar's background?"

"Plenty," he said, taking out his notebook and flipping it open. "But, so far as I can tell, none of it is going to be of any real help to us."

"Forget about that for now; let's at least try to get some idea of who the hell he really is; then we'll see if that gives us anything to work with."

Kragar nodded, found his place, and began reading. "His mother lived the happy and fulfilling life of a Dragon-Dzur halfbreed. She wound up a whore. His father, it seems, was into a whole lot of different things, but was certainly an assassin. Reasonably competent, too. As far as I can tell, his father died during the fall of the city of Dragaera. We think the same thing happened to his mother. He hid out during the Eastern invasions, and showed up again after Zerika took the throne. He tried to claim kinship with the House of the Dragon and was rejected, of course. He tried the same thing with the House of the Dzur, with the same results."

"Wait a minute," I said, "you mean this was before he fought his way in?"

"Right. Oh, by the way, his real name is Leareth—or rather that was the name he was born with. That was the name he used the first time he joined the Jhereg."

"The first time?"

"Right. It took one hell of a lot of digging to find out, but we did. He was using the name Leareth, of course, and there are no references to anyone of that name in Jhereg records."

"Then how—"

"Lyorn records. It cost us about two thousand gold to

do, by the way. And, it turns out, 'someone' had managed
to bribe a few Lyorns. A lot of records that should have
mentioned him, or his family, weren't there. Part of it was
just luck that we ran across something that he'd missed, or
couldn't get access to. The rest was clever planning, bril-
liant execution—"

"Money," I said.

"Right. And I found a young Lyorn lady who couldn't
resist my obvious charms."

"I'm surprised she noticed you."

"Ah! They never do, until it's too late, you know."

I was impressed, in any case, both with Kragar, and with
Mellar. Bribing Lyorns to get access to records isn't easy,
and bribing them to actually alter records is almost unheard of. It would be like bribing an assassin to give you the
name of the guy who gave him the contract.

"Actually," Kragar continued, "he didn't officially join
House Jhereg then, which was one reason we had so much
trouble. He worked for it on a straight free-lance basis."

" 'Worked?' "

"That's right."

"I don't believe this, Kragar! How many assassins are we
going to run into? I'm beginning to feel like I'm one of a
horde."

"Yeah. It just isn't safe to walk the streets at night, is it?"
he smirked.

I gestured toward the wine cabinet. It was a bit early for
me, but I felt the need of something to help me keep up
with the shocks. "Was he good?" I asked.

"Competent," he agreed, as he poured us each a glass of
Baritt's Valley white. "He did only small-time stuff, but
never muffed one. It seems that he never took on anything
that was worth over three thousand."

"That's enough to make a living," I said.

"I guess so. On the other hand, he also didn't spend very
much time at it. He didn't take on 'work' more than once or
twice a year, in fact."

"Oh?"

"Yeah. Here's the killer, if you'll excuse the expression:
all the time he was working for the Jhereg, he was spending
most of his free time studying swordsmanship."

"Really?"

"Really. And, get this, he was studying under Lord Onarr."

I sat up in my chair so suddenly that I almost dumped Loiosh, who complained rather bitterly about the abuse. "Oh, ho!" I said. "So that's how he got so good with the blade that he could beat seventeen Dzur heroes!"

He nodded grimly.

I asked, "Do you have any guesses as to why Onarr was willing to take him on as a student?"

"No guesses—I know exactly. It's a real sweet story, too. Onarr's wife apparently contracted one of the plagues during the Interregnum. Mellar, or I guess he was called Leareth then, found a witch to cure it. As you know, sorcery was inoperable then, and there were damn few Easterner witches willing to work on Dragaerans, and even fewer Dragaerans who knew witchcraft."

"I know all about it," I said shortly.

Kragar stopped and gave me a look.

"My father died of one of the Plagues," I explained. *After* the Interregnum, when they were pretty much beaten. He didn't know sorcery. I did, but not quite enough. We could have cured him with witchcraft, either myself or my grandfather, but he wouldn't let us. Witchcraft was too 'Eastern,' you see. Dad wanted to be a Dragaeran. That's why he bought a title in the Jhereg and made me study Dragaeran-style swordsmanship and sorcery. And, of course, after dumping all of our money out the window, there wasn't any left to hire a sorcerer. I'd have died of the same plague if my grandfather hadn't cured me."

Kragar spoke softly. "I didn't know that, Vlad."

"Anyway, go on," I said abruptly.

"Well," he continued, "if you haven't guessed it already it was Mellar who had arranged with a witch to give Onarr's wife the plague in the first place. So he comes up, just as she's dying, saves her, and Onarr is very, very grateful. Onarr is so grateful, in fact, that he's willing to teach swordsmanship to a houseless cross-breed. Nice story, isn't it?"

"Interesting. Some elegant moves, there."

"Isn't it interesting? You'll note the timing, I'm sure."

"Yeah. He started this before he tried to join the House of the Dzur the first time, or the House of the Dragon."

"Right. Which means, unless I miss my guess, that he knew exactly what would happen when he tried to claim membership."

I nodded. "That puts a bit of a different light on things, doesn't it? It makes his attempting to join the Dragon and the Dzur not so much confusing, as downright mystifying."

Kragar nodded.

"And another thing," I said. "It would appear that his planning goes back a lot longer than the twelve years we were thinking of. It's more like two hundred."

"Longer than that," said Kragar.

"Oh, that's right. He started during the Interregnum, didn't he? Three hundred, then? Maybe four hundred?"

"That's right. Impressive, isn't it?"

I agreed. "So continue."

"Well, he worked with Onarr for close to a hundred years, in secret. Then he fought his way into the House of the Dzur when he felt he was ready, and from there you know the story."

I thought it over a bit, trying to sort it out. It was too early to see if there was anything there that I could use, but I wanted to try to understand him as well as I could.

"Did you ever find any clues about why he wanted to get into the Dzur, the second time, when he fought his way in?"

Kragar shook his head.

"Okay. That's something I'd like to find out. What about sorcery? Has he studied it at all?"

"As far as I can tell, only a little."

"Witchcraft?"

"No way."

"Well, so we have something, anyway, for all the good it will do us."

I sipped my wine, as the information began to sink in, or rather, as much of it as I could handle just then. Studied under Onarr, eh? And fought his way into the Dzur, only to leave and join—or rather, rejoin—the Jhereg, and get to the top, and then lighten the whole council. Why? Just to show that he could do it? Well, he was part Dzur, but I still couldn't quite see it. And that business with Onarr, and all that plotting and scheming. Strange.

"You know, Kragar, if it ever comes down to any kind of

straight fight with this guy, I think I'm in trouble."

He snorted. "You have a talent for understatement. He'll carve you into stew."

I shrugged. "On the other hand, remember that I use Eastern-style fencing. That could throw him off a bit, since he's one of you hack-hack-cut types."

"A damn good one!"

"Yeah."

We sat there for a while, in silence, sipping our wine. Then Kragar asked, "What did you find? Anything new?"

I nodded. "Had a busy day yesterday."

"Oh, really? Tell me about it."

So I gave him an account of the day's events, the new information I'd gotten. Loiosh made sure that I got the part about the rescue right. When I told him about the bodyguards, he was impressed and puzzled.

"That doesn't make sense, Vlad," he remarked. "Where would he have sent them?"

"I don't have the vaguest. Although, after what you've just told me, I can see another explanation. I'm afraid I don't like it much, either."

"What's that?"

"It could be that the bodyguards are sorcerers, and that Mellar figures that he can handle any physical attack himself."

"But it didn't look like he was doing anything at all, did it?"

I shook my head. "No, I have to admit it didn't. But maybe he was figuring to beat the guy only if he had to, and was counting on Morrolan's guards to stop him. Which, after all, they did. With help," I amended, quickly.

Kragar shook his head. "Would you count on someone else to be quick enough?"

"Well, no. But then, I'm not the fighter that Mellar is; we already know that."

Kragar looked highly unconvinced. Well, so was I.

"The only thing that really makes sense," he said, "is if you were right originally: he had some mission for them and they happened to be off doing it when the assassin came in for his move."

"Maybe," I said. Then, "Wait a minute, I must be slipping or something. Why don't I check it?"

"What?"

"Just a minute."

I reached out for contact, thinking of that guard who I had talked to in the banquet hall. I'd made a mental note of him, now, what was his name?

"Who is it?"

"This is Lord Taltos," I said. (Let us be pretentious.)

"Yes, my lord. What is it?"

"Have you been keeping an eye on those two bodyguards of Mellar's?"

"I've been trying, my lord. They're pretty slippery."

"Okay, good. Were you on duty during the assassination attempt last night?"

"Yes, my lord."

"Were the bodyguards there?"

"No, my lord—wait! I'm not sure. . . . Yes. Yes, they were."

"No possible doubt?"

"No, my lord. I had them marked just before it happened, and they were still there when I found them again just a few seconds afterwards."

"Okay, that's all. Good work."

I broke the link and told Kragar what I'd found out. He shook his head, sadly.

"And another nice theory blown through Deathsgate."

"Yeah."

I just couldn't figure it. Nothing about this business made sense. I couldn't see why he did it, or why his bodyguards seemed so cavalier about the whole thing, or any of it. But nothing happens for no reason. There had to be an explanation somewhere. I took out a dagger and started flipping it.

Kragar grunted. "You know the funny thing, Vlad?"

"What? I'd love to hear something funny just around now."

"Poor Mellar, that's what's funny."

I snorted. " 'Poor Mellar!' What about poor us? He's the one who started this whole thing, and we're going to get ourselves wiped out because of it."

"Sure," said Kragar. "But he's dead anyway, one way or another. He started this thing, and there isn't any way that he's going to survive it. The poor fool came up with this truly gorgeous scheme to steal Jhereg gold and live through it, and he worked on it, as far as we can tell, for a good three hundred years. And, instead of having it work, he's going to die anyway, and take two houses with him."

"Well," I said, "I'm sure he wouldn't cry about taking the two Houses with him—" I stopped. "The poor fool," Kragar had said. But we knew Mellar was no fool. How can you come up with something like this, spend hundreds of years, thousands of Imperials, and then trip up because you didn't realize that the Jhereg would take an action which, even to me, seemed logical and reasonable? That wasn't just foolishness, that was downright stupidity. And there was just no way I was going to start thinking that Mellar was stupid. No, either he knew some way of coming out of this alive, or . . . or . . .

Click, click, click. One by one, things started to fall into place. Click, click, wham! The look on Mellar's face, the actions of the bodyguards, the fighting his way into the House of the Dzur, all of it fit. I found myself filled with awe at the magnificence of Mellar's plan. It was tremendous! I found myself, against my will, filled with admiration.

"What is it, Vlad?"

"What is it, boss?"

I just shook my head. My dagger had stopped in mid-toss, and I was so stunned I didn't even catch it. It hit my foot, and it was only blind luck that the hilt was down. But I expect that even if it had landed point first in my foot, I wouldn't have noticed. It was so damn beautiful! For a while, I almost wondered whether I had the heart to stop it, even if I could think of a way. It was so *perfect*. As far as I could tell, in the hundreds of years of planning and execution, he hadn't made *one* mistake! It was incredible. I was running out of adjectives.

"Damn it, Vlad! Talk! What's going on?"

"You should know," I told him.

"What?"

"You pointed to it first, a couple of times, the other day. Verra! Was it only a day or two ago? It feels like years. . . ."

"What did I point to? Come on, damn you!" Kragar said.

"You're the one who started telling me what it would be like to grow up a cross-breed."

"So?"

"So we still couldn't help thinking of him as a Jhereg."

"Well, he *is* a Jhereg."

I shook my head. "Not genetically, he isn't."

"What does genetics have to do with it?"

"Everything. That's when I should have realized it; when Aliera told me what it really meant to be of a certain House. Don't you see, Kragar? But no, you wouldn't. You're a Jhereg, and you—we—don't look at things that way. But it's true. You *can't* deny your House, if you're a Dragaeran. Look at yourself, Kragar. To save my life, you had to disobey my orders. That isn't a Jhereg thing to do at all—the only time a Jhereg will disobey orders is when he's planning to kill his boss. But a Dragon, Kragar, a Dragon will sometimes find that the only way to fulfill his commander's wishes is to violate his commands, and do what has to be done, and risk a court-martial if he has to.

"That was the Dragon in you that did it, despite your opinion of the Dragons. To a Dragaeran, his House controls everything. The way he lives, his goals, his skills, his strengths, his weaknesses. There is nothing, but *nothing* that has more influence on a Dragaeran than his House. Than the House he was *born* into, no matter how he was raised.

"It's different with humans, perhaps, but . . . I should have seen it. Damn! I should have seen it. A hundred things pointed to it."

"For the love of the Empire, Vlad! What?"

"Kragar," I said, settling down a bit, "think for a minute. This guy isn't just a Jhereg, he's also got the bloodlust of a Dragon, and the heroism of a Dzur."

"So?"

"So check your records, old friend. Remember his father? Why don't you find out more about him? Go ahead, do the research. But I'll tell you right now what you're going to find.

"His father killed someone, another Jhereg, just before the Interregnum. The Jhereg he killed was protected by a Dragonlord; to be exact, by Lord Adron. Mellar's plan *wasn't* concocted to get Jhereg gold and get out alive—the whole point of it was to get himself killed. For more than three hundred years he's been planning things so that he'd be killed, perhaps with a Morganti weapon; he didn't care. And he'd be killed, and the information he'd planted would come out about the Dzur, and he'd wash their faces with mud. And, at the same time, the two Houses that he hates the most, the Dragons and the Jhereg, would destroy each other. The whole thing was done for revenge, Kragar—revenge for the way a cross-breed is treated and revenge for the death of his father.

"Revenge as courageous as a Dzur, as vicious as a Dragon, and as cunning as a Jhereg. That's what this is all about, Kragar."

Kragar looked like a chreotha who's just found that a dragon has wandered into its net. He went through the same process I had, of every little detail falling into place, and like me, he began to shake his head in wonderment, his face a mask of stony shock. "Oh, shit, boss," was all he said.

I nodded in agreement.

15-

"Staring into the dragon's jaw, one quickly learns wisdom."

The banquet hall of Castle Black appeared the same as it had the last time. A few different faces, a few of the same faces, many faceless faces. I stood in the doorway for a moment, then stepped inside. I wanted to gather my thoughts a little, and let my stomach finish its recovering act before I began any serious work.

"Can you believe, boss, that Morrolan actually likes it this way?"

"You know Dragons, Loiosh."

Kragar had taken an hour and had verified each of my guesses as regarded Mellar's parentage. It seemed that his father had indeed been the one whose work had set off the second Dragon-Jhereg war, which Kragar had never heard of either. The references to it among the Lyorn records had been scattered, but clear. The thing had happened, and more or less as I'd been told.

Everything fit together very nicely. And I wasn't a bit closer to figuring out what to do about it than I'd been the day before. That was the really annoying thing. All of this information really ought to be food for something besides the satisfaction of solving a puzzle. Oh, sure, it meant that I knew now that certain things wouldn't work, since Mellar had no intention of leaving Castle Black alive, but I hadn't had any idea of what to do before, so that didn't really affect anything. It occurred to me that the more I found out, the more difficult, instead of easier, the thing became.

Maybe I should arrange to forget most of this.

There was, I realized then, still one more mystery to solve. It wasn't a big one, or, I expected, a difficult one, but I was somewhat curious about why Mellar had brought bodyguards with him at all, if he didn't intend to try to save his life. Not very important, perhaps, but by now I couldn't afford to overlook anything. This was what had brought me back to the banquet hall: to take a look at them and see if there was anything I could learn, guess, or at least eliminate.

I wandered through the crowd, smiling, nodding, drinking. After about fifteen minutes, I spotted Mellar. I brought up the memory of the two faces that Loiosh had given me and found the two bodyguards, a few feet away.

I moved as close to them as I figured was safe and looked at them. Yes, they were both fighters. They had that way of moving, of standing, that indicated physical power. Both were large men, with big, capable hands, and they were both skilled in observing a crowd without seeming to.

Why were they doing it, though? I was convinced, by now, that they had no intention of stopping an assassin, so they must have some other purpose. A small part of me wanted to just take them both out, here and now, but I had no intention of doing so until I knew what their business was. And, of course, there was no guarantee that I'd succeed.

I was very careful to avoid having them notice my scrutiny, but you can never be sure, of course. I checked them as carefully as I could for concealed weapons, but oddly, I didn't spot any. They both had swords, standard Dragaeran longswords, and they each had a dagger. But I couldn't see anything concealed on any of them.

After five minutes, I turned and started to leave the banquet hall, making my way carefully through the mass of humanity. I had almost reached the door, when Loiosh interrupted my contemplation.

"Boss," he said, *"tough-guy warning, behind you."*

I turned in time to see one of them coming up to me. I waited for him. He stopped about one foot in front of me, which is what I call "intimidation range." I wasn't intimidated. Well, maybe just a little. He didn't waste any time with preliminaries.

"One warning, whiskers," he said. "Don't try it."

"Try what?" I asked innocently, although I felt my heart drop a few inches. I ignored the insult; the last time I'd let the term bother me, I hadn't had any. But the implications of the statement were, let us say, not pleasing.

"Anything," was his answer. He looked at me for a few seconds more, then he turned and walked away.

Damn! So Mellar *did* know I was after him. But why would he want to stop me? Oh, of course, he didn't. He was working under the assumption that I was out for him, and that I had no idea of why he was doing this. That made sense; if I had somehow given myself away, which was certainly possible, then it would be out of character for him to ignore it. He was playing the game to the hilt. (Interesting choice of words there, I noticed.)

This made me feel somewhat better, but not a whole lot. It was a Bad Thing that Mellar knew where the threat was coming from. While the bodyguards wouldn't actually stop a direct attack on Mellar, the fact that they were aware of me seriously cut my chances of getting away with anything tricky—and whatever I came up with now, it was going to have to be something tricky. I felt the first glimmerings of the younger brother to despair stir within me as I left the hall. I forced the feeling down.

Just outside the door, I stopped and got in touch with Aliera. Who knows, I thought, maybe she and Sethra have come up with something. In any case, I felt that I ought to let them know what we'd learned.

"What is it, Vlad?"

"Mind if I come up and see you? I have some information that you probably don't want to hear."

"I can hardly wait," she said. *"I'll be expecting you in my chambers."*

I walked down the hall to the stairs and met Morrolan, descending. I nodded to him and started to pass by. He motioned to me. I stopped, and he walked up the hall toward the library. I followed dutifully and sat down after he had closed the door behind me. The situation reminded me unpleasantly of a servant being called in for a dressing down for not scrubbing the chamberpots sufficiently.

"Vlad," he said, "perhaps you would care to enlighten me on just exactly what is occurring around here?"

"Eh?"

"Something has happened somewhere that I don't know about. I can feel it. You are preparing to move on Mellar, aren't you?"

By Verra's fingers! Did the whole Empire know?

He began ticking off points. "Aliera is rather upset about this whole matter and doesn't know quite what to do. You were acting the same way, as of yesterday. Today, I am informed that you have been, if I may put it so, snooping around Mellar. I see Aliera and she is just as pleased with life as you can imagine. Then I see you walking up the stairs, I assume to see my cousin, and you appear to know what you're doing all of a sudden. Now, would you mind telling me exactly what it is you two are planning?"

I was silent for a while; then I said, slowly and carefully, "If I'm acting any different today than yesterday, it's because we just solved the mystery—not the problem. I still don't have any idea of what I'm going to do about it. I will say, however, that I have no intention of doing anything that will, in any way, compromise you, your oath, or your House. I believe I stated that yesterday, and I have no reason to change my mind. Is that sufficient?"

"Go, boss, go!"

"Shut up, Loiosh."

Morrolan stared at me, long and hard, as if he were trying to read my mind. I flatter myself, however, that even Daymar would have trouble doing that without my noticing. Morrolan, I think, also respects me too much to do so without asking first. And in any case, hawk-eyes should stay on Hawklords, where they belong.

He nodded, once. "All right, then," he said. "We'll say no more about the matter."

"Frankly," I said, "I don't know what is on Aliera's mind. As you guessed, I was heading up to see her when I ran into you. But I don't have anything planned with her— yet. I hope she doesn't have anything planned without me."

He looked grim. "I like that rather less," he said.

I shrugged. "As long as I'm here, tell me: have you checked over those bodyguards?"

"Yes, I took a look at them. What of it?"

"Are they sorcerers?"

He seemed to debate with himself for a moment. Then he nodded. "Yes, both of them. Quite competent, too."

Damn. The good news just kept piling up.

"Okay, then. Is there anything else you wanted?"

"No—yes. I would appreciate it if you would keep an eye on Aliera."

"Spy on Aliera?"

"No!" he said emphatically. "Just, if she tries to do something that she should, perhaps, not do—I think you understand—try to discuss it with her, all right?"

I nodded, as the last piece of the puzzle fell into its place. Of course! That was what Mellar was worried about! He had bodyguards so that he wouldn't be killed by a non-Jhereg. He had, indeed, heard of Pathfinder.

The solving of this last piece of the mystery put me no closer to its solution; no surprise. I took my leave of Morrolan and headed up the stairs to Aliera's chambers. I felt his eyes on my back the whole way.

"What kept you?" asked Aliera.

"Morrolan wanted to have a chat."

I noted that Aliera did, indeed, seem to be in fine spirits today. Her eyes were bright green and shining. She relaxed against the back of her bed, absently stroking a cat that I'd not been introduced to. Loiosh and the cat eyed each other with abstract hunger.

"I see," she said. "What about?"

"He seems to think that you have something in mind. For that matter, so do I. Care to tell me about it?"

She arched her eyebrows and smiled. "Maybe. You go first."

The cat rolled over on its back, demanding that its stomach be attended to. Its long, white fur stood out a little, as it chose to deny that Loiosh existed. Aliera obliged it.

"Hey, boss."

"Yes, Loiosh?"

"Isn't it disgusting how some people cater to the whims of dumb animals?"

I didn't answer.

"For starters, Aliera, the idea we had before won't work."

"Why not?"

It seemed that she wasn't too worried. I was beginning to be.

"A number of reasons," I said. "But the main thing is that Mellar has no intention of leaving here."

I explained our deductions about Mellar's plans and motives. Surprisingly, her first reaction was similar to mine—she shook her head in admiration. Then, slowly, her eyes turned a hard metallic gray. I shuddered.

"I'm not going to let him get away with this, Vlad. You know that, don't you?"

Well, I hadn't actually known, but I'd been afraid of something like it. "What are you going to do?" I asked softly.

She didn't say anything, but her hand came to rest on Pathfinder's hilt.

I kept my voice soft, even, and controlled. "If you do, you are aware that Morrolan will be forced to kill you."

"So what?" she asked, simply.

"Why don't we find a better way?"

"For example?"

"Dammit, I don't know! What do you think I've been racking my brains about for the last few days? If we can find some way to convince him to leave, we can still follow the original idea—you trace him with Pathfinder, and then we take him wherever he ends up. If I just had more time!"

"How much time do you have?"

That was a very good question. If we were very, very lucky, the news wouldn't get out for three more days. But, unfortunately, I couldn't count on being lucky. And, what was worse, neither could the Demon. What would his next effort be like? I asked myself again. And how much of a chance would I have to stop it? I didn't like the answer I got to that last question.

"Today and tomorrow," I told her.

"And what," she asked, "happens then?"

"Deathsgate opens up. The matter is taken out of my hands, my body turns up somewhere, and I miss out on a fine Dragon-Jhereg war. *You* get to see the war. Lucky you."

She gave me a nasty grin. "I might enjoy it," she said.

I smiled back at her. "You might at that."

"However," she admitted, "it wouldn't do the House any good."

I agreed with that, too.

"On the other hand," she said, "if I kill him, there's no problem. The two Houses don't fight, and only the Dzur are hurt, and who cares about them, anyway? Well, maybe we can think of some way to intercept the information about them before it gets out."

"They aren't the problem," I told her. "The problem is that you end up dead, or having to kill Morrolan. I don't consider either possibility to be an ideal outcome."

"I have no intention of killing my cousin," Aliera stated.

"Great. Then you leave him alive, with his reputation dead."

She shrugged. "I am not unconcerned about my cousin's honor," she informed me. "It's just that I'm more concerned with precedence than Morrolan."

"There's another thing, too," I added.

"Oh?"

"To be honest, Aliera, I'm not convinced that you can take Mellar. He's got two experts guarding him, both of them good fighters, and both good sorcerers. I've already told you who trained him as a swordsman, and remember that he was good enough to fight his way into the House of the Dzur. He's determined that only a Jhereg is going to get him, and I'm afraid he may have what it takes to back that up. I'm not at all sure that you'll be able to kill him."

She listened patiently to my monologue, then gave me a cynical smile. "Somehow," she said, "I'll manage."

I decided to change the subject. There was only one other thing I had to try—and that was liable to get me killed. I didn't really feel like doing it, so I asked, "Where is Sethra, by the way?"

"She's returned to Dzur Mountain."

"Eh? Why?"

Aliera studied the floor for a while, then turned her attention back to the cat. "She's getting ready."

"For . . ."

"A war," said Aliera.

Just wonderful. "She thinks it will come to that?"

Aliera nodded. "I didn't tell her what I plan on doing, so

she's assuming it's going to happen."

"And she wants to make sure that the Dragons win, eh?"

Aliera gave me a look. "It isn't our custom," she explained, "to fight to lose."

I sighed. Well, now or never, I decided.

"Hey, boss, you don't want to do that."

"You're right. But it's what I'm paid for. Now shut up."

"One final thing, Aliera," I said.

Her eyes narrowed; I guess she picked up something from the tone of my voice. "And that is . . .?"

"I still work for Morrolan. He pays me, and I therefore owe him a certain amount of loyalty. What you propose doing is in direct violation of his wishes. I won't let you do it."

And, just like that, even as I finished speaking, Pathfinder was in her hand, its point level with my chest. She measured me coolly with her eyes. "Do you think you can stop me, Jhereg?"

I matched her gaze. "Probably not," I admitted. What the hell? Looking at her, I could see that she was prepared to kill me at once. "If you do, Aliera, Loiosh will kill your cat."

No response. Sheesh! Sometimes I think Aliera has no sense of humor at all.

I looked down the length of the blade. Two feet separated it from my chest—and my soul, which had once been her brother's. I recalled a time, it seemed like ages now, when I had been in a similar position with Morrolan. Then, as now, my thoughts had turned to figuring out which weapon was closest. A poison dart would be a waste of time. My poison works fast, but not *that* fast. I'd have to hit a nerve. Fat chance. I was going to have to go for a kill—anything else wouldn't do. My odds that time had been poor. This time they were worse. At least Morrolan didn't have his weapon out.

I looked back to her eyes. A person's eyes are the first things that let you know when he is about to make a move. I felt the hilt of the dagger up my right sleeve—point out. A sharp, downward motion would be required, and it would be in my hand; an upward motion after that would have it on the way to her throat. From this range, I couldn't miss. From this range, neither could she. I'd probably be dead before she was, and they wouldn't be able to revivify me.

"Just say the word, boss. I'll be at her eyes before—"

"Thanks, but hold, for now."

That last time, Morrolan had changed his mind about killing me because he'd had a use for me, and I'd stopped just short of mortal insult. This time, I felt sure, Aliera would not change her mind—once she decided on a course of action she was as stubborn in pursuing it as I was. After all, I thought bitterly, in an odd sort of way we were related.

I readied myself for action—I would have to get the drop on her to have any chance at all, so there was no point in waiting. It was odd; I realized that everything I'd been doing since I'd spoken to the Demon had been directed either at finding a way to kill Mellar, or risking my life to prevent someone from solving my problem.

I timed my breathing and studied her. Ready, now . . . wait . . . I stopped. What the Hell are you doing, Vlad? Kill Aliera? Be killed by her? What, by the great sea of chaos, would that solve? Sure, Vlad, sure. Good thinking. All we need now is for you to kill a guest of Morrolan's—and the wrong one at that! Sure, all we need now is for Aliera to be dead. That would—

"Wait a minute!" I said. "I've got it!"

"You've got what?" she asked coolly. She wasn't taking any chances on me—she knew what a tricky bastard I was.

"Actually," I said in a more normal tone of voice, "you've got it."

"And what, pray tell, have I got?"

"A Great Weapon," I said.

"Yes, I certainly do," she admitted, not giving an inch.

"A weapon," I continued, "that is irrevocably linked to your soul."

She waited calmly for me to go on, Pathfinder still pointed straight at my heart.

I smiled, and for the first time in days, I actually meant it. "You aren't going to kill Mellar, my friend. *He's* going to kill *you!*"

16-

**"The adding of a single thread
changes the garment."**

There was absolutely no question about it: I was doing too much teleporting these last few days. I forced myself to take a few minutes to relax at the teleport area for my office building, then went charging up the stairs like a dzur on the hunt. I skimmed past my secretary before he had time to unload mundane business on me and said, "Get Kragar up here. Now."

I stepped into the office and plumped down. Time for some hard thinking. By the time my stomach had settled, the details of the plan were beginning to work themselves out. Timing would have to be precise, but that was nothing new. There were a few things I would have to check on, to make sure they could be done, but these I'd make sure of in advance, and maybe I could find a way around any problems that turned up.

I realized that I was also going to have to depend a lot more on other people than I was at all comfortable with, but life is full of risks.

I started ticking off points, when I realized that Kragar was sitting there, waiting for me to notice him. I sighed. "What's the news today, Kragar?"

"The rumor mill is about to explode—it's leaking from several directions."

"Bad?"

"Bad. We aren't going to be able to keep this under our cloaks for very long; there's too much going on. And the bodies didn't help either."

"Bodies?"

"Yeah. Two bodies turned up this morning. Both sorceresses, Left Hand."

"Oh. Right. One of them would be the one we discussed before."

"Yeah. I don't know who the other one was. My guess is that the Demon found someone else who was spreading too many rumors."

"Could be. Was she killed with a single dagger blow to the heart?"

He looked startled. "Yes, she was. How did you know?"

"And there was a spell on her to prevent revivification, right?"

"Right. Who was she, Vlad?"

"I never learned her name, but she was just what you said, a sorceress from the Left Hand. She was involved in setting up and taking out Morrolan, and he took it personally. I didn't actually know that it would be single shot to the heart, but that's how he was nailed, and he does have a certain sense of poetic justice."

"I see."

"Anything else worth noting?"

He nodded. "Yeah. I wouldn't go outside today, if I were you."

"Oh? What did you hear?"

"It seems that the Demon doesn't like you."

"Oh, wonderful. How did you find this out?"

"We have a few friends in his organization, and they've heard rumors."

"Great. Has he hired anyone?"

"No way of being sure, but it wouldn't surprise me."

"Terrific. Maybe I'll invite him over for a friendly game of 'Spin the Dagger,' and let the whole thing get settled that way."

Kragar snorted.

"Do you think," I asked, "that he'll back off if we finish this Mellar business for him?"

"Maybe. Probably, in fact, if we can do it in time—that is, before the word gets out too far. From what I hear, that isn't too long from now. I guess the council members are starting to feel the bite of digging into their own purses. They aren't going to be able to avoid giving an explanation too much longer."

"That's all right. They aren't going to have to."

He sat up suddenly. "You have something?"

"Yeah. Nothing I'm horribly proud of, but it ought to do the trick—at least part of it."

"What part is that?"

"The hard part."

"What—?"

"Wait a minute."

I stood up and went over to the window. I made an automatic glance down at the street below, then opened the window.

"Loiosh, see if you can find Daymar. If you do, ask him if he would mind putting in an appearance here."

For once, Loiosh didn't make any remarks as he left.

"Okay, Vlad, so what is it?"

"Get a message out that I would very badly like to see Kiera. Then draw off a thousand gold from the treasury, and bring it up here."

"What—?"

"Just do it, okay? I'll explain everything later, after everyone is here."

" 'Everyone?' How many should I figure on?"

"Uh, let me see . . . five. No, six."

"Six? Should I rent a convention hall?"

"Scram."

I settled back to wait and went over the plan again. The rough spot, as I saw it, was whether or not Kiera could pull off the switch. Of course, if anyone could, she could, but it was going to be difficult even for her, I suspected.

There was, to be sure, an even rougher spot, but I tried to avoid thinking about that.

Alarms. "Bing bing," and "Clang," and everything else, both psionic and audible, went off all over the place. I hit the floor rolling and had a dagger ready to throw as my receptionist came bursting in, sword in one hand, dagger in the other. Then I realized what had happened—I saw Daymar floating cross-legged, about three feet off the floor.

I was rather pleased that before he had time to uncross his legs and stand up (or stand down, as the case may be), there were a total of four of my people in the office, weapons drawn and ready.

I stood up, resheathed my dagger, and held my hand up.

"False alarm," I explained, "but good job."

Daymar was looking around him with an expression of mild interest on his face. My receptionist was looking unhappy about putting his weapons away. "He broke right through our teleport blocks like they weren't even there! He—"

"I know. But it's all right, never mind."

They stood for a moment, then shrugged and left, casting glances at Daymar, who was now looking bewildered.

"Did you have teleport blocks up?" he said. "I didn't notice any."

"I should have thought to have them turned off. It doesn't matter. Thanks for showing up."

"No problem. What do you need?"

"More help, old friend. Sit down, if you wish." I set an example by picking up my chair and sitting myself down in it. "How are you at illusions?"

He considered this. "Casting them, or breaking them?"

"Casting them. Can you do a good one, quickly?"

"By 'quickly,' I assume you mean fast enough so that no one sees the intermediate stages. Is that right?"

"That, and with little or no warmup time. How are you at it?"

He shrugged. "How is Kiera at stealing?"

"Funny you should bring that up. She should be here—soon, if I'm lucky."

"Oh, really? What's going on, if you don't mind my asking?"

"Hmmm. If it's all right with you, I'd like to wait on the explanations until everyone shows up."

"Oh. Well, that's fine with me. I'll just meditate for a while." And, lifting his legs off the floor, he closed his eyes and began to do so.

At that moment, I heard Loiosh tapping on the window. I opened it. He flew in and landed on my right shoulder. He looked at Daymar, hissed a hiss of puzzlement, and looked away.

I reached out for contact with my wife, found her. *"Honey, could you come over to the office?"*

"Certainly. I don't suppose you have work for me, do you?"

"Not exactly, but the next thing to it."

"Vlad! You've got something!"

"Yep."

"What is—? No, I suppose you want to wait 'til I'm there, right? I'll be right over."

I repeated the process with Aliera, who agreed to teleport in. This time, however, I remembered to drop the protection spells before she arrived.

She looked around. "So this is your office. It looks quite functional."

"Thank you. It's small, but it suits my humble life-style."

"I see."

She noticed Daymar, then, who was still floating some three or four feet off the floor. She rolled her eyes in a gesture that was remarkably like Cawti's. Daymar opened his eyes and stood up.

"Hello, Aliera," he said.

"Hello, Daymar. Mind-probed any teckla, lately?"

"No," he answered with a straight face, "did you have one that you wanted mind-probed?"

"Not at the moment," she said. "Ask me again next Cycle."

"I'll be sure to."

He probably would, too, I reflected, if they were both still around then.

Cawti arrived at that moment, in time to avoid any further clashes between Hawk and Dragon. She greeted Aliera warmly. Aliera gave her a cheery smile, and they went off into a corner to gossip. The two of them had become close friends in recent months, based in part on a mutual friendship with Lady Norathar. Norathar was a Dragon turned Jhereg turned Dragon, who had been Cawti's partner, if you recall. Aliera had been instrumental in returning to Norathar her rightful place as a Dragonlord. Well, so had I, but never mind. That's another story.

It occurred to me, then, that Norathar was another one who would be somewhat caught in the middle by this whole thing. Her two best friends were going to have to try to kill each other, and she had loyalties on both sides. I put it out of my mind. We were here to prevent her from having to make that choice.

Kiera entered shortly, followed by Kragar. He handed me a large purse, which I immediately turned over to Kiera.

"Still another job, Vlad? I ought to teach you the craft. You could save a lot of time and money if you could do it on your own."

"Kiera," I said, "there aren't enough hours in the day for me to learn your art. Besides, my grandfather doesn't approve of stealing. Are you willing to help me out in this? It's in a good cause."

She absently weighed the purse, no doubt able to tell within a few Imperials how much was in it. "It is?" she said. "Oh, well. I guess I'll help you out anyway." She smiled her little smile and looked at the others in the room.

"Oh, yes," I said. "Kiera, this is Aliera e'Kieron—"

"We know each other," interrupted Aliera.

They smiled at each other, and I was surprised to note that the smiles seemed genuine. For a while I'd been afraid that Kiera had once stolen something of Aliera's. Friendships do turn up in the oddest places.

"Okay," I said, "let's get down to business. I think everyone knows everyone, right?"

There was no disagreement.

"Good. Let's get comfortable."

Kragar had, without my mentioning it, made sure that there were six chairs in the room, and had sent out for a good wine and six glasses. These arrived, and he went around the room making sure everyone's was full, before sitting down himself. Daymar disdained the chair, preferring to float. Loiosh assumed his position on my right shoulder.

I began to feel a little nervous about the whole thing. I had gathered in that room a master thief, a high noble of the House of the Hawk, a Dragonlord who traced her lineage back to Kieron himself, and a highly skilled assassin. And Kragar. I was just a bit troubled. Who was I to use these people as if they were common Jhereg to be hired and sent out?

I caught Aliera's eye. She was looking at me steadily and confidently. Cawti, also, was waiting patiently for me to describe how we were going to get out of this.

That's who I was, of course. Cawti's husband, Aliera's friend, and more . . . and the one who knew, possibly, how to handle this situation.

I cleared my throat, took a sip of wine, and organized my thoughts. "My friends," I said, "I would like to thank each of you for coming here, and agreeing to help me out on this. With some of you, it is, of course, in your own best interest, for one reason or another, that this matter be favorably settled. And to you, I would like to add that I am honored that you are trusting me to handle it. To those of you with no direct interest, I am deeply grateful that you are willing to help me at all. I give you my assurance that I won't forget this."

"Get to the point."

"Shut up, Loiosh."

"As to the problem, well, most of you know what it is, to one degree or another. Put simply, a high noble in the Jhereg is under the protection of Lord Morrolan, and it is necessary that he be killed, and not later than tomorrow at that, or," I paused for another sip of wine and for effect, "or events will occur to the severe detriment of some of us."

Aliera snorted at the understatement. Kiera chuckled.

"The important thing to remember is the time limit. For reasons that I would prefer not to go into, we have only today and tomorrow. Today would be much better, but I'm afraid that we're going to have to take today to iron out difficulties, and to practice our parts.

"Now, it is important to some of us," I looked quickly at Aliera, but her face betrayed no emotion, "that nothing be done which would compromise Morrolan's reputation as a host. That is, we can't do anything to this person, Mellar, while he is a guest at Castle Black, nor can we force him to leave by threats or by magic, such as mind-control."

I looked around the room. I still had everyone's attention. "I think I've found a method. Allow me to demonstrate what I have in mind, first, so we can get the hard part down before I go on with the rest of it. Kragar, stand up for a moment, please."

He did so. I came around the desk and drew my rapier. His eyebrows arched, but he said nothing.

"Assume for a moment," I said, "that you have weapons secreted about your person at every conceivable point."

He smiled a little. Assume, hell!

"Draw your blade," I continued, "and get into a guard position."

He did so, standing full forward, with his blade pointed straight at my eyes, level with his own head. His blade was a lot heavier and somewhat longer than mine, and it formed a straight line from his eyes to mine. His palm was down, his elbow out. There was a certain grace apparent, although I still consider the Eastern *en garde* position to be more elegant.

I stood for a moment, then attacked, simulating the Dragaeran move for a straight head cut. I came at his head, just below the line of his blade, giving me a sharp angle up.

He made the obvious parry, dropping his elbow so that his sword also angled up, even more sharply than mine. Also, the strong of his blade was matched against the weak of mine. This lined him up very well for a cut down at my head; however, before he could take it, I moved in and . . .

I felt something strike my stomach, lightly. I looked down, and saw his left hand there. Had this been a real fight, there would have been a dagger clutched in that hand. Had we been alone, he would probably have used a real dagger and avoided hitting me with it, but he wasn't keen on letting all of these people in on where he kept his extra blades. I resumed a normal position, saluted him, and sheathed my blade.

"Where," I asked, "did you get the dagger from?"

"Left forearm sheath," he said, with no hesitation.

"Good. Is there anywhere else you could have gotten it from that would have worked as well?"

He looked thoughtful for a moment, then he said, "I was assuming a spring-loaded type of forearm sheath, set for left-hand use. If he has it set for a right-hand draw, which is just as common, then I'd expect a simple waist sheath would be the one he'd go for. Either way it would be fast. I can use the fact that the whole left side of your body is undefended, and I can attack with the same motion I draw with. An upper thigh sheath would mean dropping my arm lower than I have to, there isn't any reason to go cross-body, and anything else is worse."

I nodded. "Okay. Cawti, anything to add, or do you agree?"

She thought for a moment, then shook her head. "No, he's right. It would be one of those two."

"Good. Kragar, I want you to secure two Morganti daggers."

He looked surprised for a moment, then shrugged.

"Okay. How strong do you want them?"

"Strong enough for anyone to tell that they are Morganti, but not so strong that they are apparent when they're sitting in their sheaths; okay?"

"Okay, I can find a couple like that. And, let me guess, you want one to be the right size for a waist sheath, and the other to be the right size for a forearm sheath."

"You've got it. Let me see for a minute. . . ." I had looked very closely for the weapons Mellar was carrying, but I hadn't been so much concerned with how big they were as where they were. I tried to remember. . . . Where was that little bulge? Ah, yes. And when he had turned from talking to the Hawklord, I had seen how much hilt from the waist sheath? Right. It looked like a standard bone hilt. How long a blade would make it balance right? And how wide? I'd have to guess, but I felt I could come pretty close.

"Waist sheath," I announced. "Overall length, approximately fourteen inches, of which half is blade. Just a fraction over an inch wide at the widest. Forearm sheath: call it nine inches overall. The blade is about five-and-a-half inches long, and about three-quarters of an inch wide near the guard." I stopped. "Any problem?"

He looked uncomfortable. "I don't know, Vlad. I should be able to get them, but I can't count on it. I'll talk to my supplier, and see what he has, but you're being damn precise."

"I know. Do the best you can. Remember, they don't have to be untraceable this time."

"That will help."

"Good."

I turned to Kiera. "Now, the big question. Can you lighten Mellar of a pair of daggers without his noticing, and, more of a problem, without his bodyguard noticing? I'm referring, of course, to the waist and forearm daggers."

She just smiled in answer.

"Okay, now; can you return them again? Can you put them back without his noticing?"

Her brows came together. "'Return them?' I don't know . . . I think so . . . maybe. I take it you mean substituting two new ones for the ones he has, right?"

I nodded.

"And," I added, "remember that they're going to be Morganti daggers, so they have to stay unnoticeable during the switch."

She brushed it off. "If I can do it at all, the fact that they're Morganti won't make any difference." She took on a vacant expression for a moment, and I noticed her hand twitching, as she mentally went through the motions that would be needed. "The waist dagger," she said finally, "can be done. About the other one . . ." she continued to look thoughtful. "Vlad, do you know if he has a spring-loaded mechanism for the left-hand, or just a reverse right-hand draw setup?"

I thought about it. I brought up my memory of seeing him again, and the bulge that had to be that blade, but I couldn't quite pin it down. "I don't know. I'm sure he has something, I mean, one or the other, but I just can't tell which one. Hmmmm, it just occurred to me, that if he has the reverse draw type, he won't use it for what we're talking about doing, so it really doesn't matter. We can assume—"

"Say, Vlad," said Kragar suddenly. "Remember that he's been trained as a master swordsman. That means he'll figure on fighting sword and dagger. Chances are, he's got the spring mechanism, so he can just twist his wrist and have a blade pop into his left hand."

I nodded.

Kiera said, "Do you have a forearm sheath, Vlad?"

It made me uncomfortable to discuss it, but I realized what she had in mind, and it was a reasonable question. I nodded.

"Spring, or right-hand draw?"

"Right-hand draw," I said.

She stood up. "Those are easier," she said, "but that will make up for the fact that you'll be watching for it. Let's see what I can do. . . ." She crossed in front of Cawti and Kragar and stood in front of my desk. She set her wineglass down a few inches from my own. I was holding it loosely, and the cuff was open a little, which should work to her advantage.

I kept my eyes on my arm and her hand where she set the glass down. So far as I could tell, her hand never came closer than three inches from mine.

She walked back to her chair and sat down again.

"How was that?" she asked.

I pulled back my sleeve, and checked the sheath. It held the same dagger it always had.

"Fine," I said, "except for the little matter that—" I stopped. She was smiling that smile of hers that I knew so well. She reached into her cloak, pulled out a dagger, and held it up. I heard a gasp, and saw Kragar staring at it.

He gave a quick twist to his left wrist, and suddenly a knife appeared in his hand. He looked at it, and his mouth dropped open. He held it as if it were a poisonous snake. He closed his mouth again, swallowed, and handed the dagger back to Kiera. She returned Kragar's to him.

"Misdirection," she explained.

"I'm convinced," said Kragar.

"Me, too," I said.

Kiera looked pleased.

I suddenly felt a lot better. This thing might actually work.

"I saw the whole thing, boss."

"Sure you did, Loiosh."

"Good," I said. "Now, Aliera, did you see that stroke I made at Kragar, with a bind following it?"

"Yes."

"Can you make the exact same attack?"

"I suspect so," she answered drily.

"Okay. I'll work on it with you. It's going to have to be perfect."

She nodded.

I turned to Cawti. "You're going to have to do a simple takeout."

"Any particular fashion?"

"Very quick, very quiet, and very unnoticeable. I'll be providing a distraction, which should help somewhat, but we have to be absolutely sure that no one sees you do it, or Mellar will be alerted too soon, and the whole thing blows up."

"Can I kill the guy?"

"No problem. Your target is an uninvited guest, so anything that happens to him is his problem."

"That makes things easier. I don't think I'll have any difficulty."

"Remember, he's a damn good sorcerer, and you aren't going to have much time to check him over."

"So? I eat sorcerers for breakfast."

"You'll have to cook me up one, sometime."

She smiled, slightly. "Does he have any protective spells up at the moment?"

I looked over at Aliera, who had checked the two of them out after I had left her.

"No," she said. "They're both good enough to get defenses up quickly if they have to, but I guess they don't want to call attention to themselves by using spells in Castle Black unless they actually have to."

"You keep referring to 'they,'" said Kiera. "Which one am I going to be taking out?"

"That's just the problem," I said. "We don't know. It will be whichever one is on Mellar's left, and we don't know which one that will be. Does that present a problem?"

She gave me what I call her I-know-something-you-don't-know smile, and made a dagger appear in her right hand. She spun it in the air, caught it, and made it disappear. I held myself answered.

"Daymar," I said, turning to him, "you're going to have to throw an illusion at me. It's going to have to be fast, thorough, and undetectable."

Daymar looked suddenly doubtful. "Undetectable? Morrolan will be able to tell that I'm throwing a spell in his castle no matter how subtle I am."

"Morrolan won't be there, so you don't need to worry about him. It does, however, have to be good enough so that a topnotch sorcerer, who *will* be there, doesn't notice it. Of course, he'll be rather busy at the time."

Daymar thought for a minute. "How long does the illusion have to stay on?"

"About five seconds."

"No problem, then."

"Good. Then that's everything. Now, here's the plan. . . ."

"'I like it, Vlad," said Kragar, "up to the teleport. That leaves you in a pretty miserable position, doesn't it? Why don't we go back to the original plan that you worked up with Aliera at that point?"

"You aren't thinking it through," I told him. "We're really pulling an elaborate hoax. It has to happen fast enough for Mellar to act while he's disoriented and confused. In fact, we're going to have to make him panic. Someone like Mellar isn't going to panic easily, and it isn't going to last very long. If we give him time to think it through, he'll realize what happened and just teleport back. We'll be right back where we started."

"Do you think," asked Kragar, "that we can get Morrolan to put up a teleport block around Castle Black so he can't come back there? Or maybe Aliera can do it."

"Aliera isn't going to be in any condition to put up or keep up a teleport block, if you remember. And if Morrolan is there to do it, he'll interfere in the earlier part of the plan, and we won't be able to bring it off at all."

"What about," said Cawti "letting Morrolan in on it from the beginning?"

Aliera answered for me. "He'd never permit me to do what I'm going to do, even if he agreed with the rest—which he wouldn't, by the way."

"Why not?"

"Because he's Morrolan. When this is over, if it works, he'll agree that it was a fine thing to do. But in the meantime, he'll try to stop it if he can."

"What do you mean," Cawti asked, "about his not permitting you to do what you are going to do?"

"Just what I said. Even if he wasn't involved in any other way, he'd at least try to stop that part."

"Why? If you aren't in any danger—"

"I never said," replied Aliera softly, "that I wouldn't be in any danger."

Cawti looked at her sharply. "I don't pretend to understand Great Weapons, but if it isn't safe—"

"Nothing is 'safe.' This is a better chance than I'd get if I did something that forced Morrolan to kill me."

Cawti looked troubled. "But Aliera, your *soul*—"

"So what? I think I have a good chance of surviving, and this leaves Morrolan with his honor intact, and the problem solved. The other way, Morrolan and I both end up worse off, with no chance at all for things to work out right. This is our best chance."

Cawti still looked unhappy, but she didn't say anything more on the subject.

Kragar said, "What about if Daymar throws a second illusion so I can get in on it?"

"No good," I said. "Who's going to do the teleport then? We can't do it ourselves, remember, because that's using magic against a guest at Castle Black. I'm convinced that it will be one of the two bodyguards who does the teleport, so they can make it untraceable at the same time."

"Even if Mellar asks you to do it?"

I looked at Aliera, who nodded. "Even then," she said. "He has to leave under his own power, or by the hand of one of his own people, or Morrolan will almost certainly take offense."

"Well—I suppose. But there has to be some way that we can get help to you."

I shrugged. "Sure, it could be that they don't get their trace-blocks up fast enough, so you could find me then. And I expect that Aliera will be able to find me with Pathfinder—after she recovers." I carefully didn't add "if she recovers."

"And how long," said Kragar, "will that take?"

"Who can say?" said Aliera. "Nothing like this has ever been done before, so far as I know."

Cawti looked grim. "And there isn't any way we're going to be able to find you ourselves?"

"Well," I said, "it would be nice if you tried. But I'm sure that some kind of block will be put up, and the guy doing it is good. Without having Pathfinder, you'll have to spend quite a while breaking down his spell."

Cawti looked away. "From what I hear, Vlad, you aren't in the same class with him as a fighter."

"I'm aware of that. But I fight Eastern-style, remember? And my intention is to take him before he even knows that I'm not who I'm supposed to be."

"Which reminds me," said Aliera. "If it does come down to a fight, you're going to have to keep him busy the whole time."

"I expect that he'll take care of that," I said drily. "But why?"

"Because if he realizes what has just happened—and the way you spoke of him, he will—he'll just teleport right back to Castle Black if you give him the chance to."

Great. "You're right," I admitted. "He probably will. How long will it take him, do you think?"

"To do the teleport? If I'm right in my assessment, it will take him only two or three seconds."

"So I can't allow him more than two seconds of breathing time during the fight." I shrugged. "That's all right. As I said, I don't expect him to allow *me* any breathing time, if it comes down to a fight. But I'm hoping it won't."

"By the way," said Kragar, "what happens if he turns to you and tells you to teleport him out?"

"I'm hoping he'll ask the other guy—which is a fifty-fifty chance. If he does turn to me, I'll do a dumb and stupid look and pretend that I'm in a state of shock. That should be believable."

Daymar snapped his fingers. "The Necromancer!" he said. "She won't have to trace the teleport; she can use her own ways of getting to you."

"Not without psionic contact," I said. "And chances are that whatever blocks they put up against tracing the teleport will block out general tracing spells as well—and that means that you won't be able to contact me, and I won't be able to contact you."

"Oh," said Daymar.

"Well," I asked the room in general, "can anyone think of any alternatives? Anything I might have missed?"

There was silence.

"I didn't think so," I said. "All right, that's what we've got. Let's get to work."

Kragar left to procure the daggers. The others went off to practice their parts. I went into the weapons closet and found two identical knives. They were long, thin stilettos, with seven inches of blade.

I picked one up and sharpened it carefully, spending over an hour on it. I wouldn't have to coat this one with nonreflective black paint, I decided, since there wasn't going to be much sneaking around involved here after I had it in my hand.

It isn't that I'm not willing to use any weapon I can get at to finish a job; it's just that I feel that I'm better off if I have a blade in mind from the beginning and know it exactly. That is why I picked out two identical weapons. After sharpening the one, I wouldn't touch it again until I left for Castle Black tomorrow. That way, it would have very little, if any, association with me. Since it had so little of my "feel" about it, I could safely leave it right at the scene.

This is much safer than being caught later with it on me—since there is no way to disguise the link between murder weapon and victim.

I picked up the duplicate, felt the weight and balance, and held it for a while. I took a few cuts and lunges with the thing in either hand, and then concentrated for a while on using my left hand with it.

I drew my rapier and fenced a little, practicing flipping it at a target on the wall between parry and riposte. In fact, I would never plan on throwing a knife at someone if this were a standard job, but in this case, it might be necessary.

I took out a few pieces of wood, then, and set them against the wall, and plunged the knife into them several times, alternating strokes. I used every type of attack I could think of, each several times.

I was satisfied. It was a good blade. Not very good for cutting, but it was unlikely that the death blow would be a cut. It threw well enough—although not perfectly—and it fit very well into my hand for any kind of stabbing motion that I was likely to make.

I picked out a sheath for it, and, after some thought, secured it to the outside of my left leg, just above the knee. The knife was a bit too long to be concealed effectively, but my cloak would cover it up pretty well, and it was perfectly placed for maximum speed of draw if I were fencing. Well, no; around the back of my neck would have been better for that, but then I'd have it in my hand in somewhat of an overhand position, which wouldn't be as good as an underhanded grip for stabbing in the middle of a bind, for example.

Loiosh watched my preparations in silence for a while, then he said, *"There is one problem with your plan, boss."*

"That being?"

"The 'distraction' part."

"What about it?"

"If I'm busy distracting people, that means I'm not along when you take off."

"I know."

"Well, I don't like it!"

"To be perfectly honest with you, old friend, neither do I."

17-

**"No matter how subtle the wizard,
a knife between the shoulder blades
will seriously cramp his style."**

Every citizen of the Dragaeran Empire has a permanent link to the Imperial Orb, which circles the head of the Empress with colors that change to reflect the sovereign's mood at the moment.

This one link serves many functions at the same time. Perhaps the most important one, to most people, is that it allows the use of the power from the great sea of chaos (as distinct from the lesser one that Adron created), which provides the energy for sorcery. To anyone skilled enough, this power can be shaped, molded, and used for just about anything—depending, of course, on the skill of the user.

One of its less important functions, to most people, is that one need only concentrate briefly in the proper way, and one knows precisely what time it is, according to the Imperial Clock.

I have, I will admit, some small skill in sorcery. I mean, I can start a fire with it, or teleport if I have to, or kill someone with it—if he isn't very good, and I get lucky. On the other hand, I only rarely have a use for it. But the Imperial Clock has been a friend that I could count on for years.

Eight hours past noon, every other day (and today was one), Morrolan inspected his guard positions personally. He would go outside of Castle Black, and teleport from tower to tower, speaking with the guards and checking them over. There was rarely, if ever, anything to correct or to criticize, but it was very effective for troop morale. It was also one of relatively few things that Morrolan did with any regularity.

Eight hours past noon, on this day, the day after we had met in my office, Morrolan was inspecting his guard positions, and so was not in the banquet hall of Castle Black.

I was.

Daymar was there as well, standing next to me. Cawti was around somewhere, as was Kiera. Aliera was somewhere outside the hall, waiting.

I tried to be inconspicuous. I didn't drink anything, because I didn't want anyone to notice that my hand was trembling.

I looked around the room for a while and finally spotted Mellar. Kiera was standing about ten feet away from him, to his rear, and looking in my direction. I decided that I must, at least in part, be succeeding in being inconspicuous, since none of my acquaintances had yet seen me. Good. If we could just hold onto that kind of luck for another couple of minutes, it wouldn't matter.

Okay. Relax, hands. Shoulder muscles, loosen up. Stomach, unknot. Neck, ease up. Knees, loose your stiffness—it's time to go.

I nodded to Kiera. She nodded back. I was no longer nervous.

From where I stood, I had a plain view of Kiera as she walked past one of Mellar's bodyguards, reached for a glass of wine past him, and walked away. I never saw her make the transfer. In fact, I wondered whether it had been made at all until Kiera caught my eye and nodded. I looked at her right hand, which was at her side. She had two fingers out, the rest in a fist. Both weapons planted. Good. I let my eyes acknowledge.

Here we go, I said to myself.

I glanced around the room then. This was the one part that I didn't have planned out—because I couldn't know who would be here from one day to the next—or one moment to the next.

Over near a table, about twenty feet away from me, I spotted the Hawklord who had been speaking to Mellar the other day. Perfect! I owed him one. I moved over toward him, planning my part. I observed the contents of the table and fitted it in. I took enough time getting there to give

Loiosh his instructions in detail.

"Know your part, Loiosh?"

"Worry about your own lines, boss. I'm just doing what comes naturally."

I leaned on the table, briefly raised my nobility a couple of notches, and said, "I say, hand me a glass of that Kiereth, four thirty-seven, will you?"

For a minute, I was afraid I'd overdone it when he actually started reaching for it, but then he caught himself, and turned to face me fully, his voice and eyes cold.

"I don't fetch for Jhereg," he announced. "Or Easterners."

Good. He was mine, now.

I pretended amusement. "Oh, indeed?" I responded, turning on my best sardonic smile. "Nervous about serving your betters, eh? Well, that's quite all right."

He glared, then, and his hand went to his sword hilt. Then, remembering where he was, I suppose, he let go of it.

"I must ask Morrolan," he said, "why he allows inferiors to share his accommodations."

It occurred to me that I should encourage him to do so, just to see how long he lasted—but I had a part to play. "Do that," I said. "I must admit to being curious as well. Let me know how it is that he justifies your presence here, among gentlefolk."

There were a few people watching us now, wondering whether the Hawk would challenge me, or simply attack. I didn't really care, as it happened.

He felt the crowd watching too. "Do you think," he said, "to claim equality with Dragaerans?"

"At least," I replied, smiling.

He smiled back, having mastered his temper. "What a quaint notion. A Dragaeran would not think to speak to anyone that way unless he was ready to back it up with steel."

I laughed aloud. "Oh, always, anytime," I said.

"Very well. My seconds will call upon you in the morning."

I pretended surprise.

"They will?" I said. "My seconds will call upon you in the alley."

I turned my back on him and walked away.

"What?" came the enraged cry behind me. I had taken three steps when I heard the sound of steel being drawn. I continued walking briskly.

"Now, Loiosh!"

"On my way, boss."

I felt the jhereg leave my shoulder, as I continued walking smoothly and evenly away from the Hawklord. Now, at this point, was when I was going to need all of the skills Kiera had taught me years before.

I heard a cry behind me, and the shouts of "It bit me!" and "Help!" and "Get a healer!" and "Where's the damn Jhereg?" and "Look, he's dying!"

There would be no eyes on me, I knew, as I walked toward Mellar. His bodyguards, I noted, didn't seem especially alert, although they, of all the crowd, must have recognized the distraction for what it was.

Mellar's face was calm. I was taken with sudden admiration for him. This was what he'd been expecting. He figured to die here and now and was ready for it. His bodyguards knew, and weren't making any effort to stop it. Could I have stood there like that, waiting for, perhaps, a Morganti dagger in my back? Not a chance.

I smiled to myself. He was about to get a surprise, however. I continued toward him, coming around the back. I was aware of the crowd around me as I blended in with it, but no one was aware of me. I had, to all intents and purposes, vanished. The art of the assassin. It would take an exceptional skill to spot me at this point—a skill that was beyond even the two bodyguards, I was sure.

Mellar stood, unmoving, awaiting the touch of a blade. He'd been flirting with a young female Tsalmoth who was playing dumb teckla maiden, while Mellar pretended he believed it. She was looking at him curiously now, because he'd stopped speaking.

And, amazingly, he actually began to smile. His lips curled up into the barest, thinnest smile.

"Now, Aliera!"

"Here I come!"

May Verra protect thy soul, lady who was my sister. . . .

The smile faded from Mellar's face as a shrill, drunken voice rang out through the room.

"Where is he?" cried Aliera. "Show me the teckla who would dishonor my cousin's name!"

A path cleared in front of Aliera. I got a glimpse of the Necromancer, a shocked look on her face. It is rare to see her shocked. She would probably have done something, but she was just too far away.

Speaking of too far away . . .

"Loiosh?"

"I'm busy, dammit! They won't let me go! I'm trying to get over there, but—"

"Forget it. Like we discussed. We just can't risk it. Stay where you are."

"But—"

"No."

I moved in as Aliera did—she from the front, and I from the back. Of course.

Good luck, boss."

I moved into position and noticed a sudden tension in Mellar's back. He must have recognized the naked blade in Aliera's hand as Morganti. I'm sure the whole room was aware of it.

I was in position, so I could hear everything he said. I heard him curse under his breath. "Not her, dammit!" he hissed to his bodyguards. "Stop her."

The two of them moved forward to bar Aliera's path, but she was the quickest. From her upraised left hand, a green scintillating light flashed out. Then I saw something that I'd heard about, but had never actually seen before. The energy she sent at them split; forked into two bolts, which caught the two bodyguards full in the chest. They were flung backwards and fell heavily. If we'd given them time to think, they would certainly have realized that Aliera couldn't be very drunk to throw a spell like that. They were both good enough to block part of the effects and they began to pick themselves up.

And, at that moment, Cawti, my wife, who had once been called "The Dagger of the Jhereg," struck. Silently, swiftly, and with perfect accuracy.

I don't think anyone else in the room would have seen it even if they hadn't all been busy staring at Aliera, who was waving Pathfinder around drunkenly over her head. But one of the two fallen bodyguards, as he tried to pick himself up, tried to cry out, found that he no longer had a larynx to do it with, and fell back.

And then I felt a tingling sensation as Daymar's spell took effect. Daymar threw his second spell just as quickly, and the dead bodyguard became invisible.

I stood up in his place. I matched paces with my "partner," but we saw we couldn't get there in time. I strongly suspect that the other fellow was a great deal more disturbed by this than I was.

Mellar also realized that we would be too late to save him. He now had two choices: he could allow Aliera to kill him, thus dying amid the ruins of three hundred or more years of planning, or he could fight Aliera.

His sword was out in a flash, and he took his guard position as Aliera swayed toward him. He certainly knew by now that he was going to have to kill her, if he could. His mind, I knew, would be working hard now; planning his blow, estimating her timing, and realizing gratefully that he could kill her without making it permanent if he was careful. He had to make sure that she died, but he must avoid any blow to the head.

He fell back a step. "My lady, you're drunk—" he began, but Aliera struck before he could finish. Pathfinder swung in a tight arc, straight for the right side of his head. If he'd been any slower, or the attack had been any more difficult to parry, it would have all been over for Mellar right there. But he made the obvious parry, and Aliera stepped in to bind.

He was too good a swordsman to miss the obvious opening, and he didn't. The back of my mind noted that he did, indeed, have a spring mechanism for his left sleeve dagger.

There was a flash of motion by his left hand, and his dagger caught her in the abdomen.

He must have realized, even before it struck her, that something was wrong. As it hit, I could feel within my mind the sentience that identifies a Morganti weapon.

Aliera screamed. It may or may not have been genuine, but it was one of the most horrendous screams I have ever heard. I shuddered to hear it, and to see the look on her face as the soul-eating blade entered her body. Mellar moved forward and tried vainly to draw it out, but its own power held it in as Aliera slumped to the floor, her screams dying away. The blade came free in Mellar's hand.

There was a moment of silence, and lack of motion. Mellar stared down at the knife. The other bodyguard and I stood next to him, frozen, as everyone else. Realization grew in Mellar that he had just thrown away any claim to protection he could have had from Morrolan. Anyone could kill him now, with no recriminations. He would be feeling his whole plan falling into pieces, and, no doubt, could only think of one thing: escape. Try to get out of this mess and come up with something else.

And, in this moment of weakness, of near panic, the final stroke came, administered by Daymar, to complete his feeling of disorientation and push him over the edge.

Mellar felt the mind-probe hit and cried out. I didn't know at that time whether he was sufficiently disoriented that his mental defenses were down. The mind-probe might have worked, or might have failed, but it worked as far as I was concerned: Mellar turned to me. "Get us out of here!" he yelled. It was unfortunate that he chose to look at me instead of the other bodyguard, but I had known that it could happen.

I didn't look back at him; just stared straight ahead. He saw, no doubt, the stunned and stupefied expression I was wearing. I heard the unmistakable note of panic in his voice, now, as he turned to the other bodyguard. The crowd was beginning to react, and I sincerely hoped that Sethra the Younger or the Necromancer didn't get to him before we were able to get out of here.

"Move!" he said to the other bodyguard. "Get us out!"

At that moment, I think, something must have clicked in him, and he turned back to me, his eyes growing wider still. Either Daymar's spell was fading so I no longer looked like the bodyguard I was imitating, or he noticed a mannerism that I didn't perform right. He was backing away from me as the walls vanished around us.

As best I could, I ignored the nausea that accompanied the teleport and made a fast decision.

If he hadn't realized that something was wrong, if he had happened to turn to the other one first, there would have been no problem. I would have simply killed him and finished off the bodyguard as best I could. Now, however, it was different.

I had time to take out either Mellar, or the other bodyguard, but I couldn't get both before they got in a cut or two at me. Which one should I go for?

The bodyguard would be setting up a teleport block and a spell to prevent tracing, while Mellar had already drawn his blade. Also, Mellar was closer.

However, I had to make sure that Mellar was killed permanently. As I've said, it is no easy thing to kill someone in such a way that he can't be revivified. With him ready and facing me, it wouldn't be as easy as it would have been if I'd had a free shot at the back of his head. What if I took him out, but wasn't able to make it permanent? And then the bodyguard were to nail me? The latter would just teleport again with Mellar's body, and get him brought back at his leisure. If I went for the guard, I could take the time and do a thorough job on Mellar, and not have to worry about Mellar skipping off on me.

What decided me, however, was the fact that the bodyguard was a sorcerer. That gave him a bigger advantage over me in this situation than I liked.

I didn't stop to think about any of this; it just flashed through my mind as I moved.

I threw myself backward, and, as my right hand went for my blade, my left hand found three poison darts. I flipped them toward the bodyguard and mentally recited a short prayer to Verra.

Mellar's first swing, which occurred just about then, missed; I had managed to get just out of range. Gods! He was strong! I was on the ground by then, but I had my rapier out. I rolled to my left and came up . . .

. . . in time to parry, just barely, a cut that would have split my skull open. My arm rang from the blow of his heavier sword, and I heard the welcome sound of a body falling off to my left. The bodyguard was out of it, at least. Thank you, Verra.

At that point I first became aware of my surroundings. We were outside, in a jungle area. That would put us somewhere to the west of Adrilankha, which meant at least three hundred miles from Castle Black. They weren't going to be able to trace the teleport in time to help me, then; not if the sorcerer/bodyguard had been able to get his spell off. I would have to assume that I was on my own.

Mellar struck again. I fell back as fast as I could, hoping

like Hell that there was no obstruction behind me. At the best of times, I was nowhere near as good a fighter as Mellar, and at this moment my stomach was churning and it was taking a great deal of effort just to keep my eyes focused on him. On the other hand, an inferior swordsman can hold off a superior swordsman for quite a while, as long as he can keep retreating. I could only hope that he would let up enough to give me a chance to throw my dagger at him, and that I was able to hit him with it—without being nailed at the same time. At that moment, I would have let him get through to me if I could have been sure of doing a complete job on him in exchange. I looked for the chance, in fact.

He, however, had no intention of giving me any such opportunity. Whether he guessed my intentions or not I don't know, but he didn't let up for an instant. He kept hacking at my head and advancing. His left hand found a knife.

I felt a cold shiver run up my spine as I realized that he was now holding the Morganti blade that I had set him up with, one of the two we gave him, to make sure that he used one on Aliera. He noticed it, then, and his eyes widened. For the first time, he smiled. It was a very unpleasant smile to be on the wrong end of. The same could be said for the dagger. Somehow, at that moment, the irony of the whole thing was lost on me.

I kept falling back. The only thing that had kept me alive so far, I knew, was the fact that he wasn't used to a fencer who presented only the side of his body, rather than the full forward of the sword-and-dagger Dragaeran style. He, of course, was fighting full forward, with a dagger up in a position to strike, or parry, or cast spells with.

He wasn't about to cast spells with it, and he didn't need to parry because I hadn't had a chance to attack yet. Not even a simple riposte—and now he had two blades to my one. Also, he was a good enough swordsman that it wouldn't take him long to learn how to deal with my kind of swordplay.

He was quite content, meanwhile, to keep me busy until I ran up against a tree or tripped on a log, as I inevitably would in this jungle. Then it would be all over—he'd come in with the dagger, and my soul would go to feed a sentience in nine inches of cold steel.

He spoke for the first time. "It was all a trick from the beginning, wasn't it?"

I didn't answer, not having the breath.

"I can see it now," he continued. "It might have worked, too, if you were a better swordsman, or if you had nailed me when you had the chance, instead of going for my friend back there."

That's right, you bastard, I thought. Rub it in.

"But as it is," he continued, "they should know the truth by now at Castle Black. If I can figure it out from here, they can certainly figure it out from there, where they have the body and the blade to look at. What's to stop me from just going back there?"

I stopped and tried to bind him, parrying strongly. He took a cut at me with the dagger, however, and I had to jump back. I'd had no chance for an attack.

"It is unfortunate," he went on, "that I can teleport, or it might have worked anyway."

It takes you two or three seconds to teleport, my friend, and I don't intend to give you two or three seconds. Sorry, but I don't psych.

He must have realized that, too, because he stopped talking. I managed to put my left hand on the stiletto I'd selected to destroy him with, and I pulled it out. I cradled it in my hand like a jhereg holds her egg. I thought, very briefly, about trying to flip it at him, but to do that I'd have to turn full forward. If I did that, he'd have me before I could even loose it, and my head would be rolling on the ground.

For a moment, then, I considered that. If I fell to his sword, the dagger couldn't hurt me. It requires a living soul to feed such a blade. My soul would be safe, and, just maybe, I could take him with me.

I threw away the idea and stepped back again. No, he was going to have to do it all himself—that much I'd take from him. I was not about to let him cut me down and leave me here, for the wild jhereg to feed on my corpse, to complete the irony of the situation.

. . . Jhereg? Wild jhereg? I felt a sudden breeze, cool against the back of my neck, reminiscent of the feel of a knife's edge, and of other things.

A memory came back to haunt me, from years ago. This same jungle it was. . . . Could I . . .?

I was just distracted enough by the thought that I almost missed a parry. I jumped backward, and his deflected sword ripped into my side. I felt the blood start to flow, and it began to hurt. Verra be thanked, my stomach was settling down.

Witchcraft is similar to sorcery in many ways, but uses one's own psionic powers rather than an external energy source. The rituals and incantations were used to force the mind down the right path, and to direct the power. How much were they really necessary?

My mind reached back . . . back . . . back to the time I had summoned the jhereg who was Loiosh's mother from these very jungles. His mother was, quite likely, long dead, but I didn't need her. Could I do it again?

Probably not.

"Come to me, blood of my House. Join me, hunt with me, find me."

I almost stumbled, and was almost killed, but didn't, and was not. What the Hell was it? Come on, brain, think!

As my grandfather had taught me long ago, I let my arm, and my wrist, and even my fingers do all the work of keeping me alive. My mind had other things to do, the sword-arm would just have to take care of itself.

Something . . . something about . . . wings? No, *winds,* that was it, winds. . . .

"Let the winds of Jungle's night . . ."

Something, perhaps the look on Mellar's face, warned me of the tree behind me. Somehow I stepped around it without being spitted.

"Stay the hunter in her flight."

I felt myself weakening. Blood loss, of course. I didn't have time for that.

"Evening's breath to witch's mind . . ."

I wondered whether Loiosh would ever speak to me again. I wondered whether anyone would be able to speak to me again.

"Let our fates be intertwined."

Mellar changed tactics, suddenly, and his sword thrust at my chest, instead of chopping at my head. I was forced into a clumsy parry, and he caught me with the tip. Was that a rib cracking, or just a good imitation? I brought up my blade before the dagger could sweep down, and made a leap backward. He followed immediately.

"Jhereg! Do not pass me by!"

As he closed, perhaps just a touch too cockily, I tried a full-extension stop-thrust—Dragaeran swordplay has nothing like it—dropping to one knee and cutting up under his sword-arm. He was as surprised as I that my first offensive move got through, and it gave me time to get back before he countered. He bled a little from high on his right side. It was too much to hope for that this would affect his sword-arm, but it gave me more time.

"Show me where they soul doth lie!"

My side screamed with pain as I stepped back still further. Each parry caused red flashes before my eyes, and I felt that I was near to blacking out. I felt drained, too. I mean, *drained*. I don't think I had ever put that much into a spell.

I moved back out of the way of another blow that almost slit open my belly. He followed with a cut with the dagger that was almost faster than I could see, but I was moving back, so it missed. I stepped back again, before he could set himself. . . .

What? Was there . . .? Come on, brain! Mind, relax . . . be receptive . . . listen . . .

"Who?" came the thought to my forebrain.

"One who needs you," I managed, as I almost stumbled. I hung on to my consciousness with everything I had.

"What have you to offer?"

Oh, Demon Goddess! I don't have time for this! I wanted to start crying, to tell them all to just go away.

He caught my blade with the dagger, and the sword swept down; I squirmed to the side, made it.

"Long life, O Jhereg. And fresh, red meat, with no struggle or search. And, sometimes, the chance to kill Dragaerans."

All in all, one hell of a time to be bargaining.

Mellar did a fillip with his wrist that should have been impossible with that heavy a sword. He connected lightly with the side of my head—as heavily as he could, given what he was doing, and as lightly as it was possible for him to, considering the size of the weapon he had.

But I still didn't black out. I took a chance, then, because I had to, and lunged, cutting down at his forehead. He stepped back and parried with his dagger. I backed up another step before the sword came sweeping down at me again. It occurred to me that, even if the jhereg should choose to respond, it might be too far away to do me any good.

"And what do you ask?"

Mellar was smiling again. He could see that I was going, and all he had to do was wait. He continued pressing the attack.

"For the future, aid in my endeavors, and your friendship, and your wisdom. For the present, save my life!"

Once again, Mellar struck at the side of my head and got through. There was a ringing in my ears, and I felt myself start to fall. I saw him move in, raising the dagger and grinning broadly . . .

. . . and then he was turning, startled, as a winged shape struck at his face. He moved back and took a swipe with his sword; missed.

I dropped my sword and caught myself with my right hand. I heaved myself up from there until I was standing; barely. Mellar took another swing at the jhereg. I transferred the dagger to my right hand, and fell forward, walking being somewhat beyond my powers at that point. My left hand grasped his left arm, his dagger-arm, and swung him around.

He turned, and I saw panic in his eyes, and his dagger began to arc toward my neck. I tried to hold back his right arm, which was swinging forward with the sword, but it slipped from my grasp.

I thrust straight in, then, with everything that was left in me.

The stiletto took him in the left eye, burying itself to the hilt in his brain. He screamed then—a long wail of despair, and he lost interest in removing my head. I saw the light of life go out in his right eye, and I might even have rejoiced if I'd been capable of it.

I was screaming then, as well, as we twisted, toppled, fell. We landed on each other, with me face up, and the only thing still in the air was his lifeless arm, holding a living dagger in a fist that wouldn't let go. I watched it, unable to do anything, as it fell . . . fell . . . fell . . . and hit the ground next to my left ear.

I could feel its frustration, and had a crazy moment of sympathy for any hunter that loses its prey by such a small margin.

A thought, then, came into my mind and set up house-keeping. *"I accept,"* it said.

Just what I need, I remember thinking, another wiseass jhereg.

I didn't quite lose consciousness, although I don't think I was completely conscious, either. I remember lying there, feeling damned helpless, and watching the jhereg take bits out of Mellar's corpse. At some time in there, various animals came up and sniffed me. I think one of them was an Athyra; I'm not sure about the others. Each time, the jhereg looked up from its meal and hissed a warning. They backed off.

Eventually, perhaps half an hour later, I heard a sudden disturbance. The jhereg looked over, hissed, and I looked too. Aliera was there, holding Pathfinder. With her were Cawti and Kragar and Loiosh.

The other jhereg was female. She hissed at Loiosh. With the jhereg, the female is dominant. (With the Jhereg, the matter is still up in the air.)

Cawti rushed up to me with a cry and sat down. She carefully placed my head on her lap and began stroking my forehead. Aliera began inspecting and treating my various wounds. I'd be hard pressed to say which helped more, but it was nice getting all the attention.

Kragar assisted Aliera, after verifying that the two corpses were, indeed, corpses.

Loiosh had found the other jhereg. They were looking at each other.

Aliera said something then, I think it was about Day-mar's mind-probe having worked, but I wasn't really listening, so I'm not sure.

Loiosh spread his wings and hissed. The female spread her wings further and hissed louder. They were silent for a while, then exchanged hisses again.

I tried to communicate with Loiosh, but found nothing. At first I thought that it was because my mind was still too exhausted from the spell I'd done, but then I realized that it was because Loiosh was blocking me out. He'd never done that before. I got a sinking feeling.

Suddenly, the two of them rose into the air. I lacked the strength to look up and follow their flight, but I knew what must be happening. Tears blinded me, and desperation gave me a small loan against my future energy holdings. I tried to force my way into his mind, and I sent out my desperate call, trying to pierce the barriers he had erected against me.

"No! Come back!" I think I called.

Cawti's face above me began to waver, as my body and mind gave up their fight at last, admitted defeat, and the darkness that had been hovering over and around me finally found entry.

Nevertheless, the contact was as sharp and distinct as it had ever been, sneaking under the gate even as it closed.

"Look, boss. I've worked for you nonstop for more than five years now. You'd think I could have a few days off for my honeymoon!"

Epilogue

**"Failure leads to maturity;
maturity leads to success."**

On my terms, this time.

The Blue Flame was quiet at this hour, with three wait-ers, a busboy, a dishwasher, and three customers.

All of them were enforcers who worked for me. All of them, at one time or another, had done 'work.'

This time I faced the door, and my back was against the wall. I had a dagger out, lying openly on the table next to my right hand.

I wished Loiosh was back, but he wasn't necessary this time. I was making the rules, and we were playing with my stones. Somewhere, Cawti and Kragar were watching.

Let him try . . . anything. Anything at all. Sorcery? Ha! No spell would go in this place that didn't have Aliera's ap-proval. Try to bring in an assassin? Maybe, if he wanted to pay for Mario, he could come up with something I'd worry about. Other than that, however, I wasn't about to get upset.

A face appeared in the doorway, followed by another.

The Demon had brought two bodyguards with him. They stopped in the doorway and looked around. Being competent, they saw how things were and spoke to the De-mon quietly for a while. I saw him shake his head. Good. He was smart, and he was gutsy. He was going to do it my way because he knew, at this point, that it was the only way it would get done—he was too good a businessman not to realize that it had to get done.

231

I saw him signal his men to wait by the door, and he came forward alone.

I rose as he reached me, and we sat down at the same moment.

"Lord Taltos," he said.

"Demon," I said.

He looked at the dagger, seemed about to speak, and changed his mind. At this point, he could hardly blame me, after all.

Since I had requested the meeting, I ordered the wine. I chose a rare dessert wine, made by the Serioli. He spoke first while we waited for the wine to arrive.

"I note that your familiar is missing," he said. "I hope he isn't ill."

"He isn't ill," I said. "But thank you for asking."

The wine came. I allowed the Demon to approve it. It's the little touches that make the fine host. I sipped mine and let it flow down my throat. Cool, and sweet, but neither icy nor cloying. That was why I'd chosen it. It had seemed appropriate.

"I was afraid," the Demon continued, "that he'd eaten something that had disagreed with him."

I chuckled. I decided that I'd come to like this guy, if we didn't kill each other first.

"I take it the body has been found," I said.

He nodded. "It's been found. A bit jhereg-eaten, but there isn't any harm in that, certainly."

I agreed with his sentiments.

"And," he went on, "I received your message."

I nodded. "So I see. I have what I claimed to."

"All of it?"

"All of it."

He waited for me to go on. I was enjoying it enough so that I didn't even mind the pain I felt from the events of the day before. One reason that I'd arranged to have the place full of my people was that I didn't want it to get out how much trouble I had walking in. Standing for the Demon had cost me; hiding that fact had cost me even more. Aliera is good, but it still takes time.

"How did you get it?" he asked.

"From his mind."

The Demon arched his eyebrows. "I'm rather surprised," he admitted. "I wouldn't have expected him to be subject to mind-probes."

"I have some good people working for me," I told him. "And, of course, we caught him at a good time."

He nodded and sipped his wine. "I should tell you," he said, "that, as far as I'm concerned, it's all over."

I waited for him to continue. This was what I'd arranged the meeting for, after all.

He took another sip of his wine. "To the best of my knowledge and belief," he said, choosing his words carefully, "no one in the organization has anything against you, means you any ill will, or will profit from any harm that comes to you."

That last wasn't true in a literal sense, but we both knew what he meant—and he had his reputation to hold on to. I didn't think he would lie to me about it. I was satisfied.

"Good," I said. "And allow me to say I hold no ill will over anything that happened—or almost happened—before. I believe that I understand what was going on, and there is no cause there for complaint on my part."

He nodded.

"As for the other," I went on, "if you send an escort over to my office, say at the fourth hour past noon, I'll be able to supply them with your goods to return to you."

He nodded his satisfaction at the arrangements. "There are a few other things," he said.

"Such as . . .?"

He stared off into space for a moment, then turned back to me. "Certain of my friends are exceptionally pleased with the work you did yesterday."

"I beg your pardon?"

He smiled. "I mean, the work your 'friend' did yesterday."

"Yes. Go on."

He shrugged. "Certain of them felt that perhaps a bonus is in order."

"I see. Well, that I'll gladly accept, on my friend's behalf, of course. But, before we go into that, perhaps you will allow me to buy you dinner?"

He smiled. "Why yes, that would be very kind of you."

I called a waiter over. He was, actually, a lousy waiter, but that was all right; I think the Demon understood.

* * *

More than our apartment, more than my office, the library at Castle Black has seemed like home base to me.

How many times in the past had Morrolan and I, or Morrolan, myself, and Aliera, or a host of others, sat in this room and said some form of "Thank Verra, it's over"?

"Thank Verra, it's over," said Aliera.

I lay on my back on the lounge chair. As I said, Aliera was good, but it takes time to heal completely. My sides still ached, and my head gave me no end of trouble. Still, in the three days since Mellar had passed from among the living, and the two days since I'd met with the Demon to arrange for nine million gold to be returned (and to insure that no more attempts were going to be made on my life), I had pretty well made the transition back to humanity.

Cawti sat next to me, gently brushing my forehead from time to time. Loiosh had returned and sat perched on my chest, as near to the shoulder as my position allowed. His mate took the other side. I felt quite contented with life, all in all.

Morrolan sat opposite me, staring into his wineglass. His long legs were stretched out in front of him. He looked up. "What are you calling her?" he asked.

"Her name is Rocza," I said. On hearing her name, she leaned down and licked my ear. Cawti scratched her head. Loiosh hissed a jealous warning, whereupon Rocza looked up, hissed back, licked Loiosh under his snakelike chin. He sat back, mollified.

"My, aren't we domestic?" said Morrolan.

I shrugged.

He continued to look at the female jhereg curiously. "Vlad, I know as much about witchcraft as any Easterner, you must admit—"

"Yes, that's true."

"—and I don't see how you can have a second familiar. I had always understood that the relationship between witch and familiar is such that it is impossible for it to occur with more than one animal.

"For that matter," he continued, "I've never heard of making a familiar from any adult animal. Don't you have to acquire the thing as an egg, in order to achieve the proper link?"

Loiosh hissed at Morrolan, who smiled a little and cocked his head.

"I'm calling *you* a 'thing,' that's who," Morrolan said.

Loiosh hissed again and went back to licking Rocza's chin.

"Well, Morrolan," I said, "why don't you find out for yourself? You're a witch, why don't you get a familiar?"

"I already have one," he answered, dryly. He gently stroked the hilt of Blackwand, and I shuddered involuntarily.

"Rocza isn't really my familiar, in any case," I explained. "She's Loiosh's mate."

"But still, she came to you. . . ."

"I called for help and she heard. We were able to strike a bargain similar to the one a witch makes with the mother of his familiar for the egg, but it wasn't exactly the same. I did use the same spell, or a close variant, to achieve initial contact," I admitted. "But that's where the similarity ends. After I got contact, we more or less just spoke. I guess she liked me."

Rocza looked up at me and hissed. I got the feeling that it was intended to be laughter, but I'm not sure. Loiosh broke in at that point. *"Look, boss, no one likes to be spoken of as if he isn't there, okay?"*

"Sorry, chum."

I stretched myself out, enjoying the feeling that there was blood circulating, and all those other good things.

"I can't tell you how happy I was when those two let me know that they weren't going to kill each other, though," I summed up.

"Hmmmmph!" said Aliera. "You sure couldn't tell us then. You were too busy going down for the third time."

"Was it that close?" I asked.

"It was that close."

I shuddered. Cawti stroked my forehead, gently.

"It works both ways, I guess. I was also mightily pleased to see that you made it after all. I didn't tell you before, but I was plenty worried about that whole business," I said.

"You were worried!" said Aliera.

"I still don't understand that, Aliera," said Kragar, who, I discovered, had been sitting next to her the entire time. "How is it that you survived the Morganti dagger?"

"Just barely," said Aliera.

He shook his head. "When you first went over it, you said it would work out, but you never said how."

"Why? Do you want to try it? I don't really recommend having your soul eaten as a form of entertainment."

"Just curious . . ."

"Well, basically, it has to do with the nature of Great Weapons. Pathfinder is linked to me, which really means it's linked to my soul. When the dagger threatened to destroy me, Pathfinder acted to preserve me by drawing my soul into itself. When the threat was gone, I was able to return to my body. And, of course, we had the Necromancer standing by, just in case there were problems."

She looked thoughtful for a moment. "It is an interesting perspective from in there," she remarked.

"It is a rather frightening one from out here," put in Morrolan. "I thought we'd lost you."

Aliera smiled at him. "I'm not that easy to get rid of, cousin."

"In any case," I said. "It all worked out."

"Yes," said Morrolan. "I would imagine that you did rather well for yourself out of the affair."

"In more ways than one," I said.

"I suppose," said Morrolan.

I shook my head. "It isn't just the obvious. It seems that certain parties were quite pleased with the return of the gold, in addition to everything else. I've been given responsibility for a somewhat larger area."

"Yeah," said Kragar, "and you didn't even have to ask your friend to kill anyone for it."

I let that pass.

"I should point out, though," said Kragar, "that, in actual fact, you don't have any more responsibility than you did before."

"I don't?"

"Nope. You just make more money. *I'm* the one with more responsibility. Who do you think does all the work, anyway?"

"Loiosh," I answered.

Kragar snorted. Loiosh hissed a laugh.

"You are hereby forgiven, boss."

"Lucky me."

Morrolan was looking puzzled. "Speaking of the gold reminds me of something. How *did* you discover where it was?"

"Daymar took care of it," I told him. "Just before Mellar teleported me out, Daymar did a mind-probe on him. It was the only time he could have had a chance of succeeding, with Mellar completely disoriented. He caught him with his psychic pants down, you might say. Daymar found out where he had hidden the gold and found out about the arrangements he'd made for the information about the Dzur to get out. And, of course, it was the mind-probe itself that finally broke down Mellar and sent him into a panic."

"Oh," said Morrolan, "so you *did* find out about the information he had on the Dzur."

"Yep," I said. "And we suppressed it."

"How did you do that?" asked Morrolan.

I looked over at Kragar, who had actually handled the matter. He smiled a little.

"It wasn't difficult," he said. "Mellar had given it to a friend of his in a sealed envelope. We picked up this friend, brought him to the dock where we'd dumped Mellar's body, and pointed out to him that there was no reason for him to keep the thing anymore. We talked a little, and he ended up agreeing."

Best not to know any more, I decided.

"What I don't understand," Kragar continued, "is *why* you didn't want the information to come out, Vlad. What difference does it make to us?"

"There were a couple of reasons for it," I told him. "For one thing, I made it clear to a few Dzurlords I know that I was doing it. It never hurts to have Dzur heroes owe you favors. And the other reason was that Aliera would have killed me if I hadn't."

Aliera smiled a little, but didn't deny it.

"So, Vlad," said Morrolan, "are you going to retire, now that you are wealthy? You could certainly buy a castle out of town and turn properly decadent if you chose to. I'd be curious. I've never had the pleasure of seeing a decadent Easterner."

I shrugged. "I may buy a castle somewhere, since Cawti's been wanting one, and now we can afford a few luxuries like a higher title in the Jhereg, but I doubt I'll retire."

"Why not?"

"You're rich. Are you retiring?" I asked him.

He snorted. "From what should I retire? I've been professionally decadent for as long as I can remember."

"Well, there is that . . . Say!"

"Yes?"

"How about if we both retire! What do you think about selling Castle Black? I can give you a good price on it."

"Depend on it," he said.

"Oh, well. Just asking."

"Seriously, though, Vlad; have you ever thought about quitting the Jhereg? I mean, you don't really need them anymore, do you?"

"Ha! I've thought about quitting the Jhereg a great deal, but so far I've always managed to be just a little bit quicker than whoever wanted me out."

"Or luckier," said Kragar.

I shrugged. "As for leaving voluntarily, I don't know."

Morrolan looked at me carefully. "You don't actually *enjoy* what you do, do you?"

I didn't answer, not really knowing at the time. I mean, did I? Especially now, when my biggest reason, my hatred for all things Dragaeran, turned out not to have the cause I had thought it did. Or did it?

"You know, Aliera," I said, "I'm still not really sure about this genetic inheritance through the soul. I mean, sure, I felt something for it, but I also lived through what I lived through, and I guess that shaped me more than you'd think. I am what I am, in addition to what I was. Do you understand what I mean?"

Aliera didn't answer; she just looked at me, her face unreadable. An uncomfortable silence settled over the room, as we all sat there with our thoughts. Kragar studied the floor, Cawti caressed my forehead, Morrolan seemed to be looking around for another subject.

He found one, finally, and broke the silence by saying, "There is still a thing that I fail to understand, concerning you and Rocza."

"What is that?" I asked, as relieved as everyone else.

He studied the floor in front of the couch. "Exactly how

do you plan on housebreaking her?"

I felt myself going red as the odor reached my nose, and Morrolan wryly called for his servants.

About the Author

Steven Karl Zoltán Brust was born on November 23, 1955. His parents raised both their children and the household plants by the system of Benevolent Neglect (and insist that it worked with the plants). His care and supervision have since been taken over by his family: his wife, Reen; his son, Corwin Edward; and his twin daughters, Aliera Jean and Carolyn Rozsa. He presently earns his living as a systems programmer for a computer manufacturer and as a drummer for a suburban white reggae C & W band. He also plays the guitar, acts in community theatre, fences, practices pistol-shooting, studies Shotokan karate, invents traditional Hungarian cuisine, serves as vice-president of the Minnesota Science Fiction Society, and is planning to get some sleep Real Soon Now.